39

YOUR LAST

BIRTHDAY

TIMOTHY GENE SOJKA

Black Rose Writing | Texas

This is a work of fiction. Names, characters, businesses, places, events, and incidents are either the products of the author's imagination or used in a fictitious manner. Any resemblance to actual persons, living or dead, or actual events is purely coincidental.

ISBN: 978-1-68513-169-2
PUBLISHED BY BLACK ROSE WRITING
www.blackrosewriting.com

Printed in the United States of America
Suggested Retail Price (SRP) $21.95

39 is printed in Garamond Premier Pro

Other Titles from Tim Sojka

Smith Driskill is dying to prove a point...

PAYBACK JACK

TIMOTHY GENE SOJKA

Take A bribe, Meet youR MAKeR

Politikill

Timothy Gene Sojka

Author of the #1 Political Thriller,
Payback Jack

Dedicated to the incredible
Abigail Sojka
You didn't come with an instruction manual.
I did my best.
Thank God you had an incredible mother.

39

Silsbee, Texas
Grateful to be grown there.
Could not wait to get away.
Blessed to be shaped by the pines, rivers, creeks, and people.
Willingly return in my dreams, thoughts, and memories.

ac·knowl·edg·ments

An author's awkward statement of indebtedness to others, typically printed at the beginning of a book in case the writing sucks so badly you can't make it to the end. I will endeavor for that not to be the case here.

Some writers are great editors. None of those writers are me. So, blessings and thanks to the patient and incredible editors Linda Migura, Lisa Petrocelli, and Brandee Miller.

To Denise Kingham and Linda Migura, my test reader extraordinaire.

To my wife, the beautiful, intelligent, and driven Lori Sojka, the only woman I will ever love. Thank you to my daughter Abigail Sojka, the coolest and most adult person I know, which is a testament to you and your incredible mother. To my brother, Jeff Sojka, the bravest kid I ever met.

Thank you to the teachers at Silsbee Elementary, Jr. High and High School for helping a child with rampant ADHD navigate twelve years. A special thank you to Mrs. Johnson, Mr. and Mrs. Edwards, Mr. Atmar, Mr. Meldrum, Mr. Leigh, Mrs. Seabrook, Mrs. La Toof, Mrs. Voigtman, Mrs. Gaye Lokey, and all the teachers who took extra time with me. You should each be nominated for sainthood.

Thanks to the Silsbee Class of 1985, for your support, which is surprising, because let's admit it, I could be a royal pain at times, sincere apologies.

A special thanks Sherry Jacks Davis. You helped promote my book better than an advertising agency. Your organizational skills are a blessing to the entire class of 1985. To my other friends in high school, college, and ATO fraternity brothers at Texas Tech: We made terrible decisions together...*you're welcome*.

Thanks to the readers of my first two novels, *Payback Jack* and *Politikill*, for your encouragement. Thanks to author and mentor AJ McCarthy and Luke Swanson for your guidance. Special thanks to Keller Williams, Paul Crandall, the See TIM Sell Team, and Katy Christian Magazine.

Thank you to my unbelievable test and support readers, Denise Kingham, the Smiths (Brett, Mary, Steve, and Patti), the Joyners (Jenni and Troy), Kathy Girgenti, Karen Norwood, Kristen Mann, Beez Beasley, Ed Wiesner, Robert Anthony, Katie Tognietti, the Kilcommins (Joey and Jennifer), Misty Gonzalez, Jim Bob Stuckey, the Bishops (Lori and Alan), Scott and Christy White, Kathy Adams, Charlyne White, Brian Varvel, Linda Garrett, Tracey Ross-Watmore, Paul Crandall, Ed Kampf, Zack Kampf, Bill Holt, Joel Matthews, Kem Sandifer, Gaye Lokey, Diane Morgenroth, Heath Hardin, Leroy Johnson, and Jeff Erwin.

I bet I forgot someone, so if I did, call me! I will set you up with a free book or mention you in the next novel. Unless of course you decide to duck your contributions, which may be smart.

Thank you to *Payback Jack, Politikill* and *39* publisher, Minna and Reagan Rothe of Black Rose Writing. Your partnership is invaluable.

Finally, thanks to Laura Hoffpauir and *The Best Little Bookclub in Texas*, Chris Kerth and the Happy Day Daiquiris' Book Club, and the Longwood Book Club (and hostess Jeanne Remik and coordinator Diane Morgenroth). Your encouragement meant so much.

Readers, let's be bros. You can follow me or reach out to me at timothygenesojka.com

Book clubs – Let me know if I can hang out with your crew one day.

Eight Days 'Til I Die

Tuesday, July 20, 1999, Chicago

I die in eight days, on my 39th birthday. I've known that fact for twenty-four years. Knowing changes things. Hell, it changes everything.

Before I step into the taxi, I turn to the apartment that served as my residence for eighteen months. Not a home, more domicile, stopover, way station—like each uncluttered, undecorated, barely unpacked one-bedroom for the last twenty years. A quick adieu, then I lower my head and fold myself into the back seat.

I pass the driver my destination scribbled on an envelope, a trick to circumvent conversation. I breathe in, embracing my chosen life—grass diamond gypsy, second-tier talent, baseball journeyman. Traded home, against my will, after decades away.

Why now, so close to the end?

The magnetic draw washes over me, so sensual. She beckons me home. Not Charla James or the sun-kissed beauties of my youth, but the Neches River. I feel her pull, the current appearing soft, playful on the surface, romancing the foolish. I grew up a child of her waters, cypress knees, and rope swings.

Swimming with Rooster, sunbathing with Braelyn Ryan, tanning near the riverbanks. Fishing for channel cats and blues.

I haven't seen her, the Neches, I mean, in two decades. Ah, the cool water she offers freely, the embrace of her sandbars, the beauty of her ever-changing banks, the dancing of fireflies at night. The peaceful death. Most of us survived her wicked enchantment…most.

I left her waters and never returned; my bewitchment tainted by unforgiveable memories.

Yesterday, against my will, edicts, and request, the Chicago White Sox traded me to the Houston Astros—a commodity, a product, a bargain-basement bat. Houston, not my childhood home, but just a short drive from the soaring pines and dark caramel-colored rivers of my hometown. Too close for avoidance and excuses that served me well in the past.

The Neches predicted my homecoming. She started sharing twisted memories via nightmares weeks ago.

Waking in hotel beds, traveling with the team, to images of the of Devil's Oak branded in my skull. Bolting up in unfamiliar beds. Wearing blue jeans to sleep every night…to this day, for the protection the denim offers. Awakening to the putrid smell of death engulfing my nostrils, even though I roomed alone.

The dark legacy somehow directed my return. The hanging man awaits me. He always has. Always will. "Not much longer," I whisper in the taxi's back seat.

"'Scuse me?" asked the driver, not turning. Two words telegraph his Chicago cadence.

"Nothing, talking to ghosts."

"Should I charge for the extra passenger?"

"Passengers," I stated.

Returning in my mind to the Old Place, I pictured Rose Petal, too ornery to die, rocking on her porch, venting at Uncle Two Bucks, waiting…for me.

When others speak of beauty, they refer to sunsets and ocean views. After witnessing dozens of beach sunsets, they offer nothing special to me. Only open water and an orange globe cliff-diving toward horizon.

With full authority, I promise, nothing rivals sitting, feet in the Neches, surrounded by dense forest, listening to mockingbirds' melodies and crickets' cadence. The distinctive smell of pine trees comforting your soul. The setting sun, painting margins between the trees, darkening shades of orange, pink, then purple. Purple promising the fireflies' arrival, fireflies surrendering to stars.

Despite my unwillingness to return to her, I admit the Neches' lure. She and her sister, the Piney Woods, the unbridled romances of my youth. Each sibling's charm enhanced by proximity to her counterpoint. Each with her secrets.

The Piney Woods dark, sprawling beauty, intertwined with fatal missteps. However, her secrets pale in comparison to her deadly sister. The Neches River's rushing water so intimately resembles the laughter of long-lost children. I hear their giggles now echoing through me.

Do you?

I'm not a researcher. Far from it, I'm a professional baseball player. One traded kicking, screaming to my hometown team. Still, because of my past, drownings fascinate me.

Before we start, I need to dispel a myth.

Ready?

Think of drowning. Close your eyes.

Tell me when you're done...I'll wait.

Embrace the image, make it real. Experience the swimmer's final lunge to the surface, then their inevitable surrender, their fingers the last thing seen before...

Take a moment, we're in no rush...

You thought of the ocean. Most do.

Fact: *Drowning*
1) The leading cause of injury death to young children;
2) Third leading cause of death for teenagers;
3) About one thousand children die from drowning every year;
4) Less than 4% of those children die in the ocean;
5) Over 80% of children drown in rivers, lakes, and ponds;

The waters surrounding my childhood home, Rose Petal's domain. These waters appear less dangerous than the ocean, a toxic misdirection, fooling generations of mothers and fathers.

The stories haunt childhoods. Of course, they do—classmates there one day and then gone. We all know stories of random tragedy.

Imagine...

The Pee-Wee Ponies, celebrating a first-place season, splashing in the seemingly innocent beauty of burnt-sugar brown river water, surrounded by crowding pines and knotty-kneed cypress, the king of river trees.

Travel with me into imagination. Teammates taunting, wrestling, giggling, splashing, slinging river bottom mud. Unconcerned parents talking—translate gossiping—about Friday's cakewalk fiasco or the deputy's wife's affair. Usually responsible adults, lulled by serene surroundings, pay token attention to their offspring. Guardians, senses dulled by alcohol, as generations before, who reveled on the same sandbar. Because things almost never happen.

Almost.

I spy the *one* perfect protector, the nurturer every child deserves. The mom who maybe holds too tight, okay, way too tight. She hawk-eyes her kid, hell, every kid, worrying about all, but especially hers.

The mother sews clever outfits for the first week of school, ensembles to ensure her son stands out. She assembles lunches, not thrown together at the last minute, but crafted. Homemade brownies wrapped in foil, BLTs constructed to maximize crispness (bacon gets soggy next to tomatoes, just saying). Others begin to hang out with her son, not because they like him, which they do...a little...but because they hope he trades lunch. He never swaps, but often shares.

Teachers station him front row in class photos, smaller than the other kids, but adorable, dressed to impress. Over time, the others adopt him. The worst player on every team, but no one cared because his mom stepped up as team mother, passing out homemade brittle before the first game. I taste the browned butter and sugar intermingled perfectly with pecans.

Can you?

The kid steps on the field occasionally, mostly because the twice divorced coach secretly crushes on the kid's mom.

Back on the sandbar, fathers gather grill-side. Mothers mingle on tailgates.

But not the nervous mom, the team mom.

She stands steadfast at river's edge, protecting her wards. But Red Face badgers the protector. My memory sees Red Face. Saw her my entire childhood, crimson of cheek and nose. I overhear Red Face, "Honey, boys'll be boys, nothin's gonna happen."

Most of the time, Red Face would be correct.

Most of the time.

Let's call the protective mother Molly. Don't know if her name is Molly, just like the name. Everyone likes her. I am positive her name's not Brandy because my mom never attended a Little League game in her life.

The drunken Red Face badgers. "Eat a hot dog, honey, relax."

Molly rotates a millisecond to wave Red Face away.

And he's gone.

Her boy, of course.

Claimed by the Neches.

Everyone searches the waters in horror. Shrieking women point from the bank. Dads, the bravest of them, diving through the killer current, testing her depths.

The small dead boy floats for days. Invisible, jerked to the muddy bottom, spirited away. Then Thursday, a search leader, Molly's mailman, finds the bloated corpse resting, wedged between cypress knees.

We read the stories in the *Silsbee Bee*, our local paper, repeated them, remembered them. We watched the local broadcast out of Beaumont. So, despite the river's romantic pull, I recognize the dangers of her awaiting waters. The perils of my trip home.

Before I return to evergreens, packed so tightly light battles to reach the pine straw-coated forest floor to the Neches River, Village Creek, and the folk of my youth, you need to decide if you want to ride shotgun, because not everyone survives the trip.

Leased Gulfstream /
Cruising at 42,300 Feet

914 Miles from Houston

Despite the beauty reclining across from me, I drift in and out of dreams. Eyelids heavy with sleep deprivation and abundance of bourbon, bat up and down to the jet's rhythm. Brief moments on the jet, smiling at the beautiful creature redlining a contract, then drifting into a Piney Woods dreamland.

No...not again...my eyelids drop...seconds too long.

Charcoal night surrounds me. Stars illuminate my hands in syrupy darkness. The night woods, usually bustling, offer only silence, tribute to death's presence. Arms burn from exertion. Then, the why offers herself to me. I— correction, we—started carrying it twenty minutes ago.

The dead body.

A voice a few feet ahead orders, "Grab his boots again or come up here and help me drag 'im."

"Ahhh," I mutter before jolting awake.

Not in the Piney Woods, but the sleek comfort of the most modern convenience, my agent's jet. Napping no longer occupies my agenda.

"Bad dream?" my cabin-mate asked.

"I wish."

"Excuse me?"

"Sorry, nothing."

"Doesn't seem like nothing."

I do not respond, choosing silence and a sip of bourbon. She waits momentarily, but I offer nothing. She nods accepting the subject's close, but opening another, not understanding the topic's interconnection.

"Dad tells me you're from the Houston area but had no desire to move back," said Elora Banks, concurrently crossing her tan legs.

"Correct," I answered, unsuccessfully ignoring distraction.

"Hate the Astros?"

"No, love 'em. Love Houston too. Just never desired to play baseball there."

"Well, that's a conundrum, Mr. Detals, since you're expected to be the starting shortstop at the Astrodome, for the home team...tomorrow."

"Yes." I surveyed the flight attendant, an attempt to look anywhere, anywhere, but my agent's daughter's legs. "Call me Tails. Everyone does."

"But your name's Stephen."

"Tails is fine."

"Okay, Tails, why don't you want to play in Houston?"

"Memories."

"Bad memories?"

"Great memories, bad memories, haunted memories. Everything."

"Haunted memories?"

"Long story."

"There's time, Stephen...sorry, Tails."

Raindrops pulled across the jet's stylish window, valiantly trying but invariably failing to keep hold. Lightning decorated the night sky, illuminating infantries of daunting clouds. I spent my adult life flying city to city, usually at night. Few phenomena rival torpedoing through a thunderstorm or prove more terrifying.

Few.

"So, Tails."

"Yes."

"I can move to another seat. Bet let's be honest with one another."

"Oh...ahh...okay."

"You like my legs."

Busted.

"Before today, you haven't seen me since I was eleven. You were eighteen or nineteen. Twenty years ago. I solved algebra equations at Dad's desk while you signed your first contract. Hell, I still wore pigtails. So, you're battling guilt. But I'm thirty now. Move past it."

Staying silent served me well.

"Still, based on our time together and your cursory glances in my general direction, you would rather look at my legs than not."

She did not need her freshly polished law degree to make that assessment.

"Tails, I like haunted houses, scary movies, goose bumps crawling across my skin. So, why don't you want to return to Texas?"

I pondered my options. I never told anyone. I listened to the tale, usually in pieces. No one ever shared the whole truth because no one dared cross Rose Petal Details.

She forbade the story's telling. My grandmother, not Grandma or Granny, always Grandmother, reminded no one of the delicate image her name invoked. With Rose Petal, you got the thorns, not the petals.

I collected the story—bits, drops, and dollops—overhearing a cashier inhaling Tiger Drive-In's Frito-Pie, listening to whispers from the next aisle, while buying *Fantastic Four* comics at O'Bannon's, or eavesdropping while sitting under the bleachers at a Little League game. Everyone knew the story, everyone but me. Over time, I ingested the story, details becoming as much a part of me as hair color, freckles, or my batting stance.

Pausing enough for her to be unsure if I still obsessed about her legs, I did, I decided *what the hell.*

"I, ah...never told anyone."

"Okay." Elora shrugged.

"I mean, everyone where I grew up knows. But I never..."

"How much longer until you get to it?"

"All right," I answered, perturbed.

"All right," she mocked, but I found myself entertained.

"I grew up in the Piney Woods, or Big Thicket, of Southeast Texas. Perfect for ghost stories. Soaring pines are packed so tightly, they allow mere strappings of light to force their way through. Thick air sits on you, viscous as motor oil, keeping you within its grip. The interplay of light and shadow, mimicking mockingbirds, crunching pine straw underfoot, cracks of fallen limbs hint someone or something's behind you, watching.

"If you brave the woods at night, discomfort often blooms into fear. Picture walking through pines and undergrowth, muted moonlight fights intermittently into your field of vision. Move, and the cracking and popping of each step follows. Or stand still, chirping frogs, caroling crickets, and hooting horned owls fill your ears. Each step sets off a cacophony of sounds while silencing others.

"That's my childhood landscape. Add family dynamic, and…"

"Scary?"

"One word for it. Anyhow, I grew up outside of Beaumont, a small town called Silsbee. So, ahh…Grandfather lived like a local celebrity at most, a beloved oddity at least. Still, over time, stories of his University of Texas football glory, World War II misadventures, gambling conquests, and his tumultuous marriage faded into the collective ether, recalled less and less by even the proudest local.

"Stories of his death never faded. Not even today. Campfire whispers, sleepover stories, and drunken discussions turn to Buddy Detals' death. Small towns embrace their ghost legacies. For instance, Saratoga, Texas, boasts Bragg Light Road."

"What?" she asked.

"Look it up, famous haunting. *National Geographic* published a photo proving the lights existed in the '70s. According to legend, a train crash decapitated a brakeman. Searchers located the body, not the head."

"Creepy."

"Legend goes, the brakeman carries a lantern searching for his head. I've been on Bragg Road late at night. Sometimes, you can spot the brakeman looking for his head or at least a floating light. There're all kinds of explanations, glowing swamp gas, distant headlights merging into one…"

"But the headless brakeman theory, much cooler."

"Much. Well, the Bragg Road Ghost Light belongs to Saratoga, Texas. But my hometown embraces its ghost. My grandfather, Buddy Detals, the Hanging Man."

"Hanging Man?"

"Yeah, so, October 31st, 1954, was Grandfather's 39th birthday."

"Your grandad was born on Halloween?"

"Yes."

"Nice start."

"Thanks, I thought you wanted to get to it."

"Sorry, yes, before you do, did you know him?"

"Only through stories. Larry was nineteen when Grandfather died."

"Larry?"

"Technically provided the sperm…"

"Your dad?"

"Your words, not mine." I ensured no further interruption. "The story goes, the day Grandfather died was perfect in every way, except of course for the fact that he hung himself. Grandfather was the picture of health, farm boy strong, rail-thin. Grandmother made an extra big breakfast for his 39th birthday. He ate three pancakes, four eggs, six strips of bacon, emptied two cups of coffee, and downed a glass of milk.

"As he stepped outside, heron shades of blue-gray only seen before sunrise colored the sky. Grandmother watched him stretch and yawn. She swore to the police she heard Buddy's back pop from inside the house. He stepped off the porch and headed to the field.

"Buddy talked to a neighbor at the fence line about noon. He, Grandmother, my Uncle Two Bucks, and Larry brought in the last of the crops weeks earlier."

"Did you just say your uncle's name is Two Bucks?"

"Yes."

"I'm going to need an explanation," said Elora, recrossing her legs.

I really need her to stop doing that. Taking a deep breath, I looked into her perplexing green eyes. As they did when I first met her years ago, her eyes telegraphed ever-ready intelligence. Her softly muscled body leaned toward me, giving the tale momentum.

"If I stop every time we come across interesting nicknames or quirky consequences, we'll never finish."

She stayed silent, waiting for answers.

"My grandmother…"

"Rose Petal…"

"Yes."

"Sorry, that's hilarious."

"Are we going to get to this or what?"

She nodded.

"Larry traveled, and Brandy…"

"Brandy, your mom?"

"If you must."

"There's a pattern emerging, huh?"

"Want me to continue?"

"You bet."

"Brandy showed no interest in motherhood. My grandmother and Uncle Two Bucks raised me. Rose Petal called my uncle Two Bucks because he was lazy. The story goes, she complained at the dinner table, if he had two bucks in his pocket, he wasn't willing to do a damn thing. If his pockets jingled enough to buy beer, flirt with girls, and light up, Uncle Two Bucks was content. So, where were we?"

"The crops were brought in."

"Larry drove home from UT when he could, but they didn't need him. Crops were in. Two Bucks slipped out early, headed for a bar outside town, avoiding Grandmother, a trick he mastered. Grandmother went to town for supplies. Grandfather surveyed the property that day alone.

"The melons and sweet corn, both bumper crops, sold the week before. My grandfather, wealthy, healthy, and 39, could step away, cash out. Rumors imply he itched to try something new.

"Grandmother loved running the farm. She saved every spare penny; they were both Depression kids. My grandparents weren't millionaires but reigned as small-town Rockefellers. Grandfather won the farm in a poker game."

Elora said, "Wait…"

"Before you ask, we'll cover that later."

She looked miffed but allowed me to continue.

"The farm equipment had been paid off. No debt. Buddy Detals was beloved. One son in college and another to work the farm. Grandmother loved the farm and negotiated with neighbors to buy more land.

"Minutes before sunset, as the blue sky surrendered to night, Buddy Detals walked to the only oak tree on our property, threw a rope over the strongest limb, tied the rope to the trunk. A red-and-rust tractor rested under the tree, died there decades before. No one ever hauled it off. Grandfather climbed the tractor, put the noose around his neck, spat in the Devil's eye, stepped off the tractor, and hung himself."

Leased Gulfstream /
Cruising at 42,300 Feet

Closer to Houston

"The old Case tractor's still there, what's left at least. It and the oak served as our cracked closet door at midnight, our entry into nightmares.

"I never played there, kept my distance. Hell, I spent my childhood working the farm, tossing a baseball, or sitting in the shade. Hard to oversell shade's value in Southeast Texas. But I never sat under that oak, not for a picnic, to court girls, to read a novel.

"Grandmother caught high school kids trying to spend the night there on a bet, or for bragging rights. Two Bucks busted a couple mid-stroke, if you know..." I stopped before completing the sentence. "I apologize. Sorry. Too much?"

"Little early in the relationship maybe..."

"Sorry." Did this elegant creature just mention the word *relationship*?

"Try skipping ahead a few beats." A wry smile pushed her right cheek upward.

Trouble. "Smart."

"Yes, smart."

Selecting a return-to-story as an infatuation defense, I continued. "Anyway, locals snapped Polaroids before we ran 'em off. For all the kids we caught, I can't imagine the kids we didn't. Pictures under the Devil's Oak—they called it that—became collector's items."

"Okay, you just mentioned the Devil's Oak. You said your grandfather spit in the Devil's eye."

"Legend is Grandfather made a deal with the Devil."

"Excuse me?"

"Yep. Deal with the Devil. In eighth grade, he was a skinny runt. Full head shorter than his classmates, awkward, stuttered. He wore Coke-bottle glasses and battled asthma. He played football but mostly got splinters in his ass from bench-warming. No one saw him that summer. Not unusual. He lived on a farm a few miles from town.

"He showed up his freshman year, no glasses, no breathing problem, a foot taller. Still skinny, but the team's strongest kid. Started on both sides of the ball, cornerback and tailback. Buddy led the league in yards, interceptions, and tackles his sophomore, junior, and senior year. In one summer, Buddy Detals went from geek to most sought-after boy in school.

"After high school, he played football at UT, big deal for a Texas boy. He won our farm playing poker, married the state's prettiest girl, according to locals, and ran the county's most profitable farm. The chatter didn't start immediately, but each Buddy Detals' success planted the seed of rumors."

"Nice setup."

"Thanks. Anyway, the gossipmongers decided someone with Buddy's luck must've made a deal with the Devil. Some small-dicked, superstitious shit-shoveler started the story, and it spread like mono at a kissing booth. When I was twelve, at a church camp marshmallow roast, north of Dallas, a *four-hour* drive from Silsbee, a camp leader told everyone a ghost story."

"No," she said.

"Yes, about a guy from Silsbee who sold his soul to Satan."

"Did you tell him?"

"No. Besides, I can list dozens of similar stories."

"Exaggerate much," Elora challenged.

"Challenge accepted. Okay, on my first road trips, right after I hit the big leagues, we played the Dodgers. Nat Guillory..."

"I remember him, competent backup infielder, from Texas too, right?"

"So, the Cardinals charged him with looking out for me. He grew up on Lake Livingston, an hour or so from Silsbee. Nat took me to a great Cuban sandwich shop. We enjoyed a perfect day. Bougainvillea decorated the outside of the shops. Smells of jasmine and smog intermingled, L.A.'s calling card. We sat minutes from Chavez Ravine. We couldn't be further from the Piney Woods. Nat knew nothing about my past. When I mentioned I grew up in Silsbee, he asked if I heard hanging man stories."

"I see why you're not dying to get home."

"That's not the reason."

"No?" asked Elora.

"No." Being honest, I admitted, few things offer intrigue more than a beautiful woman's interest. Even if her interest related to my family's warped past.

"Buddy's death seeped into Silsbee's collective conscience. He died in '54. As the Devil's Oak became part of lore, the stories bothered a local preacher. He gathered the heads of the local congregation. First, small-town churches seldom agreed on anything, except their unspoken desire to steal each other's parishioners. The preachers petitioned to cut down Devil's Oak. Grandmother argued the tree stood on private property, outside the pastor's purview. Locals pressured our family to no avail. But Rose Petal— and I am using her given name here for irony—fought back with her entire arsenal. Then it came to a head.

"One night our preacher and some deacons tried to chop the Devil's Oak down. Rose Petal ran 'em off with her shotgun. The story spread all at once. Sunday, frequent churchgoers arrived early to secure the best seats. Even the CME crowd showed."

"CME crowd?"

"Oh, I forget you're not from the South. Church members you only see on Christmas, Mother's Day, and Easter."

"Okay, funny."

"I remember the whispers and energy that morning. When service started, Grandmother sat on the front row glowering at Preacher Talemore. After church, life got interesting. A chunk of the congregation surrounded the preacher's truck. One deacon ran his hands across the tailgate. The preacher's tailgate and bumper looked like it had chicken pocks in reverse, peppered with tiny dings."

"Your grandmother shot the back of a preacher's truck?"

"Bingo."

"No one got killed?"

"If Rose Petal wanted them dead, they'd be dead."

I watched Elora engage her lawyer brain. "The preacher, the deacons, no one sued?"

"They were on private property. In the '60s, Grandmother gets off scot-free. The judge or jury would pin a medal on her for protecting her property."

"Wow."

"Yes, wow. There're still scars on the oak from the axe marks. Ugly, ragged, but the damned thing's still standing. That was '63. I remember because Oswald shot Kennedy that year. But, in Silsbee, even today, people talk about the damned oak more than Lee Harvey Oswald."

"You're kidding?"

"I'm not, because a year later, someone set the damn tree on fire."

"What?"

"Someone watched the house, I guess; no one knows for sure. Rose Petal stopped by the library, then shopped for a new dress at Birdwell's. Me and Rooster watched a movie at the Pine's Theatre."

"You have a friend named Rooster?"

"He was my best friend until... Charla James. I haven't talked to him in ten years."

"Over a girl...she must be special."

"Special's the wrong word for Charla James. Manipulative, gold-digging, and controlling fit better."

"Wow, lot of venom, Tails."

"You bet. Had a best friend. Then didn't. Had a girlfriend. Then didn't. It's more than that. I'm always on the road, so is Rooster..."

"On the road...?"

Watching her process proved more entertaining than staring at her legs.

"Baseball player?" she asked, knowing the answer.

"No."

Again processing. "But he's on the road a lot?"

"Yes." I enjoyed watching her search for the answer.

"Your best friend is Cole 'The Rooster' Brewster?"

"Or was, but yes."

"My old boyfriend's a fan. Rooster's from a small town, smaller than yours?"

"Yes, just north of Silsbee."

"What the hell? Don't bury that. Lead with it, Tails."

"I'll remember next time. Rooster's a big part of my life. But we haven't talked for ten years. So, I can't get VIP tickets or anything. Want me to finish or not?"

"You'll get back to the Rooster thing?"

"The flight's only so long, Elora."

"Dinner after the game tomorrow?"

I considered her proposal. First night in a new town, meeting new teammates, getting an apartment set up, all stood before me, weighing on me. So, of course I said, "Sure."

"Look, I'll hang around. Dad asked me to set you up anyway. I already leased an apartment for you, all utilities, etcetera. You rented your place furnished in Chicago. Dad said you live like a monk."

I remained quiet, not knowing how to respond.

"I'll furnish your place, equip the kitchen, pick out some art."

I stared at her, confused.

"It's what junior agents do."

"I'm not one of your dad's star clients. Never had a personal shopper."

"This one time you do. I'll just need your credit card."

I reached for my back pocket.

"Not this second, stupid. Our hotel's near the Astrodome. Give me your card after you check in."

"Sure."

"You'll stay at the hotel while I set you up. Your apartment will be fully functional before the Astros hit the road. Okay?"

"Sure."

"So, late dinner tomorrow night, you tell me about Rooster. For now, back to the story. Someone tried to burn down Devil's Oak."

"When Rooster and I left the movie, Silsbee's Volunteer Fire Department's siren greeted us. The baying resembled a World War II bombing siren. Still echoes in my head. That call is as much a part of childhood as baseball and chicken fried steak fingers."

"Was it scary?"

"In a way. But the alarm signaled help was on the way. I remember the sound as strangely reassuring. Most of my local heroes served as volunteer firefighters. Rooster and I wanted to bolt to the fire station from the theatre. We looked at each other. If either of us sprinted there, the other'd follow. The old station was blocks from where we stood, near the water tower and Silsbee's Little Theatre. We wanted to watch the red engines, sirens blaring, leave the station, manned by friends and neighbors.

"But a whupping awaited if we did not meet Rose Petal as promised. So instead of running to the fire station, as our bodies beckoned, we walked to meet Grandmother at Birdwell's, the local boutique. The tinkling shop bell greeted us as we entered a different type of fire. Rose Petal, back to us, roared at the saleswoman. She explained the dress could not possibly be a size seven because Grandmother wore a size seven, and the dress didn't fit.

"The shop owner stood, saying nothing. Disagreeing with Rose Petal remained the opposite of a survival tactic in Silsbee. After incessant berating, the shopkeeper agreed the dressmakers mislabeled the dress.

"I watched for entertainment value. Knowing the shop owner, hell, we knew every shopkeeper on the square. Still, Rooster and I understood an utterance would turn Rose Petal in our direction. We selected silence. Grandmother lost steam, selecting another Sunday dress, and we left. The excitement of the fire alarm forgotten, we piled into Grandmother's Chevy and headed home. We passed 418, where 5th Street became 92, when we spotted the smoke. Even miles from home, Grandmother knew—we all knew—the fire originated on our property. My eyes locked on the smoke tower. Grandmother drove the same pace she always drove, seemed calm, but uttered two words, 'Someone'll pay.'"

"Sorry to interrupt but that's three words, someone will pay." Elora seemed pleased to add comic relief.

I smiled. "Two words where I grew up." I waited for commentary. Seeing none on the horizon, I continued. "When we drove up, the fire truck idled in front of our home, nowhere near the former fire. Sixty yards of grass smoldered around Devil's Oak. Firemen stood inspecting the tree. From my seat I spotted the oak's blackened trunk. Pastor Talemore's now blackened axe scars appeared eerier. The oak's lower limbs took fire damage, but the damned tree looked invigorated by the test, more terrifying.

"We stepped out of the truck, as the fire chief explained, 'Old man Caine called. Said he saw smoke from your field near the Devil's...' Rose Petal glared. He corrected, 'near your oak. But when we got here, the fire already burned out. Arson, for sure, the guys smell gasoline. Not sure who set it or why it tapped out so quickly. Maybe a thunderstorm blew through. Damndest thing I ever saw, the Dev...the oak I mean, shoulda burnt, but it didn't.'

"News of the fire spread 'round town. Locals claimed no fire could burn the Devil's Oak, because a Devil's tool, like the oak, must be fireproof. Pastor Talemore went missing two weeks later."

"That's it?"

"Excuse me?"

"The preacher disappearing. Too far."

"Okay," I said.

"Okay."

"Didn't want to rehash this shit anyway."

Elora dissected me, looking for signs of misdirection or bullshit. The attendant delivered another Jim Beam and filled Elora's red wine.

I sipped my poison of choice, letting the vanilla caramel tones soothe my soul. I'm going home, like it or not. Going home.

She sipped her wine, looking over the glass at me. "You're not going to try to convince me?"

"I wasn't trying to convince you. You asked, I told you."

"I want to hear the rest."

"Why, if you don't believe me?"

"It's entertaining."

"My family misfortune amuses you?"

19

"Not what I meant."

"Okay, no more interruptions."

"Promise."

As if on cue, the pilot announced our approach into Houston.

"Hey, that wasn't me," said Elora.

"Ready for the big finish?"

"If you ever get to it."

"Okay, but you asked for it."

She laughed.

"I'm not sure who started, but I remember the first time."

"First time?"

"Yea, country kids got driven into town on Halloween. Two Bucks dropped us off on 7th Street near the old Catholic church. My bag was half-full of Sweet Tarts and M&M's, when I turned the corner and saw him. Someone created a full-size diorama. Fake tractor made of boxes, tree decorated with charcoal and chalk to mimic burning and scarring. My grandfather hanging from the tree."

Elora Banks got her wish. Goose bumps rippled across her arms and legs.

The Limousine

Houston, Texas; Minutes from the Hotel

"You mean in effigy?" Elora asked.

Houston landmarks passed through the tinted limousine window.

"I spent little time in Houston during childhood. My parents, Brandy and Larry, lived near River Oaks Country Club. Brandy played tennis at the club. Larry golfed on weekends. I visited sometimes, correction—seldom—okay, almost never.

"I tell people I'm from Houston because Brandy and Larry lived there. Also, people never heard of Silsbee, Texas. Beaumont, the closest town of any girth, represented the big city to me. If I saved my allowances, I got dropped at Parkdale Mall or watched a movie at the Gaylynn.

"Houston was Oz, otherworldly. As teens, Rooster's mom once dropped us at the Galleria, another time at Astroworld. Once Larry brought me and Rooster to an Oilers game. As an adult, I played ball in most US cities. Still, Houston touches me because the weather's so similar to Silsbee. Reminding me of rocking on Rose Petal's front porch, fireflies wafting lazily in the night air. Reading by yellow porch light. Swatting mosquitos. Recalling what Braelyn Ryan wore to school. Bullshitting with Two Bucks. The heat surrendering to its superior tormentor—humidity. The stickiness of your clothes, the line of sweat forming across your back, supergluing skin to shirt. Funny what you get used to, what becomes part of you. Toes touching the painted planks, guiding the porch swing back and forth. Creaking chains supporting my weight, complaining with each pass. The screen door cawing open and Rose Petal walking out, ending my evening. Pointing me bedward, my room with the view of the Devil's Oak. Not opening the curtains at night, never."

"You listening?" asked Elora.

"What?" I answer, now mentally back in the limo.

"On Halloween, when you trick-or-treated, the hanging man. It was an effigy, not the real thing of course."

"Just a stuffed scarecrow. First year, that's the only one I saw. Following year, I spotted three variations of the hanging man. The next year, a dozen. My grandfather, the hanging man, became Silsbee, Texas's, wraith, local nightmare, and legend wrapped into one."

"Sorry."

"Yeah, thanks."

"How far's your hometown from Houston?"

"Not far enough."

"More specific, please."

"Coupla hours. An hour and a half if you're haulin'. So, why'd my agent, your dad, do this to me? I never wanted to play here."

"How much *honesty* you up for, Tails?"

I winced before saying, "Release the Kracken."

"You're 38 years old, you turn 39 next week. Twice an all-star, but a decade ago. You're one of baseball's better contact hitters, but how many home runs did you hit last year?"

"Four," I answered, annoyed.

"Baseball used to be a station-to-station game. But you saw the commercial, 'Chicks dig the long ball.' Pitchers and home-run hitters demand premiums. You're an above-average shortstop, below par arm, you get by on craft. You steal ten or twelve bags most seasons. You haven't been caught stealing in four seasons. Gold star for you.

"You were the Cardinals' top shortstop project, then they traded you for Ozzie Smith. You received a World Series ring because you pinch-hit in '82. The Cardinals kept you around while Ozzie got settled to make sure he fit. He did. Boom, you're expendable. You've bounced around the league since then. You keep your mouth shut, work hard, and take the extra base.

Consistently a good player on bad teams, but you haven't been back to the playoffs since '82.

"You've finished second for the batting title four times. Three times you went into the final weeks leading the race, then collapsed. People think you're a soft finisher, afraid to win, inflicted with Number Two disease."

I asked, so I swallowed my medicine.

"You're 38. Teams don't grant no-trade clauses to aging journeymen. You pounded out a .278 batting average, with a .353 on-base percentage last year. Above league average, not exceptional."

"Seventh at shortstop, in both categories," I had to add.

"Sure, but not for a winning squad. People that matter don't think you're a winner."

"Shit." I ran both hands through my hair.

"Let's go deeper. Six glasses of bourbon on the flight, and two since we've been in the limo."

"I showed up on time, every time. Never missed practice."

"Sure, you showed up on time, smelling like stale booze but never late."

"That's not a crime."

She shook her head. "Never married, no kids or pets, never settle in...anywhere. Teammates like you, but you never try to lead. Some teams think you're bad news."

"Harsh."

"San Diego's blue chipper, Juan Pablo Tejas, their hottest prospect in decades, loved you. Followed you everywhere. Kid bounced out of baseball because of drinking problems at 25. The Padres blamed you."

"I took him for drinks but..."

"Look, Tails. The Astros play in the Astrodome. Power hitter's nightmare. A contact hitter's wet dream. They're in a tight playoff race with the Reds. The 'Stros don't need you to lead. They need you to get on base and stay off the sauce."

She paused, allowing me to understand my situation's gravity.

"The Astros move to their new stadium next year, a power hitter's park. I'd bet they cut you after the season. This is your chance, probably last chance, for another World Series run. Everyone, and I mean *everyone*, knows about your drinking. Most heard rumors."

"Rumors," I mumbled.

"Don't make me say it."

"I didn't try to kill myself."

"Okay, drink yourself to death, you pick the verbiage. Despite multiple missteps and an affinity for self-destruction, you possess a skillset the Astros need. Someone to get on first so their bats can bring you home. So, stop whining, collect your checks, and play a game most men would play for free."

I wanted—needed—another glass of bourbon. The carved crystal bottle in the limo's minibar taunted me. But I did not give her the satisfaction; she would not see me drink again, at least tonight.

The limo pulled up to the hotel. I exited the limo and slammed the door. The driver handed me my bag. I took Elora's bag too. Years of small-town upbringing disallowed my mood to override my gentlemanly training. A vested man standing behind the bar walked over to greet us. Bart, per his name tag, played the role of late-night bartender, front desk manager, and concierge. "Mr. Detals, I've been waiting for you. No need to check in."

Bart extended his hand and offered my room key.

I took my key and forced a smile. Trying not to telegraph my only want—get to my room's minibar and inhale the tiny bottles of booze. Drinking without judgment offered immense appeal.

Bart spoke before I turned. "Mr. Detals, management arranged a morning massage in your room to loosen you up. Details on the notepad on your desk. The hotel's limo will deliver you to the Dome tomorrow."

"Thanks."

Bart said nothing but presented a baseball and Bic. I obliged, signing the ball. Even exhausted, the joy the simple act gives a fan gives me a boost, and it gave me a boost now. Maybe even the desire *not* to empty every bottle in my minibar. Maybe.

Elora and I walked to the elevator, and despite her appeal, I longed to be alone. She stepped into the elevator, and we rode up together. I remembered to hand her my AMEX.

She got off on seven before the elevator closed and said without turning, "Meet at the lobby bar for dinner."

I watched her walk away, mindful most men would think of nothing else, but understanding a minibar battle awaited me when I reached the room. Unfortunately, or fortunately, I was wrong.

Seven Days 'Til I Die

Wednesday, July 21, 1999, The Astrodome
(Astros Trail 2-0 / Ninth Inning)

"*Striiike two*," the umpire howled. I turned as he popped two fingers skyward. Unhittable pitch, low and tight, but possibly grazing the strike zone's nether regions.

Not one damn thing tipped my way tonight or last night.

Last night, my hotel room minibar stood as empty as this umpire's soul. I walked down for a nightcap, and Bart, the very pleasant late-night bartender/front desk manager/concierge explained the person who arranged my room specifically requested no minibar. To pile onto my predicament, the stunning woman (Bart's words) I arrived with heavily tipped him not to serve me alcohol.

I considered hitting the streets and locating a drink(s) via my booze-dar. The bartender's forced smile, communicating his pity, propelled me back to my room. After an internal tantrum, I climbed into bed, admitting that showing up at the ballpark clearheaded seemed a solid concept.

I arrived at the Astrodome early for batting practice. Systematically spraying the ball everywhere, the Dome offered herself to me, a slap hitter's Shangri-La. The manager, Lonnie 'Butz' Butzkowski, showed up just after me. We played together in St. Louis, me a rookie, he a grumpy old backup catcher.

"Good to have you, Tails," he said.

"Good to be here, Butz."

"Haven't seen you in person in a while. You look much younger on TV."

"Thank you...or go to hell."

"Either works."

"Nice crew you got. Your first baseman can crush."

"Whew, can't he. He'd have twenty more RBIs with you batting in front of 'im."

"You sure know how to flatter a girl," I returned.

We caught up. His family moved to Los Angeles after the Dodgers promoted his oldest. Butz introduced me to his guys. Buncha' kids really, but a great young team. Likely these guys make a serious World Series run if they managed to slay the mighty Braves.

My first at-bat for the frigging team, I bounced into a double play. Then lined out sharply in the fourth and seventh innings. Liriano, our pitcher, tossed eight strong innings, surrendering two runs. Most nights, he would earn a chance for a win, not tonight. Diamondbacks pitching dominated with twelve strikeouts, no runs. Hell, no runners past first base. With their bullpen, hopelessness started an unwelcome pass through our dugout. With two outs in the ninth, I stood as the only obstacle between us and shut out.

So far, I offered exactly nothing to my team. Arizona brought in their cannonball kid to close out the ninth. He dismissed our first two batters on seven pitches. The kid brimmed with the confidence of a man sporting a 98- to 100-mph fastball.

Diamondbacks promoted Gallegos to closer last month. The league failed to decipher him to date. One thing for sure, the kid packed a flamethrower.

After blowing the two fastballs by, he tried to strike me out with a whiplash curveball that missed the strike zone. He threw another, missing by a mile, not tempting at all.

Lucky me. A sliver of hope. Gallegos didn't bring his curveball with him to the ballpark. The kid knew it; I knew it. Two balls, two strikes, no time for deep philosophical thoughts.

Gallegos could not control his curveball. I had no chance against his fastball. Stalemate. But I needed to help my team. With luck, I burn into

Gallegos' pitch count, waste this kid's pitches. Tire him out, piss him off, get on base somehow...anyhow. Give our next hitter a chance.

Gallegos proved hard to square up, but I fouled off the next three fastballs, knowing it was his only pitch. Next...curveball, missed by a mile. I noticed Gallegos paused slightly to re-grip the baseball in his glove. The pause telegraphed the curve. The Diamondbacks would pick up Gallegos' tell soon, train it out of him. But that offered no help to their stud tonight.

The count stood at three balls and two strikes. No one on base. Two outs. Gallegos bulleted four more fastballs. I fouled each offering. Not a challenge, when certain of the fastball's arrival.

Gallegos went to the well once more, fastball, inside corner, unhittable. I swung; my bat shattered. The baseball ricocheted bat to forearm to chin. I fell, but honestly felt tossed, to the turf.

Just a foul ball, wasted pitch. No glory, no trip to first. At least I was still alive, in the baseball sense. The count remained three balls and two strikes.

From a physical standpoint, pain is enhanced by lucidity. Yep, alive and hurting. Crimson gushed from my lip. I spit, tasting copper and iron in the blood now bathing my teeth. I rose to an elbow, grinning at Gallegos for effect. He looked unimpressed.

"Tails, you okay?" asked Carlson, the Diamondbacks' grizzled catcher.

"I'm roses."

The trainer and Butz raced out of the dugout. I attempted to wave them off, but they kept coming. "Tails, I'm going to..." started Butz.

"I got this," I said, standing, using my bat and Butz's body to balance.

"You can hardly stand up, Tails."

"Let's finish this." I spit blood to the outer edge of the batter's box. I winked at Gallegos. The Diamondbacks' ace glowered back.

"Looks like you're finished," said Butz.

"Got 'em right where I want 'em."

The trainer made me walk to prove I could. I surprised myself by pulling it off. After a full minute debate, the trainer and Butz headed to the dugout.

I did not tell anyone about my forearm turning purple under my long-sleeve T-shirt. Adrenaline may tote me through this at-bat, but pain promised hell to pay tomorrow. I swung the bat funkily a few times, hoping to hide the pain. I burnt another minute, dusting and adjusting myself before venturing back into the batter's box. Praying Gallegos spent time in his head, evaluating, overthinking.

I stepped to the plate and Gallegos fired. This time, his offering drifted center cut. I smacked the shit out of it. The ball bulleted toward the fence. A missile darted toward a fan's mitt. Slowly, painfully, the ball banana'd foul. A 360-foot foul ball. Crap. My lip ached, but the true problem presented itself. I could barely grip the bat without vomiting. Every fiber of my being engaged to let the pain focus but not control me.

Gallegos' hometown probably worshiped him like a god, setting the template for his arrogance. Six-foot-four-inches of muscle, testosterone, and hubris. Nature fitted Gallegos with Zeus' arm, nurture insured a spoiled man-child brain.

I just smacked his best pitch. Mostly because he missed his mark, but he might not know that. I watched as he wrestled doubt.

The Diamondbacks' catcher, Luke Carlson, long ago proved himself a steadying influence for young guns like Gallegos. But the pitcher shook off his batterymate. Stupid.

Gallegos looked spent. He wasted seven to 10 full-effort fastballs on me. Gallegos shook off Carlson again. I pictured Carlson's fingers begging for a fastball. Gallegos' curve did not concern me.

Carlson understood Gallegos' inability to deliver the curve over the plate, even if he walked it up in a stroller.

My brain was electrified with the onslaught of information. I stepped out of the batter's box, buying time. Gallegos shook off fastballs. No chance curveball returned to the mix. The kid wanted something new.

Earlier, I studied the Astros' scant scouting report on Gallegos. He had yet to develop a third pitch. I thumbed through my mental filing cabinet, opening the Diamondbacks' pitching philosophy folder. The D-backs liked guys born with big heaters. Then the pitching coach taught the change-up to throw off hitters.

The change-up's secret—pitchers use the same arm slot and motion as a fastball. The change-up releases slower and sports a funky movement. The kid wanted to test his change-up.

If I predicted the change-up and missed, the kid's fastball blew me away. Still, I bet change-up and pushed my chips to the middle. Gallegos sneered at me over his glove as I stepped into the batter's box. The kid's dark stare promised aggression, selling fastball. He wound up, uncurling all of his six-foot-four frame, telegraphing 100-mph heat.

A fastball meant the game's last out happened with the bat resting on my shoulder. A terrible look.

I felt foolish, but the ball tailed just slightly. Then the damn thing cratered, bouncing off home plate, past Carlson. Change-up. Ball four. I could walk to first, but the ball's trajectory coaxed me to sprint. My ears informed me the ball clanked off the backstop, promising a chance for second...if I hustled. The first base coach's arm windmilled as I rounded first and raced to second. I wanted to glance toward Carlson to see if he corralled the ball yet. But a glance toward home would cost time. Instead, I churned my legs and dove to the bag, beating Carlson's throw by a millisecond. My forearm screamed as I collided with the bag.

"Safe," shouted the second base ump.

I stood, dusting myself off with my left hand, my right now useless. I attempted to look cool but fought to control my agony. Gallegos turned, considering me with disgust. I winked again as he pounded his fist into his glove.

I owned this kid now. After Gallegos returned to the mound, I screwed with him. I took large leads, danced off second, and taunted him to try to pick me off. He tried...twice. I dove back safely both times, but each dive back took something from me.

Still, I wanted—needed—the kid to lose focus on the hitter.

The mind game between me and Gallegos allowed me time to process. If Gallegos re-gripped, boom...curveball. A curveball meant I steal third base. Our batter, Perkins, crushed fastballs. So, Carlson might call for Gallegos' weak-ass curve again.

Gallegos re-gripped. Curveballs take longer to get to home plate than fastballs. Also, curves drop or slice, pulling catchers out of throwing position. My chances of stealing third off Carlson and this rocket-armed pitcher were slim, on a fastball. On a telegraphed curveball, the odds shifted to my side.

Gallegos started his motion as I darted to third. Gallegos' wonky curve pulled Carlson glove-side. The catcher yanked the throw to third. I slid into the bag as the third baseman dove over me, failing to corral the off-target toss. I watched the ball dribble into left field before I stood and coasted home, scoring an unearned run. Astros trailed 2-1.

Perkins high-fived as I trotted by, and the dugout celebrated my return. Three pitches later, Perkins hammered a ball to the right-field corner and rounded second for a stand-up double. Our number four hitter, Jackson, jacked the first pitch to dead center. The ball screamed off his bat, but the Diamondbacks' greyhound centerfield tracked it down at the wall. Game over, we lose, pack up, head home.

However, we left the game with momentum, which means everything in a playoff run. Momentum I created.

After the game, Butz greeted me with a resounding butt smack. He put his hand on my shoulder, whispering, "Stay sober, Tails. We need you, asshole."

Sobriety, although problematic, presented the lesser of my concerns. My right arm hurt, likely broken. I considered cueing the trainer, but it was my first day with the Astros. Maybe tomorrow. MLB veterans know the system and understand how to game it.

To hide my pain, I showered one-handed, dressed quickly, and asked a relief pitcher to drop me at my hotel. Luckily, before the Astros' trainer or team doctor cornered me.

Once clear of the Astrodome, my thoughts turned to a beautiful woman. A woman eight or nine years younger than me. A woman waiting in the hotel lobby interested to see if I could grant Butz's wish.

The Hotel Lobby

Thirty Minutes Later

When I arrived at the hotel, a gray limousine idled outside. After a deep breath, I shook my head and trudged into the lobby. As expected, a beautiful woman awaited, unfortunately, the wrong one. Wrong in *sooo* many ways.

Even with one eye swollen shut, I recognized her. "Hello, Brandy."

"Would it kill you to call me Mother?"

"Not if you acted like one."

Studying the drama queen who called herself my mother when convenient, I admitted she lost a few physical tools. Still the fabled hostess of Houston high society, despite one embarrassing secret—her negative bank balance.

"Tails..."

"Brandy, I'm not giving you a fucking cent. Besides, I spent my money..."

"On whiskey, women, and wrong decisions."

"Thankfully, yes. But who the hell are you to rank decisions?"

"Son."

I spotted Elora seated in the bar. I decided to mute my voice, attempting to keep some secrets from my dinner companion.

"Stop it, just...stop. You burned through Larry's estate in ten years. He left you millions, Brandy," I said.

Angry, I continued. "Your dad left you his home in Austin, 40,000 acres, and three car dealerships. What the hell happened to those?"

She studied her stilettos.

"Spent too, you irresponsible..."

"Don't talk like that to your mother," she hissed in return.

"If you utter that word one more time, I'll call your country club crowd and inform them how broke you really are."

Her eyes reflected my hate.

"Your cronies angling for free tickets to ball games. Oh, and peach of a new boyfriend. He flew first class to Chicago, wearing a $5,000 suit to beg me for $10,000 so your condo wouldn't get foreclosed."

I started to walk away.

"Tails, you still have the trust, the trust your father set up," her voice elevated.

I motioned to quiet the conversation. "Not all of it's my money, and none of it's your money."

"Yes, but some of it is yours. You've never tapped into it, not once. It's worth millions. My lawyers will help you fix it, push the other beneficiaries out, make sure you get..."

"No, Brandy."

"Then my lawyer will crack the trust open without you. Larry was my husband. It's my money, not yours."

"My sweaty balls, you will. You've tried multiple times and failed. Not much of a threat. Oh, and thanks for your concern about my appearance. I'm fine, thanks for asking."

"Still a whiner."

I looked over Brandy's shoulder as Elora waved from the bar. I signaled one minute.

Brandy's bile bubbled over. "Who's that, one of your whores? I'll tell the tramp all about you."

"That's my agent's daughter. She knows more of my past than you do, Brandy."

"Want to bet on that? I got stories, Tails, stories that will..."

"Take your stories and pile-drive them up your rock-hard ass."

As I turned to escape, Brandy screamed, *"You'll pay for this!"* her decades-cultivated outer shell cracking to allow a glimpse of her true form.

"I have, Brandy, most of my life. Send me the bill."

"You can't afford it, Tails."

I passed the bar, as Bart mouthed *whew*. I shrugged; no other response leaped to my frontal lobe.

Elora stood awaiting my arrival, puzzlement decorating her face.

"Old girlfriend?" asks Elora on approach.

"Eww," I convulsed. "No, that's sick."

"Who, then?"

An explanation for the screaming foyer fiend seemed a reasonable request. Maybe after salad, I thought to myself. I weakly proposed, "Later, maybe?"

Elora's crossed arms and shifted hips offered her response. My guess, based on limited data, was this was Elora's "I want answers now" stance.

"That's Brandy," I said as a peace offering.

"Wow, that answer leads to a million more questions."

"Million, huh?"

"That's your mom?"

I nodded, or disgust nodded for me.

"Sorry for calling her that...Brandy, I mean...she looks great."

"Unbridled passion to fund plastic surgeons, trainers, and dieticians delivers amazing results," I answered.

"I overheard parts of the conversation, couldn't help it."

"Sorry."

"You have a trust fund?"

"My lawyer says so."

"I didn't suspect..."

"Good."

"I don't need your money, Tails; you know Dad, and he..."

"We rode here in his jet."

"Your money doesn't interest me. But *you* get more intriguing daily."

"Ahhh...thanks."

She downshifted from the "I want answers now" stance, relaxed, and motioned for us to sit.

"Epic at-bat in the ninth," Elora said. I tried to imagine all the games she attended with her dad. A sports agent's only offspring, her dad's sidekick. Intelligence deemed Elora intriguing, her form equally taunting. However, Elora Banks understood baseball. God completed a perfect package, then placed her in my periphery.

I harbored no faith she shared my interest.

She considered me, my swollen lip and blackened eye. I tried not to give her more to pity. My possible broken arm or gurgling stomach, for instance. Tasting your own blood curbs your appetite. None of my maladies mattered. Elora Banks merited my best effort.

"Thanks," I answered.

"You look like you survived a boxing match, not a baseball game. You okay?"

"Sure, I'm lovely," I lied. Exaggeration seemed the better part of valor.

She laughed. "The restaurant closed, but I tipped Bart. He'll have something for us to eat."

"Not much of a date," I answered.

"Never said it was a date."

I tried not to show my disappointment.

"Never said it wasn't either," she added.

Now, conversely, I tried to quell my excitement.

"FYI, Rooster's on one of the late-night shows."

"Just like Rooster, trying to steal my date."

"Or not dates," she said. "Anyhow, Bart, you met him last night, a few times, I believe." Elora considered me sadly.

"Yes," I confirmed. I battled mixed emotions. First, I appreciated Elora trying to limit my alcohol before my first day on a new team. I warmed, knowing someone cared enough to try. Also, her job as my agent's representative, to maximize my income, which in turn maximized her income.

But I "lone rangered" life for twenty years now. Having someone, even a beautiful someone, involved in my personal business annoyed me. I weighed emotions while she watched, seemingly understanding my battle.

She waited for my brain to re-engage before finishing. "Bart turned on the TV, so we can check out Rooster."

"Sure."

"If I remember correctly, you owe me a story."

Bart over-delivered, dropping two spinach salads, drizzled with hot bacon dressing, on our table. Next, he surprised us, or me at least, with warmed bread and Irish butter. When he asked for our drink order, Elora smiled and said, "Water."

The thought of alcohol passed over my busted lip, the searing pain squelched by a desire for my favorite sin. Elora's carefully selected words earlier influenced me as well. However, after she ordered water, her beseeching glance in my direction finalized the decision. "Water for me too."

I stared longingly at the amber-colored elixir at the bar. Each bottle backlit, an old bar owner's trick to make each bottle appear more appealing. An unnecessary endeavor. You could roll a bourbon bottle in pig shit, display it in a used toilet plunger collage, and I'd want it...need it...drink it.

Years of abuse dulled preferences. Some purists prefer bourbon, Irish whiskey, or scotch. Tennessee whiskey and Canadian whisky enchant others. I like them all, neat, on the rocks, with cola, in an old-fashioned. Two fingers deep, or three, or seven.

"Can you even eat? Your lip..." Her voice pulled me back to the present.

I berated myself. An enchantress, who may or may not hold a mild interest in me, sat in front of me, and my demons distracted my attention. "I don't know. I hope so. Even if I can't, I'll keep my promise."

I never felt Bart's presence or interruption...smooth. My mostly uneaten salad disappeared, replaced by a beautiful lasagna slice. I considered the tomato sauce's acidity and my split lip, opting instead for another cut of crusty bread.

"Before we discuss Rooster, tell me something—anything—about you."

"You know I'm Stanley's daughter. The first day we met, it was Bring Your Daughter to Work Day." She smiled. "The female staff buzzed about your arrival. They thought you were so handsome."

Did she think of me that way? Handsome. Hope made me forget my throbbing lip...and arm.

"Dad and I did everything together until I turned into a teen monster. We were buddies; baseball bored Mom. It's all Dad talked about. Most girls go to bed with stories of princesses and elves. Dad told tales of the Babe, Bobby Bonds, and Bob Gibson. Stories of perfect games, the mechanics of a perfect pick-off move. We spent a weekend comparing the greatest outfield arms of all time."

My raised eyebrows encouraged continuation.

"Roberto Clemente, no question."

"I'd argue Al Kaline."

"Sure, and you'd be wrong. Great arm, though. No one touched Clemente."

I stayed quiet, hoping for more.

"Then I hit my rebel stage. Terror, brat, spoiled, any word you wanted to wrap it in. I went to USC to be a screenwriter, a *screenwriter*. Do you get more stereotypical? But Mom and Dad supported me completely. I got credited on one small independent movie while still in school. When I graduated, I struggled, lived on friends' sofas, worked as a cocktail waitress, tended bar, and looked for writing assignments."

"You tended bar?"

"I loved tending bar. Wonderful place to find stories. Screenwriter's heaven."

"But..."

"Dad offered to pay my living expenses...if I got a law degree."

"Sneaky."

"Not really, I knew his endgame, and I railed against it."

"But..."

"But if I got my law degree, I could represent actors, screenwriters, and directors. At least I'd be in the industry. And agents sometimes transition to producers or even screenwriters. So, I went to law school. But out of defiance, rearview mirrored baseball. I hadn't attended a game in years. Even when Dad flew into town, I refused."

"Ouch."

"Yeah, terrible. Then, my law professor gave his Dodgers tickets to the cutest boy in class. Cute boy asked me to go with him."

How could he not? I thought. Attempting to keep her talking, I added, "Chavez Ravine to this day, my favorite place to play baseball."

"Perfect weather, Dodgers' Dogs, Dodgers played the Giants."

"Doesn't get better."

"Unbeknownst to me, my law professor represented the Dodgers for trademark infringement. So...great seats."

"And the cute boy?"

"Funny. I didn't tell him my history, or about Dad. Anyway, cute boy..."

"Forgot his name..."

"Yes, that seems important to you. Can I continue?"

I nodded.

"Cute boy tried to impress with his infinitesimal baseball knowledge. I stayed quiet, didn't keep a scorecard, didn't want to give away too much."

"But?"

"But Brenden Banes played left field for the Giants. Dad represented him. Brenden lived on Long Island during the off-season. Few blocks from my house. I attended private school with his son and babysat the Banes twins. Brenden spotted me in the stands and waved me down after the game. I fell right back into it. Brenden introduced me to his teammates, I got a few autographed baseballs."

"What happened to cute boy?"

"I don't know. Once he dropped me off, I forgot him. I dreamt of Yankee Stadium and scorecards. I remember Dad's pride when he told me Johnny Bench was the greatest catcher of all time and I disagreed."

"What? Bench was the best?"

"Bench won two MVPs. Roy Campanella won three and leads all catchers with a 57% caught stealing percentage."

Laughter overtook me. Debating a lawyer birthed into baseball, not the brightest move.

"I'm right." She waited for debate; raised hands signaled my surrender.

"So, dreams of Dad, smells of freshly cut grass, and the game's symmetry tugged me back. I attended eight games in the next few weeks, not because I had to; I wanted to. Going back to baseball became going home."

"And..."

"Since I graduated law school and loved baseball, who better to schlep for..."

"Than your dad," I finished. "All part of his evil plan."

"Likely." She smiled.

"Do you miss screenwriting?"

"I miss interesting storytelling, hence me buying your dinner."

"That's my cue."

Before I started, the TV's volume increased. I turned to the screen. There stood Rooster and the Curs, the rocking-est band in country music. Rooster revved his guitar and strutted the stage. More attitude than his cockiest barnyard namesake.

Not seeing him in years, in person at least, saddened me. Like Elora's Dodger Stadium visit refreshed her, watching Rooster's set spirited me. I marveled as Rooster reigned.

After the thunderous finish, his fans cheered, knowing what came next. Rooster handed his roadie Chicken Little, Rooster's signature guitar. He waited as the applause amped. At the apex, Rooster backflipped, his signature move.

"Did he just backflip in cowboy boots?" Elora asked.

"Show pony," I answered.

The host waved Rooster up for questions. Only five minutes left. Musical guests appear as late-night programming's finale.

Rooster offered a dramatic bow, then strutted toward his host as the director cut to commercial. Bart turned down the TV, proving his perfect touch as our waiter.

"Has Rooster always walked like that?"

"Like what?"

"Like a Barry White album's on repeat in his head?"

"Who's Barry White?"

"You don't know who Barry White is?"

"I'm a country boy."

"Dr. Love, the Prince of Pillow Talk."

I shrugged.

"A tip, Tails, if a girl plays a Barry White album after dinner, you got a shot."

"Wow, so Rooster…"

"Struts like he just had sex and is about to again."

"Hmm."

"Can't believe you don't know Barry White."

"Oh, I do."

"You asshole."

"I wanted you to explain it, in detail."

"Worth it?"

"Oh, hell, yes. But to answer your question, he's always walked that way."

No one had seen anything like Rooster before or since, despite dozens of imitators and emulators.

"No bullshit, he's your friend."

"No bullshit."

"How'd you two meet?"

"We didn't meet. We just were."

"What?"

"His mom, Larry, and Uncle Two Bucks played together as kids."

"Rooster's mom lived a mile away, but in another school district. Chic's family struggled because her dad…had allergic reactions to work."

"For Rose Petal's faults, and there were many, she treated Chic like one of her own."

"You're telling me Rooster's mom was named Chic?"

"She was small, is still I'd bet. A beauty too. Had the biggest crush on her."

"Your best friend's mom?"

"I was eight. Cut me a break. Anyhow, according to Two Bucks, Chic was so exotic and smart. Because she attended another school, she had mystery. Two Bucks and Larry snuck off with Chic anytime they finished chores.

"One day, Rose Petal asked Two Bucks to round up a crew to gather pumpkins. Most kids wanted no part of bringing in a crop. Only Chic showed up. Chic just started turning up and taking over chores. Over time she joined the family at lunch, then dinner, and finally breakfast. Rose Petal welcomed her.

"Chic saved her money from helping around the farm, never spent a penny. She attended a small college, paid her own way, worked at the farm in the summers. She graduated as an accountant. Rose Petal signed up as her first client. Because it was the early '60s, and Chic did not look accountant-ish..."

"Not a word."

I shrugged and continued, "She didn't pick up clients at first. Rose Petal recruited her first few, then Chic was off and running. She still works part-time at our farm too."

In the background, the TV volume increased. Elora and I turned our attention to the screen.

"Rooster, how are you?" asked the smooth host.

"I feel almost as good as I look, but not as good as I played. Hell, no one feels that good."

"Drenched in modesty tonight I see." The crowd laughed.

"As always. I'm so modest, you find the definition in Webster's Dictionary, boom, picture of me."

"So modest, they named the award for modesty after you."

"Exactly, and at the Modesty Awards Ceremony..."

"Of course, an awards ceremony for modesty is long overdue in Hollywood." The host rolls his eyes, and the crowd laughs.

Rooster paused, well trained not to step on laughs. "You're spitting the truth now. At the Modesty Awards Ceremony, the Lifetime Achievement Award for Modesty..."

"It would go to you," the host played along magically.

"Screw that, they'd name it after me. The Rooster Brewster Lifetime Achievement Award for..."

"Modesty," they pronounce in unison.

Hearing his voice, his banter, his cadence, soothed my soul. I wondered if he thought of me occasionally. Few days passed when I did not remember him and smile, despite our friendship's implosion.

"Rooster, we're short on time, tell us about your latest album."

"*The Rooster Crows at Night*, in stores now, boys and girls, buy it anywhere, and a couple for friends, give them away at weddings and quinceañeras ."

"Anything else, Rooster?"

"Shout out to my boy, Tails—Stephen Detals—just got traded to my Astros. Way to take one on the chin, brother. Miss ya, love ya, see ya soon."

Olive branch?

The host projects over the house band's exit music, "See you tomorrow night when our guest will be..." Bart turns off the TV.

I raise my eyebrows.

"Wow," she says. "Time to address your nickname. Tails, where did that come from?"

"Order dessert, we'll be here a while."

Dessert

How much to admit? How much to keep ferreted away? Opening memory's door for Elora seemed harmless.

After the Cardinals and Mariners, each successive team put a rider in my contract requiring therapy sessions to address my drinking. Most required I attend AA meetings.

Any team mandating Alcoholics Anonymous attendance possesses a poor understanding of the program. You must choose AA for yourself or you resent the person or organization that forces you to attend. All your emotional energy goes to resentment, not getting better.

In hundreds of mandated therapy sessions, I recount the recent past—breakups, benders, bar fights, and overnight jail stays. Despite psychologists, psychiatrists, and the counselor du jour's best efforts, the mental doors that led back to the Big Thicket, the Neches, and the Old Place stayed shut.

I never managed extended sobriety, but AA saved my life. Sponsors and AA brothers helped me cope. But no trips down memory lane made it into my first step disclosure, despite my sponsor's prodding. Honestly, the twelve-step climb would remain unfinished without facing that dark monster.

For the unindoctrinated, AA has twelve steps. I have never made it past number seven, humbly asking God to remove my shortcomings. My shortcoming: letting go of the hate, forgiving them, all of them, for their deeds.

Give them a free fucking pass...

Nope, can't cut that loose. Can't let the evil empress get away with her deed.

Screw her. Maybe they end up like…

Use my tools, use my tools, use my tools, use my tools.

One valid gift, even if you never complete the twelve steps, the AA mental tool belt. Tips to handle anger, your need to drink, to fight the bottle's…gravitation.

Closing my eyes, I called for those tools now. *Stay here*, I demanded. *Don't surrender the now. Remain present* with Elora and Bart. Breathe, *let anger go*, breathe. Inhale, exhale, and stay in this room. Breathe and stay with her.

I hyper-focused on Elora. She looked nothing like her father, Stanley. For the record, Elora bore no resemblance to her mother either. Asking Elora about the dissimilarity reeked impropriety at this stage of our relationship, or *not*-relationship.

Now just her, just here, hate's umbilical cord cut…for now. I pictured the hate floating into space.

Then Elora caught me staring.

"What?" she asked.

The realization hit. I already told Elora more about my past than anyone. She knew about Buddy Detals. None of my managers or teammates knew about Rose Petal, Two Bucks, Brandy, or the Devil's Oak.

I already opened the door, unwittingly, for my tablemate. Keeping it open, just a crack, felt easier. She peeked into the haunted house inside my head and stayed.

So far.

Elora only breeched the entryway so far. More to conquer. Could she survive it all? Could I? My life choices presented damning evidence of my chances.

Again, her voice stepped into my thoughts. "Well?" she prodded.

"Sorry. I should offer a disclaimer before I start."

"Not needed. Tails, most people's lives look normal. But we're all messed up inside. Anyway, I paid for dinner. You promised a story. You owe me."

"Okay, last chance to run away."

"I see the pattern. Your stories come with a warning label. I still want the five minutes back you wasted before you started your grandfather's story. Tails, you're moderately handsome, but I'm impatient."

"And?"

"And in the name of all that's holy about baseball, cut to it."

"Sorry, I overthink sometimes."

"Ya think?"

"Okay, fair, but when the warped contraption labeled my brain is right, it explains why, at 38, I'm still playing major league baseball. The bulk of guys that started with me got booted from baseball five or ten years ago."

"Still stalling." She held her watch face to me. "Tails, it's midnight. One more delay, just one, and I'm leaving."

A threat since I had zero desire to go to bed...without her, at least. *She's your agent's daughter, dumbass,* I repeated to myself three times.

"It starts with the banshee from the lobby. Brandy Detals."

"I love that name."

"Brandy knocked the luster off the name for me."

"What do you mean?"

"Most people don't know about brandy...the alcohol."

"Hmm," she mumbled.

"Most people think brandy is for cooking. It's distilled wine, so it's sweet."

"Distilled?"

"Makes it stronger, adds viscosity. The alcohol level of wine, 'bout 12%. The alcohol level of brandy is 30 to 60%, higher sometimes. You get drunk fast."

"I didn't know that."

"It's sweet and sneaky. Some brandies possess more punch than whiskey or vodka."

"Oh."

"According to booze buffs, brandy inflicts the worst hangovers. That's the woman who claims to be my mother. Looks elegant, like a nice glass of burgundy, but trashes you quicker and leads to skull-splitting headaches."

"Well played."

"Thanks."

She smiled, claiming another small piece of my heart. I comprehended this was not the first piece, recognizing that's how it happens. You fail to recognize when a woman captures the first piece of your heart, even the second. By the time your heart informs your brain, the chance to undo your predicament passed—the heart's plan all along.

"What's Brandy have to do with Rooster?"

"Everything. But let's step backward to Larry..."

"Your dad?"

"Hhhh." Air left my lungs in surrender. "You're consciously choosing to give me shit now."

"Correct."

"A little more parental than Brandy. Not much."

"Sorry, Tails."

"Larry was 23-ish. Working on his MBA. With my grandfather dead, Larry traveled home to help Two Bucks, Chic, and Grandmother with the farm. One weekend, Larry brought a woman home and announced her as his fiancée, Brandy Winthrop."

"I'm not a Texas history buff, but there's a political dynasty with that last name."

"Charming."

"Texas beauty queen, tall, long, like you. She swam at the University of Texas, alternate for the Olympics her junior year in backstroke. Larry played linebacker at UT, graduated summa cum laude. UT gave him a full-ride scholarship for his MBA. He possessed his father's looks and penchant for luck. Until he met Brandy, then his luck ran out."

"Harsh."

"And true. Brandy could've married any man—let me restate that, *ruined* any unsuspecting fool's life. She picked Larry."

"Brandy got pregnant; Larry married her in an old-fashioned shotgun wedding. You add the Winthrop political firepower, and 'shotgun' may be understating. After my parents got married, Rose Petal noticed Chic's baby bump."

"Who was the father?"

"Two Bucks is the likely candidate. Chic could pick any man in town. Single, married, clergy, you name it. Two Bucks swore every time she went walking through the square, a fender bender ensued. But she stayed single."

"Grandmother treated Chic like a queen, took care of her, never asked Chic who fathered Rooster. Chic and Rose Petal, those women are more mother and daughter than anything. They keep each other's secrets."

"What did Rose Petal think of Brandy?"

"Not much. Brandy grew up Texas royalty, with housekeepers, limo drivers, and estates. God granted her beauty, guile, and intelligence, but not one drop of work ethic or motherly instinct. Chic and Brandy, both beautiful but opposite as grease and glue.

"One thing in common though, Rooster and I, born the same day. Hours apart. Me, born in the finest facility Winthrop money could pay for. Rooster born at the Old Place, with Rose Petal serving as midwife. The Old Place—that's what everyone called our home. Really, it's as much Rooster's home as mine. After Rooster's birth, Rose Petal...persuaded...a banker to give Chic a mortgage. Chic moved out of her parents' home and into a small one-bedroom cottage. We lived north of Silsbee on FM 92, Chic and Rooster lived south of Fred."

"Wait, Rooster's town's named Fred?"

"You bet," I said and smiled, reminding myself of Elora's limited Texas indoctrination.

"Bizarre name."

"Not by Texas standards, I can top it. Kermit, Texas."

"Like the frog?"

"Sure, but I can do better. Cut and Shoot, Jot-Em-Down, Gun Barrel City, Ding Dong, Muleshoe."

"Okay, point made," she said, chuckling.

"So, Chic and Rooster lived south of Fred, so Rooster and I only had the bottoms between us."

"The bottoms?"

"The Neches River bottoms. Like a swamp, but not really. Lowlands that fill when the Neches overflow. Dangerous in ways. I did a report on it in high school, it's called a baygall. World's largest. But Rooster and I created a path to each other's home. We littered the trail with forts, tree houses, landmarks, and hideouts. Night or day, fog or clear, we could find each other."

"Alligators?" Elora asked.

"Sure, snapping turtles, foxes, rattlers, raccoons, nutria, water moccasins, etcetera. But I'm off topic. I lived in Silsbee with my grandmother. When Chic came over, Rooster tagged along. If she didn't, Rooster and I would meet up near the Neches. Except for the farm, which someone cleared before Grandfather won the place, we were surrounded by ponds, swimming holes, woods, wildlife, and rivers."

"Sounds magical and ominous."

"Both..."

Then I heard words pour from my mouth. Despite my tools, I surrendered to the sisters' pull, the Neches and the Piney Woods calling me back to the Old Place...

The rows of corn swayed. I stood, still at first, eyes searching fruitlessly, sight lines blocked by seven-foot sprouted green and yellow tops, feeling lost. Surrendering trust to my feet, I allowed them to guide me forward. The Devil's Oak twisted into view, at once welcoming me and daring me to swallow my scream. Then the Old Place appeared, and the Oak lost all menace.

I weighed in my head if my proximity to home comforted me, removing my fear. Then, understanding washed over me. The Devil's Oak failed to match the horror inside that home.

The Old Place sat on cinderblocks, lilting to the west. Rose Petal, the wealthiest farmer in the county, prided herself on living without most modern conveniences. Upgrading her home, surrendering to the present as foreign to her as soccer to an East Texas kid like me. The Old Place's residents spent more time maintaining the crops than our home, and the neglect showed. Faded, chipped white paint conceded to grayed wood underneath. Two wall AC units jammed into windows cooled most of the home. A few rooms stayed dank year-round.

I yielded to the pull. The wraparound porch remains the home's best feature, emblazoned by yellow light, to keep away bugs. Rocking chairs seesawed in the rhythm of my approach. The porch swing matched the chair's rhythm, despite the lack of an occupant. I looked to the left. Darkness coated the windows of Two Bucks' room, probably barhopping outside the city limits.

My head whips back to the porch and I hear the creaking screen door opening. This will sound like bullcrap, but the creak sounds different when she opens it.

Rose Petal Detals steps into the threshold, in all her glory.

She waited up for me.

The matriarch of my past gave way to the beauty in my present.

"Sounds creepy," Elora said, breaking my trance.

Still in the Hotel Bar

Childhood trauma causes fracturing or splits a person. Not necessarily full-throttle multiple personalities, like *The Three Faces of Eve*. Still, often one personality develops to protect another. "Protector" personalities rise to hide the true self's fear.

Protector personalities vary, from dominant over-the top manliness to comedian, to avoider. The form protectors assume is unpredictable. For me, perfection volunteered as my protector. Not in school, mostly in physical activity. Motion gained importance, finding the proper form to chop wood, an efficient process to load hay bales. I obsessed with smoothly fielding grounders, perfecting my throwing motion, owning the purest swing. Perfection protected me from questions, questions my true self remained ill-equipped to answer.

Another side effect of fracturing, maybe not for everyone, but for me—blackouts. Forgetting whole dayparts or mere moments.

Realizing my brain logged no register of the last few minutes, I grappled with which mental wounds laid exposed, bleeding, in front of my agent's daughter.

"Creepy," I repeated before steering the conversation toward my favorite person. "But I...ahhh...promised a Rooster story. We played pitch together every day."

"You mean catch?"

"Call it what you want, I call it what I want. Most days we tossed the ball, fielded grounders, shagged pop-ups. Occasionally, we recruited kids, which took work in the country, to play makeshift games. Me and Rooster raced, climbed trees, explored trails. Everything together. Rooster named me Tails because I always seemed a step behind, tailing him."

"You're a professional athlete, I doubt you lost often."

"I'm a professional athlete because I lost. I pushed to beat Rooster at everything. We attended different high schools because technically he lived in another city. But we competed in every way possible. Ready for your story?"

"I'm still here," she answered.

Traveling in my mind proved dangerous. I pictured my brain as filing cabinets. Doors slid open, accessing the relevant memories as needed. Cabinet upon cabinet crammed with baseball factoids, player preferences, and field layouts. Rooster occupied multiple memory filing cabinets himself.

Opening one drawer of Rooster memories seemed safe.

For my sanity, other drawers remained locked, keys hidden from all but the architects of my nightmares. Somehow, Elora unlocked the "hanging man" drawer, a locked drawer before yesterday. Rose Petal, like Rooster, took up multiple cabinets. Unlike Rooster's files, Rose Petal's cabinets remained locked, hidden, drawers wedged against the back wall, chain wrapped, covered by dusty blankets, surrounded by mental rat traps to injure anyone who dared approach.

I shook off Rose Petal and returned to Rooster.

"So, like I said, Rooster and I competed at everything. He patrolled center field. I can still see him there, hat barely hanging on his head. Great instincts, read the ball off the bat instantly. He caught every fly ball and most line drives. Cannon for an arm. Runners didn't dare take an extra base on him, ever. Our best pitcher, base runner, batter."

"Did you give him the nickname?"

"I wish I could take credit..." But credit belonged to someone else. "Chic hated her nickname, but she could not escape it, especially in a small town. When she got riled, which was seldom, she resembled a baby chick.

"To avoid her son having a backwoods nickname, she researched endlessly. Remember, Chic got an accounting degree. She read every baby book in the library and selected the name Cole. Very uncommon name at the time, especially in small-town Texas. In her mind, nickname proof. But circumstances laid her plans to waste.

"Cole Michael Brewster burst into this world, at sunup, screaming at the top of his lungs. The Old Place's roosters crowed, announcing the rising sun and the birth of a son. Cole Michael Brewster out cock-a-doodle-dooed 'em all, drowning out the roosters, a tough task. Rose Petal said offhandedly, 'Chic, that's quite a little rooster you launched into the world at the crack'a dawn.' So, Rooster stuck. Nothing Chic could do. Two Bucks ran with it. Name got a life of its own. Cole Michael Brewster strutted like a rooster, stood cocksure like a rooster, and over time had his run of the hens.

"I play professional baseball and live around alpha males, met no one more confident than Rooster. Not even a close second. Chic loved him with everything she had, and that one woman understood how to love a son. Rooster's day rose and set with Chic. Uncle Two Bucks, despite his faults, stood in as father figure for Rooster. Cole Michael Brewster never doubted his place in the world."

But you did, you do, you always have, my inner dialogue added. *Stay clear of the Old Place*, I reminded myself. *For God's sake, stay clear.*

I spun the roulette wheel of Rooster memories, sorting each by appropriateness and my mental stability. Elora's smile encouraged me. Her love for baseball selected the story for me.

"Rooster and I were about twelve. We played for the Little League Giants, dressed in orange, top to bottom. I usually played shortstop and Rooster patrolled center field, but we both pitched when needed.

"The previous Friday night I took the mound. Our team rocked that night. We put up five first-inning runs. By the time I stood on the mound, I was pretty relaxed. The other team hit a few balls hard, but right at Rooster. Grounders seemed to jump into infielders' gloves. I struck out a few but issued no walks. Nothing special. I just kept grooving the ball to the catcher. No better or worse than other nights I pitched. Our team sweetheart that year, Braelyn Ryan, stopped by."

"The way you say her name, she must be something."

"Yeah." I paused, taking a moment to refocus my thoughts. "Jealous."

"You'd like that," she said.

I continued, ignoring her response. "Anyway, kids lose track of the game. I remember the tactile stuff, pink cotton candy fingerprint stains on baseballs, the taste of cherry Fun-Dip. The feel of the raked infield and the smell of grass clippings. But I remember little about that game.

"I wouldn't have known anything special happened, but after the last pitch, the coach slapped my back and said I just threw a perfect game. The *Silsbee Bee* ran a feature on the game. I heard about no-hitters but never a perfect game. Two Bucks explained it to Rooster and me. No hits, no walks, no errors, nothing.

"Yeah, Chic read the article around the dinner table. Rooster seemed especially interested. The following game, the coach slotted Rooster to pitch. When Rooster warmed up, the ball sizzled out of his hand. The catcher's glove popped each throw. After the first five throws, the catcher waved off Rooster and ran to the dugout, shaking his gloved hand. Seconds later, Coach hollered to Henry's mom. She just had a baby. I heard the word 'diaper', but assumed I heard wrong. Sure enough, Henry's mom brought a diaper and handed it to the coach. Coach took out his pocketknife, carved the diaper, and stuffed it in our catchers' glove for extra padding."

"Holy crap," Elora said.

"Exactly," I said and flowed back into the story. "No catcher needed extra padding for me. I walk to the mound to chat up Rooster, manage any nerves. Rooster says, 'You will not be the only one with a perfect game, Tails.' I tell him that was luck. 'No luck needed tonight, Tails,' he replied.

"The first batter came up for the Little League Rangers. Rooster fired a fastball three inches from the batter's nose. The kid crumpled to the ground. The kid got up, dusted himself off, shaking like a hula girl on vibrate. Rooster rocketed three strikes. The bat never left the kid's shoulders."

"Poor kid."

"That's nothing. The next kid came up and Rooster hummed a fastball behind 'im. Ball clanked into the fence with authority. The umpire gave Rooster the stink eye, no warning, just a look. Again, three fastballs, three strikes. The batter hound-dogged to the dugout, head hanging.

"Rooster hit his growth spurt a little ahead of most. He struck out the last kid to finish the first inning. Rooster threw eleven pitches in the first inning, the two wild pitches, nine strikes.

"The Rangers remained shaken. Rooster struck out every batter the first four innings, each batter returning to the dugout looking like their dog died. In the fifth inning, the first batter dribbled a ball to me, and I gunned him out. Rooster struck out the next kid. The inning's last batter popped up to our catcher.

"Rooster strutted to the dugout. He called a perfect game, and through five innings, his prediction proved correct. Even though I pitched a perfect game, our two outings possessed little common ground. My performance relied on luck and happenstance. Rooster dominated. Next inning, Rooster blew away the first two batters. We had only scored three runs, so the game looked close, 3-0.

"Let's back up, Little League's different. When it's right, it's more about building character than winning. Like all sports, they get it right mostly and blow it sometimes. Usually, kids' dads end up umpiring, an essential but flawed formula. The Rangers' last hope jittered in the batter's box. His dad umpired first but also encouraged the kid to swing away.

"Rooster blew a fastball over the plate, and the batter made weak contact. The ball dribbled to me, but I snatched it and gunned the batter out by a step and a half. Out, perfect game, Rooster a prophet."

"But that's not what happened," Elora said.

"Batter's dad, first base umpire, called his kid safe."

"No."

"Rooster crowed to the heavens. The umpire tossed our coach for calling the first base umpire something that rhymes with rock chucker."

Elora giggled. "Not okay."

"Our assistant coach gets tossed next for a tangent that made our coach's rant seem like an after-school special."

"Oh."

"Hindsight, I get it. The first base umpire thought he did something special for his son. Teaching a terrible lesson in my opinion, but I get it. Rangers didn't have an ounce of hope all night. The first base umpire/dad felt sorry for them. He wanted them to have a small win and give his son a moment."

"The dad screwed a perfect game. I'm on Rooster's side."

"Agreed."

"This story's about to go sideways."

"Correct. Let me set this up. Two Bucks sat in the stands, alternately hiding and sipping his hooch. I still see him, stupid drunk smile on his face, cowboy hat pulled down to hide bloodshot eyes. But not missing a minute of the game. Our assistant coach called Two Bucks in from the bleachers to coach. I still remember Two Bucks tucking his flask in his boot.

"He lumbered to the mound, swaying to the right. I cohabitated the mound with Rooster, who glared at the first base umpire. Two Bucks' smile lit a room, usually a barroom, but in this case a baseball diamond. Two Bucks slurred. Pissed Rooster."

"Yeah."

"Pissed enough to risk missing a couple of games."

"Yep. Two Bucks waved over our first baseman. Thick kid, don't remember his name. Two Bucks slurs, 'Don't cover the bag, kid.' He protests, 'But there's a runner on...' My uncle tells him to let the runner take a big ole lead. Two Bucks nods to Rooster. Rooster nodded in return. I remained in the dark, but Two Bucks and Rooster were tuned.

"Next, the runner at first takes a huge lead, because our first baseman ain't covering the bag. The runner smiled like he deserved his spot. Kid did nothing wrong, his father, however..."

"Shit."

"Yeah, the kid's smile pushed Rooster more. He looked to first. The runner retreated to the bag. With no first baseman covering, the runner danced farther off. Rooster spins and hums a pickoff move to first base. Hardest ball he threw all night."

"But there was no first baseman."

"Nope."

"Then...oh." Realization washed over her face.

"Rooster launched his hottest throw at the first base ump. Belly high. The ump couldn't duck, or the fastball bounces off his noggin. The dumbass jumped the fastball. Too slow."

"I see how this ends."

"Rooster's fastball delivers a testicle tattoo, laces included at no extra cost."

"Ow."

"First base ump collapses, writhing in pain. Other dads rush to him. The home plate umpire bolts toward Rooster to toss 'im from the game. But Two Bucks beat him to the mound. Before the ump tosses Rooster, Two Bucks stepped between. Two Buck belts, 'What's our pitcher supposed to do? Their runner took a lead, Rooster tried to pick him off.' My uncle tossed his hands in the air, in fake/full denial. 'No one was covering the bag,' the home plate ump argued. 'Our pitcher didn't know,' Two Bucks lied. 'How's my pitcher supposed to know, Dan? Kid pitched his heart out.' The home plate umpire looked at Two Bucks, looked at me, and finally considered Rooster. He knew, absolutely knew, Two Bucks was lying, but couldn't prove it.

"I watched other dads shepherd the former first-base umpire off the field. Once he cleared the fence, the cheating son of a bitch dropped to his knees and hurled. A minute later, another dad stepped in to take the cheater's place. The new first base umpire's hands dangle in front of his...ahh...family jewels, protecting them. The home plate umpire started back to the plate, when Two Bucks added his two cents, 'Just a mistake, Dan. Like that call at first.' The home plate umpire turned back as Two Bucks laughed. 'Ain't karma a bitch.'

"Two Bucks winked right at the umpire, seconds before the umpire tossed him and Rooster. On the drive home, Two Bucks spouted, 'Rooster, you showed that man religion.'"

"I don't understand," said Elora.

"Nothing like a fastball to the nutsack to inspire a man call to God."

Elora's head flopped back as she laughed. My first time experiencing her full laugh, and I hoped not my last. It was all-encompassing, everything. I can't explain it any other way.

"We're just getting to know each other, I apologize."

"Worth a nutsack reference for your most colorful baseball story?"

"Not even close to my most colorful baseball story."

"How could that be?"

"There were no dead bodies," stumbled out of my mouth before I caught it. Someone, or something, pulled open a long-ago locked drawer. A drawer in one of my brain's most dangerous filing cabinets.

"Excuse me?" she blurted.

Six Days 'Til I Die

Friday, July 23, 1999, The Astrodome
I showed up to the Astrodome resembling a battered raccoon. Darkened eyes, swollen lip, both from the ball that ricocheted off my face yesterday. Thankfully, Butz benched me. My long-sleeve T-shirt hid my mangled arm, an arm featuring battling shades of purple, blue, and black.

The facts presented themselves:
1) my season ended yesterday...absolutely;
2) my tenure as the Astros' shortstop in question...probably.

Both facts paled to the grand finale. The big question: was my baseball career over?

None of that matters because my 39th birthday approached. A birthday my grandfather and father failed to survive.

One more day, hanging with the boys of summer, seemed a fair request. Or by some miracle, I could fight through the injury and add value.

As a big-league veteran, I knew the tweaks in the system. Using Butz benching to take a day off, I begged off infield drills and skipped the batting cage. My participation in either activity telegraphed the inevitable. I could not currently and may never play baseball again. Using every veteran trick in my arsenal, I dodged, misled, and lied to the trainers, waving off their efforts to see my injury. "No big deal, take care of Kominski, he's hurting, I'll be ready tomorrow, I'd tell you if something was wrong, looked worse than it is."

When Butz strolled by, I bluffed.

"Look, Butz, I can play." He posted the lineup card already, so my lie seemed safe.

"No one wants that face on the field," Butz joked. I longed for the game, the game I took for granted too often. I mistreated my body, taking my talent for granted.

Cruelly, the game moved on. Sitting on the bench, tears trickled down my cheek. I played baseball my entire conscious life. You seldom cherish something more than the moment circumstances jerk your beloved away. Looking to my right and left, I ensured no one shared my moment. A tear while sitting on the bench may prove difficult to explain.

No more spring training, drinking beers with the boys, coaching the rookie to spot a pitcher's tics and tells. No more kids waiting for autographs, bullshit sessions about the perfect swing.

No need for an agent, for Elora.

As batting practice continued, that thought hit me hard.

But maybe...

I tried to grip a baseball; pain shot through me. Gripping a ball was an important skill if you planned to play professional baseball.

During batting practice and warmups, my new teammates, soon-to-be former teammates, slapped my back. Most said, "Great at-bat." One rookie said three words, "Huge balls, dude."

Once the game started, I crept to the bat rack. I removed a bat with my left arm, the one not screaming in pain. I turned away, making sure no players witnessed my test run. Then I gripped the bat with my right hand. Pain whispered to me, remained tolerable, but explained the idiocy of my action.

I swung the bat gingerly. A scream formed in my throat and remained there, swaddled by my secret need for one more day in the sun. Pain's whisper roared to berserker's rage. My stomach gurgled.

Lunch threatened departure. Involuntarily, I pictured the vomit gurgling in my stomach. Light-headedness attacked next, and I swayed back, then forth.

The sound of a bat, the bat I formerly held, ricocheting off the concrete dugout floor brought me back, focused me. A few teammates turned my way. I waved them off, then returned the bat to the rack left-handed.

I spent the first few innings brooding. Resentment built, anger, then sadness. In the sixth inning, I demanded myself to enjoy my seat. The best seat in the house. Most men never experience the joy of watching major league baseball from the dugout. Embracing the game's beauty pierced the anger.

Last night, my face and arm throbbed, but the extent of the damage remained unsure. The adrenaline or newness of the injury masked oncoming problems.

I awoke understanding the ramification. Refocusing on my last conversation with Elora offered relief.

After Rooster's ball-to-testicle tale, and my slip, Elora pressed for more, but Bart announced he clocked out forty-five minutes prior.

Elora signed the bill, and we met again in the elevator. She inspected me, analyzing my words, deciding if I chronicled true events or shoveled shit. "I want to hear the rest."

"You can come to my room," I offered.

"Bad idea, I think."

"Depends on your point of view."

"Let's add clarity. Not in a million years!"

"Give me that kinda time, I'm thinking I gotta chance," I answered.

"You don't. But..."

"Hoping for a but..."

"I'm staying in town to finish your apartment's décor. Make you an official Houston resident. Let's meet again tomorrow night."

"Look..." I started.

Her hand rested on her hips, a posture comical and fetching. "Tails, I'm in town for you, getting your life set up, at least you can keep me entertained."

My brain calculated all the reasons to say no. This beautiful woman was my agent's daughter. She worked on his staff. I felt myself falling hard. My track record in that department not stellar. I failed dozens of times at anything resembling real relationship. Elora lived in New York. I now lived in Houston. The Astros needed my best effort; Elora, although alluring, qualified as distraction. My brain manufactured multiple reasons for rejecting her offer, but my mouth said, "Sure."

The Padres led early, but we dropped four on the board in the eighth inning. The Astros bested the boys from San Diego 7–4. After the game wrapped, I appreciated every moment, smiled, and joked in the clubhouse.

I considered the clubhouse upon my departure, embraced the smell of sweaty men, mint soap, and Icy Hot. My eyes drifted around the room for the last time. A man leaving his life's greatest love affair. Nevermore. I sighed.

Surprisingly, the night's next engagement presented a welcome distraction.

For the third consecutive evening, this battered, bruised, baseball vagabond would converse with a woman out of my league. Allowing a moment to adjust physically and mentally seemed important.

Southeast Texans spend their life scrambling from air-conditioned vehicles to air-conditioned domiciles. The action's frequency automates mental and bodily acceptance of the function. Sweat beads form on even the most physically fit specimens in Houston's heat and humidity.

Pay attention and you will witness burly men transition from dry to sweat-lathered within moments of stepping outside in May, June, July, or especially August.

My childhood was spent living, working, and playing in the summer soup. The Old Place's window-mounted AC units offered limited relief. But sweat-dampened, dirt-decorated clothes filled my dirty clothes hamper. Residents endure, become accustomed, then embrace the humidity.

Can you miss a sensation and abhor associated memories concurrently? Conundrum.

So, for some idiotic reason, walking to the hotel seemed a cogent action. The unindoctrinated assume, incorrectly, night air offers complete relief from humidity's attack. Wrong. Evening only lessens humidity's grip. The walk granted me time to consider the stars, look inside my soul, and admit my return to Southeast Texas comforted and terrified me...equally. A Harvey Wallbanger of mixed emotions.

I approached the hotel slowly, readying for body whiplash. The glass entrance of the hotel, frosted by moisture, in deference to humidity kissing one side and cool, conditioned air romancing the other. Entering the building invoked a quick bodily response.

Warmed sweat beads greeted by the hotel's cooled air caused goose bumps to cascade across my body. Transitioning from sauna-ing in sweat to shivering in damp clothes tickled memories. My brain felt raw, exposed, active.

My addict brain, developed over decades, called for a drink to stop memory's onslaught. Terrible plan. Still, sometimes terrible plans with numbed senses...

Then I saw her. Elora smiled, not seeing the addict. The addict wanting—scratch that, *demanding*—a drink...okay, drinks.

I walked over as she turned and leaned over the bar to engage Bart. This subtle movement caused my heightened senses to sizzle. My brain power-shifted from the past to now.

Her handshake reminded me of our professional—not personal—relationship status. I held her hand a beat longer than necessary. She said nothing and turned to our table.

I considered the amber elixir taunting me from the bar. My favorite liquid friends, Johnnie, Jim, and Jack, awaiting an invitation to join my table. White-knuckling, I requested water.

I navigated dinner left-handed, grateful for chopped chicken salad. The thought of engaging my right hand to cut steak or chicken breast offered the promise of pain. Bart once again attended to us.

Elora remembered meeting Mickey Mantle, Willie Mays, and Duke Snider the same night at an awards function as a child. No mention of last night's conversation slip, no kudos for staying sober, no transition to my appearance. She reached down to her purse and removed an envelope.

"What's this?" I asked.

"A list of AA meetings near your apartment."

"Thanks," I answered, not opening the envelope.

"You're welcome," she answered, ignoring my sarcasm. "I included AA meetings close to team hotels for the next road trip."

Sadness enveloped me, knowing road trips represented the past, not the future. I stayed silent. Elora continued.

"I included the substance abuse counselor the Astros recommended."

I said nothing to avoid sounding like a bigger asshole.

Small talk took over. I questioned her about baseball legends she met, current players she counted among her friends. Then I asked, "Do you miss screenwriting?"

"Sometimes...okay, lots of the time. Life granted me two loves. Baseball, my childhood romance, forgiving, awaiting my return, even if I pursue others. Dad's clients love me because they love him. Stepping into baseball is like coming home, where family awaits with hugs and homemade apple pie. Screenwriting proved a brief white-hot romance. A lover unforgiving of absence. An industry of recency, now or never. You're the hot thing or nothing. If I start up again, I start over. No safety, family legacy, or open arms. You have a way..."

"What?" I answered.

"Avoiding talking about yourself."

"Fair."

"There you go. A one-word answer to a wide-open invitation to talk. I'm a lawyer, we can do this the hard way or easy way."

"I vote the latter."

"Perfect, I can interrogate you about the dead body you mentioned last night. Or you can just tell me everything."

I ruminated, offering no entrée into my nightmares.

"You never told anyone; I get it."

My head nodded without my consent.

"And you like me...maybe a little."

A lot.

"You have problems...addiction."

Bingo.

"If there's any chance, which I doubt."

Crap.

"The only chance is you opening up to me, me understanding... everything."

No chance then.

"I need to understand why you never married. Never got close."

Why share a life with an expiration date?

"You throw away money partying, drinking, and carousing. You live like you're planning to die tomorrow."

Intuitive. Not tomorrow but...next week.

"What you don't spend on stupidity, you donate to children's causes!"

How does she know?

"Per your direction, our press team never promotes your donations. The only area in life where you show consistency, besides baseball and booze, is your propensity to spend money stupidly or give it away generously. You don't operate paycheck to paycheck, but it's close sometimes. I'm dying to know what that means."

Dying—funny choice of words.

"Honestly, part of the reason..."

Her pause piqued my interest.

"I've had a crush on you since we met."

I beamed.

"Don't get cocky. Also, you're the most reluctant storyteller I know, but also the best."

"Ahh...thanks."

"You're still an attractive man, despite your poor decisions. But beauty fades, Tails. Interesting stories don't."

I considered my wasted right hand, subtly, to avoid notice. I wiggled my fingers, hoping the pain lessened with time—no luck. The same probably held true for my memories.

The Hotel Lobby

Opening this door, taking this trip into my past, reeked of a one-way ticket to instability, insanity, suicide, or worse, a reintroduction of Rose Petal Detals.

Still, sharing it, regurgitating the traumas in this place, so close to the origin story, tempted. As a practicing alcoholic, I am unfortunately aware of the relief vomiting offers when worshipping at the porcelain altar of idiots. Head inhabiting the cool porcelain toilet rim, after rejecting last night's poison into the place, someone's ass-cheeks occupied moments before my residency.

Stale urine and excrement populated my nostrils as I embraced my inanimate savior, flushing proof of stupidity, excessiveness, and addiction. When considering vomit, most focus on the abhorrent aroma, displeasing appearance, terrible aftertaste, the wrenching sounds, or the twisting stomach pain. The lowest point, however, is the request you regurgitate to higher powers. "God, let me survive tonight and I'll never-ever-ever-never drink again."

I hope my graphic overview dissuades you from excess drinking. Hopefully, the picture proved graphic enough to deter others' overindulgence. I wanted to hammer home the point and pray I did. To be fair, I admit affinity for the aftermath.

Most forget the education offered by misdeeds. Your body begging, "Dude, terrible idea. Whew, let's not do that again." This is one man's opinion, but the greatest benefit of vomit is fifteen minutes after. You feel better, better than you ever believed you would again. Your body free of toxins left in the toilet's care.

So, Elora now offered me the absolution of the technicolor yawn. She asked me to vomit out my emotional bile. Vomiting in her direction reeked of unfairness. Elora weathered a few stories, haunting and colorful, a small sample size of the backstory that built me. But opening up the filing cabinets in my head offered unsupervised power tool problems to the listener—flying mallets of mental mayhem.

For better or worse, cheesy songs stick. I wish a meaningful George Strait ballad or powerful Billy Gibbons riff stuck in my head. However, I find lying to yourself a debilitating endeavor.

No great balladeer invaded my soul. Instead, the 1987 dance tune, "Catch Me (I'm Falling)" repeated in my head.

Catch me, I'm falling
Catch me now, I'm falling
Catch me, I'm falling
Catch me now, I'm falling
Falling in love [*]

Not because I felt myself falling for Elora. Which I did. More so, because of the incredible kinship with the Road Runner's nemesis, Wile E. Coyote, of Looney Tunes fame. In the recurring animated short, the cartoon canine found himself propelled off a cliff, staring down into a canyon, anticipating a fall to oblivion.

Catch me, I'm falling
Catch me now, I'm falling

I fell or started talking...a strangely similar experience.

•   •   •

" 'You either gotta beer in your hand or a bug up your ass, Two Bucks,' Rose Petal shouted as my uncle slammed his truck door. The gravel kicking from beneath Two Bucks' tires resonated a song of freedom. I watched Two Bucks pull away, shit-eating grin adorning his face, wishing I sat shotgun in that beat-up truck, instead of battling through a mess of chores. I was young, young because I still lived with Larry and Brandy sometimes."

"Your mom and dad."

"Sure."

"You're a smart-ass."

"Half right, we won't define which half.

"With Two Bucks gone, chores in front of me, and Rose Petal's thorny personality in my periphery, I bared down and powered through my task. After a few moments, the birds quieted. Then I noticed Bob White's flush from their hiding spots, near the field's edge. I listened for their approach before Chic and Rooster stepped from the woods onto our property. Ahh, saviors arrived.

"Chic started toward the Old Place, and I ran to her, hoping for a kiss. 'Dear sweet, honey child.' She called me honey child because my cartoonishly yellow hair. Her smell passed through me, lavender intermingled with sweat, from a hard day's work. 'Hey, Tails, ya'ant to play long toss?' said Rooster. 'Can't, Rooster, gotta finish up chores.' I told him. I watched Chic walk into the house, something I enjoyed even back then."

"Again, gross, your best friend's mom," Elora added.

I ignored Elora's tug back to the present and stayed in the past, continuing.

"Rooster helped me hunker through chores, so we could toss the baseball. I slopped hogs, he delivered trash to the burn pile and started the weekly fire. Chic's singing served as the soundtrack to my childhood, painting my memories. That day, she chose 'Amazing Grace.' By the time Rooster and I finished my chores, the night sounds of Texas began their orchestration, the low hum and rhythm of field crickets, bullfrogs, and birds' music to me then, as their memories are now. The burn pile, hungry at first, devouring the weeks' newspapers and refuse, simmered. The rising orange ash decorated the impending darkness. The flames' rhythmic sound almost as beautiful as the site. Rooster and I positioned ourselves where we could watch the fire, to ensure the flames did not spread. Now, the thought of kids in charge of a trash fire startles me. Still, different times, I guess.

"The sun lollygagged in the sky, offering remnants of light. Rooster and I started long toss near the house, but clear of the windows and Rose Petal's wrath. We zipped the ball to each other with all the mustard we could muster, our manliness or lack thereof on full display. Gloves pop now, much louder in my memory than reality. Still, I remember being impressed by our efforts.

"Rooster's balls sizzled. I tried to return toss with equal authority. To approach Rooster's zip, my throws added a degree of wildness. The approaching evening, fading sunlight, and my poor throw invited disaster.

"Rooster dove for the errant throw that warped my life, but the baseball ricocheted off his glove. The ball bounced once off hardened dirt before squirting toward Rose Petal's home. The Old Place sat on cinderblocks, a tin skirt protecting the home's underside. The ball found a sliver where the tin surrendered its duty to rust years earlier. The ball rattled off some discarded pots Rose Petal put under the home, in case there was a future use, nothing wasted on a farm.

"Rooster and I didn't own ten baseballs. Like most farm kids, Rooster and I shared one. If we owned another baseball, zero-point-zero chance of what happens next. Rooster stood head shaking before I asked him to go after the ball. 'I might go with you, but ain't going alone,' he stammered, a slight tremble in his non-gloved hand. Like me, Rooster knew something felt off-center, like nails on a blackboard. Several times, the weeks and days before, Rose Petal threatened to beat us within an inch of our life if she caught us under the house."

Disgust showed on Elora's face. "Why would you *ever* go under there?"

"Prime earthworm territory, big fat ones for fishing."

"Eww, okay, continue."

"Rooster and I both received our fair share of butt whoopings. Funny, I'm a 38-year-old male, and spankings from my grandmother remain some of my worst memories. If you stood still, Rose Petal blistered your bottom. You couldn't sit for entire dayparts. Got worse. If you wiggled, the belt wrapped around legs, arms, or shoulders. Post-whooping, I walked whomperjawed. Loose pants and long-sleeve shirts hid the evidence of my wrongs and ensuing punishment. Once, when Rose Petal whooped me hours before, butt still smarting from my last infraction, I unwisely mouthed off again. Rose Petal rallied her strength for another, more extensive session. You've heard the quote, 'my mouth wrote checks my butt couldn't cash'?"

"Never as literally, but yes," Elora said.

"I wiggled, 'cuz my butt got used up in the last session. The belt lashed my legs, my back leaving a map of each swing. One misdirected wallop left a rattler-shaped bruise coiled around my neck the next day. No hiding the evidence. Today, Child Protective Services shows up. Back then, my homeroom teacher asked, 'What'd you do to deserve that?' Again, different time. Not saying which is better or worse, just different.

"Back to our conundrum. As country kids, before Rose Petal's warning, we went under the home for lots of reasons. For instance, our cat Maybelline would go missing for weeks. Rose Petal and Two Bucks knew her location. It took Rooster and I a few rotations around the earth to figure it out. First, I'd hear weeping, like a baby. Days later, kittens crawled from under the house. Adorable. Kittens passed baseball and fort-building as my favorite pastime for weeks. The kittens crawled out to greet us but retreated when scared or hungry. As boys, we'd follow them back under the house.

"After a few weeks of kittens, Rose Petal announced, 'Talk to your friends at school and the folks in town. Give them kittens away 'fore they end up in a burlap bag in the river.' Rooster and I rallied to find each kitten a home."

"You're stalling again," Elora prodded.

I sat in the hotel lobby. Surprised to be there. Knowing physically I resided in this hotel, Bart taking care of our needs. Half-eaten dinner in front of me. Mentally, I lived thirty years in the past.

"Probably," I answered, remembering the kitten's sandpaper tongue licking my face, avoiding discussing...the crawl. I let myself enjoy kitten purrs, fluffy soft fur, and new-kitten smell.

I looked at Elora, knowing, despite her prodding, she needed a frame of reference.

"City folk fail to fathom the consequences. Climbing under a home and retrieving a baseball sounds simple. But even without Rose Petal's recent warning, many factors deterred the faint of heart. The Old Place, like many country homes, sat on cinderblocks, 'bout two feet off of the ground. A mini-ecosystem survives under a country home's shadows. When Maybelline gallivanted through the woods, the home's damp underbelly offered a rodent retreat, field mice and rats foraging for water or scraps. Snakes slithered under the home to capture the rodents and to escape the blistering sun when they got overheated. Roly-poly bugs, cockroaches, and worms thrived there. Maggots feasted on remnants left by the rats and snakes."

"Ehhh," Elora utters in the present.

But I remain pinned in the past. Standing, hands on my side, Rooster to my left, considering my ascent into the home's undercarriage.

"I dropped my baseball glove where I stood, looking to Rooster for confidence, finding none. I dropped to my hands and knees, the crisscrossed St. Augustine grass under palm. Fresh grass fragrance intermingled with rot wafting from under the Old Place.

"I considered Rose Petal's warning, the risk of battered backside, a frequent occurrence for me. Despite the phantom ass pains that enveloped me briefly, the desire to retrieve the lost baseball proved too strong. Rooster pulled a section of the tin border, allowing room to crawl through. I traveled on palms and knees into darkness. The moist dirt and cooler temperature proved intoxicating. As was the pull of the forbidden. I paused, allowing my eyes time to adjust to their new setting. To my left, an old metal bed frame, dumped long before my birth, now rusting or...rusted. Directly in front of me, the pots my baseball rattled off moments before.

"If my errant throw's rattle failed to draw her foreboding presence, Rose Petal must be snoring in her recliner. Other Old Place residents considered Rose Petal's naps a time of refuge. Rusted spots dotted the tin sheets serving as the home's underbelly protector, allowing my eyes to adjust, aided by light shards. I looked right and left. Rooster whispered. 'You okay, Tails?'

"My skin enlivened in a primal way. The temperature dropped, the atmosphere communicated mischief. The scent of incoming thunderstorms remains magical but not that day. Another attack to my already overloaded senses seemed unfair. The first hint of rain, the hissing, as droplets assaulted the trash fire. Next, the rains patter across the Old Place's tin roof. A romantic sound, if you occupy a covered patio's rocker, but terrifying if you reside on all fours under a home. I said, 'Don't leave, Rooster...don't leave, okay.' Rooster replied, 'I won't.'

"Rain's soft melody transitioned to a downpour. I imagined Rooster, soaked head to toe. My environment offered refuge from rain's onslaught. I thought Rooster may join me, but he stayed on guard. The trash fire's gasping signaled surrender to the storm's liquid onslaught.

"I returned focus to my task. Finding the baseball, then escaping the home's underbelly posthaste. Lightning struck yards from the house. White light electrified the scene. I spotted the wayward baseball resting near a discarded pair of boots. Because of my circumstances, I forgot the lightning's follow-up act—thunder. Enjoying thunder in the comfort of a recliner inside your home, beautiful and haunting. Thunder rattling you, while encased in darkness, offers heart-pounding terror.

"Forgetting my place, I jumped, or tried to, but head-butted the home's underside. Reality swirled in front of me. Near nausea reminiscent of the carnival Tilt-A-Whirl overwhelmed me. After steadying myself I fumbled forward. Wanting nothing more than escape, I scurried to the boots and baseball I spotted moments before. Lighting again illuminated my path. While reaching for the baseball, darkness reclaimed my surroundings. Instead of baseball, my hand found one of the two boots. Thunder rattled the home. I jumped back, inadvertently pulling on the boot. Oddly, the boot didn't budge, as if still worn.

"I froze, wrestling back terror. *Just a pair of boots, just a pair of boots*, I repeated. Still holding the boot, I reached with my other hand to discover what anchored the boot. My hand rested on molded denim then my fingers mushed a maggot buffet. The next lightning strike illuminated a rotting face. A face, despite deterioration, I recognized. A man I listened to from the pulpit every Sunday. Until he vanished.

"Between thunder strikes, when I thought nothing offered more terror, Rose Petal spoke, 'What are you fools doin' out in this reckoning? Get inside 'fore I tan your hides six ways to Sunday.' Rose Petal broadcast from the porch, so she could not see Rooster...yet. 'Tails, come on,' Rooster begged.

"As I jerked back both of my hands, staring into the dead pastor's face, a moment of clear understanding enraptured me. Step by step solved the rubric of Rose Petal:

1) Rose Petal will kill me for being under the house.
2) She knows everything that happens on her homestead.
3) The pastor trespassed before.
4) Grandmother dusted up with the pastor over the Oak.
5) The pastor went missing post-dust-up.
6) The pastor's corpse resided under our home.
7) Rose Petal knows his dead body is under the home because...
8) She killed him.
9) If Rose Petal discovers I'm under her home, refer to #1.

"I didn't crawl, I prize-pony galloped toward the tin girdle wrapping the home. Rooster held back the sheet metal, motioning for me to hurry. I burst through the opening and stood prepared to sprint, my eyes not adjusted to the barrage of light after my rebirth from the darkness. I began my escape, not sure of my destination. Far away seemed appropriate. After my second step, I tripped over my baseball glove and face-planted into the propane tank. *Dooonnnggg*. A bell being struck, or more accurately, my head ramming a propane tank.

"I woke up, disoriented, on the couch, to Chic's humming and Grandmother's heavy steps leaving the room. Chic dotted my forehead with a washcloth, her beautiful face inches from mine, my head rested in her lap, and despite everything, for a moment I experienced safety and love. 'Hey honey child,' she whispered. 'Rooster said the lightning struck right next to you boys, scared ya bout to death.'

"I looked past Chic to Rooster, his eyes communicating volumes. He raised a solo finger to his pursed lips, signaling the lie he told to cover our stupidity could be ruined with one wrong word."

Later: The Hotel Bar

"What happened next?" Elora's voice dropped me back into the bar.

"And like that, I never lived with my Brandy and Larry again."

"What?" Elora asked.

I stared into Elora's electric eyes while contemplating the tawny temptresses of liquid courage at the bar. I refreshed the math problem in my mind.

Liquid courage + more liquid courage = liquid stupidity.

Liquid stupidity = liquid regret.

Liquid regret > face-sampling toilet rims

My voice continued. "The one person you should be able to trust is your mother."

Those words hung in the air.

"I told her—Brandy—everything."

"Why'd you tell her?"

"Because I still left chocolate chip cookies for Santa. I told Brandy because I believed the biggest lie of all. She wanted to be my mother, that she wanted *me*. That *anyone* wanted me."

Elora remained trapped in her chair. The words, or the rawness of them, sat in her lap like a boulder, immobilizing her. Life spun in front of her. Elora bathed in the love received from her parents, grasping the value.

"When I told Brandy about the pastor's body under the Old Place, she listened, processed, then taught me the most important lesson of my life."

I looked again at the bar. My comfort, my assuager, my sleep aid, my tension reliever, my memory eraser, mere steps away.

Her snapping fingers brought me back. "Damnit, Tails, I'm here, right now for you. Tell me. Let it go."

"I could trust nobody but myself, no one."

"You father..." she offered.

"He let her do it."

"Do what?"

"Brandy Detals blackmailed Rose Petal."

"For money?"

"No, Grandmother would've killed her."

"Was your grandmother afraid of Brandy's family?"

"Phew, not Rose Petal. You haven't figured it out?"

"No."

"It's obvious."

"To you."

"Brandy Detals told Rose Petal that if she didn't take me off Brandy's hands, she'd go to the cops."

"If Rose Petal wasn't afraid, why'd she agree?"

"Three reasons. First, I'm blood, Larry's blood. Second, my grandmother understood at that moment that a monster was raising me. Maybe she took pity. Pity's a terrible decision-making emotion. You just regret it, take it out on people. Mom secured some type of proof, a finger or body part to ensure she had leverage."

"Who told you?"

"No one had to."

Silence dominated. Elora started but stopped talking multiple times.

"How often—"

I cut Elora off. "Larry dropped in a few times a year to help with the crops. Later, to watch Rooster and I play baseball."

"Your mom...sorry, Brandy?"

"I...ah...don't know. Only if she needed me at an event or for family photos. After the Cardinals drafted me, Brandy's dad coordinated a party to show me off. First time I'd seen him in a decade. He bragged to friends, pretended he had an impact on my life...he didn't. He took a picture with me; it was in his study, above his desk when he died."

"There...he must have loved you."

"His grandson played in the majors, that's all he loved. He held it over his drinking buddies' heads. He showed up at games, with friends to impress them. Hell, he didn't even know me. I remember Larry dropping me off at the Old Place. 'Tails, I travel so much and your mom's so involved...'

"I still called Larry's dad then. I remember sayin', 'Dad, I'll do anything. I'll take care of myself...just...'"

"You didn't tell him about the body?"

I shook my head.

"Larry Detals sat my bag on the grass, a suitcase containing everything I owned. An indicator I would never live with him and Brandy again. He half-hugged me. 'Now, Tails, it's best for everyone. Grandmother'll teach you so much. And Two Bucks, well, he'll...'"

"Okay."

Coming back to the present, I said. "He left me outside, like a bag of garbage. He didn't even come in and face Rose Petal. He reversed his car out, drove away, the dust rose under his tires; I waited as it settled. I considered every sound offered by the environment surrounding me. The call of field crickets, the rustling of pine needles, wind chime on the porch, even the snorting of the pigs. 'You coming or gonna stand there pouting? Your choice, guess the skeeters need to eat too,' Rose Petal said from behind the screen. I made out her sturdy silhouette.

"I started drag-carrying my bag to the front door. Jilted by my parents. Abandoned at a home where a dead man still rests under my room. Left in a murderess' and drunkard's care. 'Two Bucks, help Tails with his belongings. Brought enough to redecorate the White House.' Two Bucks stumbled out to open the screen.

'Hey, Two Bucks.'

'Let me grab that.'

"Two Bucks, despite patent laziness and ongoing mistreatment of his body, inherited his father's and mother's genes. He lifted the bag, tossing it from the front door toward my room. My suitcase clanked, crashing into the threshold. Most of my favorite toys did not survive the landing. He shrugged before returning to his recliner. Grandmother retreated to the kitchen, rattling pots marking her residency. 'Pull down your pants. Bend over,' she belted from the kitchen. 'I'll be there in time. Don't ask why, you know.'

"I dropped my pants and bent over the ottoman, waiting. With Rose Petal, the wait was part of the punishment. Rose Petal entered a half-hour later. A half-hour spent with my bare ass welcoming flies."

"Sounds like an exaggeration," said Elora.

"It's not. I checked Rose Petal's plastic dime-store clock. Grandmother asked, 'Paddle, switch, or belt?'

'Don't matter.'

'Don't be like that, or it'll be worse.'

'Doubt it.'

"Her soft chuckle the room's only sound. 'You are a smart boy...sometimes.' I heard a tipping bottle as Two Bucks finished his beer. He burped, then retrieved another, quietly admitting he did not want to bear witness to my bare-ass beating.

"The air whistled with the belt's woosh, Rose Petal's weapon of choice. I remember the sting of the first swing. I don't remember when it stopped. But Two Bucks gulped another beer, walked outside, and drove away. Because no one else was there when the whooping finished. Just me, Rose Petal, and a dead pastor under our home."

Five Days 'Til I Die

Saturday, July 24, 1999, My Hotel Room

Dreaming again.

Probably.

The most beautiful creature in God's menagerie entered my room last night, despite my clumsy invitation. I laid in bed, eyes closed, ill-prepared to greet the day, for once wanting to live in memories.

Last night's memory, watching Elora undress, may not currently fall under Webster's definition of Heaven, but wait for the next printing. The only proof last night happened on earth, the screeching arm pain.

I spent a career playing with injuries, but sex with a possible broken arm proved problematic. I hid my injury by encouraging...sorry, certain things must be left to imagination.

Soft smells of gardenia toyed with my nose, arousing me. Her scent.

Then it hit, like a 95-mph fastball off your batting helmet, no reason not to repeat last night. One part of me seemed steps ahead.

Locked and loaded.

So, with all of me ready, I reached over...kept reaching...she was gone.

A petite indention beside me and the warmth of a spot recently vacated, greeted me.

"That sucks."

Saddened, I climbed out of bed in my jeans. Besides the indention and the whiff of perfume, no proof of her residence in my bed existed. She left no clothing, no note, no dampened toothbrush.

After a moment to channel blood flow to my brain from body parts less inclined to think, I turned on the news, redirected my thoughts, and started a pot of coffee. I remembered everything, all of it. Grateful, I remained sober to catalog every moment, smile, and bounce. The perfection. After the final aerobics endeavor, I left bed, pulled on my jeans, and tightened my belt.

"Strange. You sleep in blue jeans?"

"Yes."

"Looks uncomfortable."

"Not to me. Long story."

"You're full of stories."

"Yes, but I'll tell you more tomorrow."

She looked sad after the word "tomorrow." To distract myself, I refocused on today's plan.

Night game, so I wasn't due at the Astrodome for hours. I looked in the mirror, raccooned eyes and bloodied lip on the mend. Next, I stretched the fingers in my right arm, my throwing arm. Pain answered all questions.

My career ended two nights ago. No one knew yet, but I did.

I wanted to tell her first, me...no one else. Own it, nothing to hide. Except for Rooster, Elora understood me more than anyone. Bonus points for the fact she did not bolt from the hotel bar screaming. Most people's first response: run from the alcoholic with Mommy issues, Daddy issues, abandonment issues, a flailing career, and an impending date with death.

Well, hell, I'm the complete packet of *disfunction*.

I spotted the hotel phone's blinking light. I selected messages, hoping for Elora's voice. No luck.

"Mr. Detals, checkout is at 11:00 AM. Your bill's been directed to the team. Oh, and someone left you an envelope."

Okay, my Astros' funded hotel stay ended today. Elora probably coordinated with the team. I chose not to call her, deciding to order breakfast. I showered before breakfast arrived, mainlined huevos rancheros, and fortified my aching body with a third cup of coffee before heading to the front desk.

Locating Elora seemed the most logical course of action. I wanted to disclose my injury, wanted her to hear everything from me. Last night, she rocket-shipped to my favorite person, even before participating in my preferred pastime. Also, she decorated my new apartment, and per the message, my hotel stay ended at 11 a.m.

After collecting my envelope at the front desk, I would find her for a tour of my apartment. The front desk clerk retrieved the envelope, smiled, and said, "Mr. Details, reminding you checkout is at 11 a.m."

I checked my watch, 10:15 a.m., plenty of time to pack and find Elora. Deciding I killed enough time to not appear needy, the desire to find her overtook me. "I need to dial a guest, where can I do that?"

"We're slow this morning. Do you want me to connect you from here?

"Sure."

"The guest's name?"

"Elora Banks."

A full sixty seconds later, he said, "Strange."

"I'm sorry?"

"We don't have anyone by that name."

"Oh, probably under her dad's name, Stanley Banks."

"I checked the last name. No one here with that last name."

"B-A-N-K-S," I spelled.

He looked at me like I was an I-D-I-O-T.

"Yes, sir, I checked that spelling of Banks." Polite, professional, and smart-ass at the same time.

"Nicely done." I appreciated the joke at my expense.

"Thank you, sir. I'm only here to serve," he deadpanned, adding a raised eyebrow for effect. A true *sarcastamaster*.

"Probably under their company. Top Talent, Inc."

The keyboard clicked, then, "Hmm."

"Well."

"Sir, are you positive Ms. Banks stayed here?"

I nodded. "Have you manned the front desk all morning?"

"Yes, sir."

"Did any beautiful women check out this morning?"

"It's Texas, sir, so yes...half-dozen of them. Some guests leave the key in their room and take the bill. So, I wouldn't see them."

"Okay."

Confused, I walked ten steps before the front desk clerk called, "Your envelope, sir."

"Oh, yeah, thanks."

My eyes volleyed from the front desk clerk to the envelope. His look communicated, *Open the envelope, Einstein.*

The envelope contained a key, parking pass, a high-rise apartment brochure, a map, and a lease contract. No note from Elora, no phone number. Just the contract.

I looked back, hoping he possessed sage advice. Disinterested in the role of my personal shaman, he shrugged before walking away. What the hell do I do now?

Following the map and key in my hand seemed logical. Elora awaited in my new apartment. I returned to my room, packed, and wrote the address of my new apartment on the hotel's stationery. Having no interest in re-engaging the front desk cynic, I left the key in my room, took the elevator, and walked to the taxi stand.

I handed the address to my driver.

"Ah, Lamar Tower, nice place."

"Thanks."

The driver dropped me at the Tower's entrance. I grabbed my bag with my left hand. A doorman greeted me. "Welcome, Mr. Details, we've looked forward to your arrival. Lots'a Astros fans here."

"Oh, great."

I checked in at the Tower's reception desk. "Welcome, Mr. Details."

"Hello"—I looked at his name tag—"...Nathan."

"Sir?"

"Did you meet the woman who arranged my apartment?"

"No, sir."

"She spent a few days here. You didn't...?"

"Sorry, no."

"She's a woman you'd remember."

Nathan nodded, not answering.

"You think someone saw her? The night staff or cleaning crew?"

"Not sure. A woman arranged for me to Fed Ex the key and parking pass to her. Residents can enter and exit without checking in with me. I remember your décor arriving. The movers checked at the desk. But no young woman."

Strange.

Nathan pointed me toward the elegant elevator. I rode to the 14th floor.

I located my apartment. Beauty greeted me. Unfortunately, not in Elora Banks' form. Grays, blacks, and blues highlighted my apartment, manly and elegant. Tasteful art highlighted the living room.

Someone arranged my Cardinals and Royals jerseys in the short hall. I walked to the bedroom and found framed pictures of myself with Ozzie Smith, Tony Gwynn, and Cal Ripken.

No one ever made me feel this special before.

I stood, flabbergasted.

I walked to the bar. Someone stocked tea, coffee, creamer, and sugar. No sign of Johnnie, Jim, Jack, or Old Grandad for that matter. Not one damn bottle of whiskey, bourbon, or scotch. "We'll take care of that, if necessary," I promised my empty apartment. My words seemed to welcome the addict to run rampant. I scoured the apartment for booze. While exploring every nook and cranny, an epiphany overwhelmed me.

Someone, an angel maybe, stocked the entire place.

Artisan breads and crackers decorated a charcuterie board on my new countertops. The refrigerator featured fresh fruit and vegetables, destined to go bad, based on past dietary choices. Boar's Head cold cuts and high-end cheeses stuffed the deli drawer—now those would get eaten.

Specialty mustards, picante sauces, and condiments filled the fridge's side doors. My benefactor equipped the cabinets with manly cups, glasses, bowls, and plates. Even the cutlery conveyed their owner possessed refinement.

"Hmm," again conversing with an elegant but empty apartment. No sign of Elora, nothing to do. An addict's disaster recipe.

Strange, I just realized, Elora never offered me her card or phone number. I possessed no proof she existed. Trapped in my thoughts, I flopped into my gray recliner, threw my head back, and screamed.

I repeated the Serenity Prayer, begging my brain to engage.

God, grant me the serenity to accept the things I cannot change,
courage to change the things I can,
and wisdom to know the difference.

Calmness overcame me. One person possessed my answers.

I picked up the phone, dialed, and was greeted by a familiar voice.

"Top Talent, Inc., 'ow may I 'elp," answered my agent's long-suffering assistant.

"Hi, Pilar."

"'ello, Tails."

Two words to recognize me. Thanks, Pilar, I needed that right now.

"Pilar, can I talk to Stanley?"

"Why j'es, Tails, un momento."

Then...elevator music.

Several minutes later: "You settled in, Tails?" Stanley Banks' Long Island tone, a perfect contrast to Pilar's rhythmic Latin cadence.

"Yes, thank you. My apartment looks great."

"Okay," he said sounding confused.

"Thanks for letting Elora come into town and set everything up for me."

"What the fuck do you mean?"

"Elora, your daughter, she flew in with me and set my apartment. Got me settled."

"Tails, drop the fucking bottle."

"What?"

"Stop drinking before you transition from functioning to nonfunctioning alcoholic."

"I haven't had a drop since I hit Houston."

"Love you, but bullshit."

"Anyway, thank Elora. My apartment looks fantastic."

"Elora's been on the West Coast for a week, meeting scouts and coaches."

"But..."

"Even if that wasn't true, and I mean this with love...I wouldn't let you within ninety feet of my daughter."

"Stanley?"

"Gotta go. Enjoy being an Astro."

Click. The phone lingered near my cheek until the disconnection tone traumatized my ears. Dropping the phone in its cradle, I mumbled, "Fucking crazy."

Was *this* fucking crazy or was *I* fucking crazy? Based on my past, the second option seemed likely.

The Astrodome

Flickering florescent lights jerked me awake, an unpleasant wake-up call. Crusted eyes opened reluctantly. I fell asleep—check that, passed out—wedged into a corner of the Astros' manager's office earlier. Butz slammed his clipboard on his desk. He stopped cold, like a soldier on patrol, sniffed the air, shook his head, and turned to me.

"Drunk?" demanded Butz, arms crossed and pissed off.

"No...I mean...not really...or at least not this second."

"Been drinking?"

I remained silent.

"Hell, I smell it. Anyone else see you like this?"

I shook my head.

"What the hell are we gonna do, Tails?"

"What the hell are we gonna do about this?" I held up my arm, rolling back the sleeve.

"Damn. Broken?"

"Think so, yeah."

"From the other night?"

"No, arm-wrestling contest."

"Sorry, stupid question. Why'd you hide it?"

"For one more day in the show. Tell me you wouldn't do the same."

"I can't because I would. How bad?"

"Can't grip a baseball or hold a bat."

"If brass discovers you came in drunk..."

"Yeah."

"Say hello to Mr. Coffee in the corner; I'll start a pot. Drink it dry. Once the game starts, sneak to the showers and clean up. Brush your teeth ten times, gargle ten more. Sober the hell up. I'll tell the team you're getting your arm checked out, be running late."

"Okay."

"Then suit up. 'Bout the fifth inning, come out and show 'em your battle wound. Tell 'em you won't be around for a while. Get help, get bone-dry sober, Tails. Not a drop."

"Got it."

"Do you really got it? Because it doesn't seem like it, asshole."

"Sorry."

"It's my job, Tails. I fought too hard to wear this uniform. Oh, and I begged the GM to trade for you."

"Sorry."

"Shut up and listen. I don't owe the favor I'm granting you."

Message received, listening not speaking, the best chance to survive this.

"When you're sitting in the dugout, enjoy the rest of the game. Encourage 'em, pat the kids on the back. Coach 'em up. Give 'em life lessons. Pay it forward."

I nodded.

"After the game, Doc will X-ray you, make everything official. Put together a game plan." Butz paused. He probably wasn't passing a kidney stone, but his face mimicked the act. "You can't be around the team."

"What?"

"You came to my office smelling like a strip club shit out of a bachelor party."

"Butz..."

"Not another word, or I'll tell the GM myself."

I nodded.

"I'm putting you on the disabled list, publicly. Privately, go work your shit out. I don't want to see you, except next season, sober, in the stands, as a ticket holder, you *got it*?"

The pregnant pause spoke volumes. Butz led a playoff-bound team. He did not need rent-a-player drama.

Butz marched to his Mr. Coffee and opened a can of Maryland Club. Luckily the coffee's aroma overtook my stench as Butz scooped grounds into the filter and started the drip.

"Pay attention to every syllable. You're 38. This was your last rodeo. I'm giving you a choice. Listen, and leave baseball a wounded warrior who sacrificed his body for the team. An inspiration."

"Or?"

"Or go out a drunk, who I suspended for coming to the Astrodome inebriated."

Butz shook his head, exhaled, and walked out of his office. But before the door slammed, he said, "Either way, your time here's over. And get to an AA meeting, dumbass."

Four Days 'Til I Die

Early Evening, Saturday, July 24, 1999, The Banks of Buffalo Bayou
My apartment bar now stood fully stocked. Well, not as fully stocked as yesterday. A few empty soldiers littered my garbage can. My baseball career, over. My dream girl may or may not be a figment of my imagination. Presenting the possibility, my brain boarded the bananas boat.

I called the hotel to find Bart, our bartender. He saw Elora and me together. My efforts proved unfruitful because Bart started vacation yesterday. Hotel policies disallowed sharing employees' personal information despite my begging. Locating the crew of the private plane that flew Elora into Houston crossed my mind, but the plane belonged to her dad's company. No go.

My crazy train ticket punched, like my father and grandfather, remained a secondary problem. The primary and more terrifying thought, Rose Petal, awaited me, too stubborn to die without firing her parting shot.

Weeks before the White Sox to Astros trade, my nightmares started. Each horror movie projected in my brain promised a return home. Subconscious informed by the universe before my conscious by the White Sox general manager.

I stumbled from my apartment to this spot on the banks of Buffalo Bayou, sporting a bourbon bottle. A cast now enrobed my throwing arm, so I long tipped the bottle with my left. Burping, I flopped down, removed my shoes, and stuck my feet in the cool water, wiggling toes like a toddler.

The Nestle Quik colored water, tumbling over and around my toes, calmed me. Not surprisingly, ranting, jag-drinking, and passing out proved untherapeutic.

Watching ESPN, Sports Center, for any baseball highlights added to my anxiousness. So, I unplugged the TV, vowing never to watch it again. Why waste my last days, the final wrinkles in my brain, with mass-produced refuse?

Thinking about my looming 39th birthday, and how I would do it—kill myself—fought into my frontal lobe.

My grandfather hung himself and Larry Detals drowned. No need to repeat territory the family already covered. Originality seemed important.

➢ *Balcony diving* from my new apartment presented itself as an option. I weighed the pluses and minuses.

    Pluses:
      • Splashy, newsworthy. The story would make quite an impact. Similar to the impact of my body bouncing off the pavement.

    Negatives:
      • Tough to lease the apartment after that. What'd the landlord do to me? Nothing. Added bonus, diving to your death sounded painful. Laying on concrete with my femur shoved through my anus, shish-kabobbing my rib cage sounded excruciating.

Balcony diving: Out.

➢ *Swallow a bullet*, a revolver-cicle, a lead breakfast?

    Pluses:
      • Sounded quick.

    Negatives:
      • I don't own a gun. So, there's that. Also, seemed to lack creativity.

Revolver-cicle: Out.

➤ The old unreliable—*Overdose*

Pluses:

• Painless, if done properly. One of the most commonly attempted methods of suicide, due to pill availability.

Negatives:

• Unreliable, considered a cry for help. Horror stories of stomach-pumping littered my research. Also, if I lived, I'd overdose on the nonstop lecturing from the Debbie-do-gooders.

Overdose: Out.

I eliminated other ideas, such as: cutting my wrist (seemed dramatic); leaving the gas on in my apartment (not a play, my apartment was all electric); stepping in front of a moving vehicle (I didn't want the driver to deal with the trauma).

Then it hit me. *Drinking myself to death*. I trained my entire adult life for that one. I owned the proper ammunition, eight surviving bottles of 80 proof. Decision made.

Of course, I ruled out today. Tradition mandated I kill myself on my 39th birthday just like unlucky Larry, and good-ole Grandad. A fucked-up family tradition if I ever heard of one.

Predestined, fated, slated.

I considered the irony. Buddy Detals, my granddad, the most successful farmer in the county, a local legend, died at the top of his game. Larry Detals, a multimillionaire investor and trader, died the president of an international conglomerate.

And me, an alcoholic screw-up, who failed at everything...but baseball. No wife, of course. No kids. I didn't want to risk passing my tainted seed to another generation. Thankfully, I excelled in wrecking every relationship. Ensuring my failure to procreate.

Score one for me.

Tilt bourbon, long swig, empty bottle, burp. I reared back to toss the bottle into the bayou, but those damn "Don't Mess with Texas" ads stopped me. I decided not to fail the environment like I failed in life. I stood, stumbling to the trash can.

There he was, bigger than life, Cole "The Rooster" Brewster, smiling at me from a billboard.

The Rooster Crows at Night Tour
1999's Highest Grossing Tour Comes to Houston
Rooster and the Curs
Sunday, July 25, at the Astrodome
"Of course," I mumbled to myself. "Why not?"

Three Days 'Til I Die

The Astrodome–Rooster's Stadium Tour
Sunday, July 25, 1999, 7:57 PM
Rooster's 60-foot-high face graced the Astrodome's edifice.

I marveled. The Astros pounded the Padres 5-2 in the Dome last night. After a rare Saturday night flight, they rocked the Rockies in Colorado, 8-5 earlier today. I know what you're saying, sports fans. Teams don't switch venues between Saturday and Sunday. But the Astros did. Check it, seriously, go ahead, I got time. Hop on the Internet if you must.

Now that we established I'm a reliable narrator, welcome back. The Astrodome's crew converted the stadium into a music venue in one day. Unbelievable.

I've not talked to Rooster in years. Sure, we grew up tighter than a belt after a BBQ buffet, but things...or a person...or specifically, a girl, wedged between us. Before we parted ways, Rooster tracked me better than I tracked him. His late-night talk show comment implied as much. So, he might know about my busted arm and the premature implosion of my season. Rooster's people catered to his whims...most of his people.

Naively, I hoped tickets would show up at my apartment. No luck.

So, now I planned to buy tickets at the box office. Wrong. *Sold Out* flashed above the ticket windows. I allowed myself a prideful moment. My wayward best friend sold out 66,000 seats. The only open windows flashed *Will Call*.

I waited in the Will Call line in case Rooster left a ticket for me. Nothing. Frustrated, I stood near the east entrance staring at the Eighth Wonder of the World, the Houston Astrodome, with a stupid look on my face.

Then someone bumped into me.

Cap and sunglasses obstructing his face, the bumper whispered, "How many?"

"What?"

"How many tickets, dumbass?"

"Oh, sorry, one."

"I sell 'em in pairs."

"How much?"

"250."

"For the pair?"

"Apiece, dipshit."

"Are the tickets good?"

"Nope, but they're legit."

I reached for my wallet when someone yelped my name, or nickname. "Tails, why you hanging outside, bro?"

I looked up and spotted Biscuit, Rooster's former high school left tackle, now head of Rooster's security. "Hey, Biscuit."

I looked, the former bumper now nowhere in sight. Biscuit affected people that way.

Biscuit waved. "Follow me, bro, I'll escort you past security."

I coasted in Biscuit's wake. He slowed to let me motor beside him. The hulk slapped me on the back, bucking me yards ahead. I turned. "Still one biscuit short of three-hundy."

"Phew, I wish. That ship sailed, bro. I'm closer to three-fiddy."

"Look's good on ya."

"Don't kiss my fat ass, bro. I'm already walking you in for free. Half Rooster's crews scouting for you."

"He guessed I was coming?"

"Bro, sent the Escalade to snatch you. Just in case."

"I wanted to arrive early. Rooster knows where I live?"

"It's Rooster. He's all-knowing, all-seeing, and already two drinks ahead, bro."

"I bet."

"Why ya talking to a scalper? Rooster sent passes."

"I didn't get 'em. Who's he put in charge of...?"

"Charla," we said in unison.

"Girl still hates you, bro," continued Biscuit. "Can't blame her. Kinda a dick move, bro."

"She started it, Biscuit."

"What are you, five?"

Rooster assembled most of his crew before Charlageddon divided us. So, the crew greeted me with hugs, smiles, and handshakes. Biscuit high-fived his way through the Astrodome's infrastructure. Hearty backslaps or "Ready, bro," his most common greeting.

Biscuit signaled a similarly sized staffer. "Hey, bro, call off the search, found 'im." Biscuit approached a door marked, not with a name, but a four-foot animated Rooster.

I chuckled.

"What can I say, bro? Boss ain't subtle."

"No."

Biscuit spun me back toward him. "I'm signing the cast, bro."

"Sure, Biscuit." I offered my arm.

"What the hell, bro? Looks like I'm slaying the virgin."

"Yeah."

"Plenty of white space." Tongue sneaking out of pursed lips, Rooster's head of security block-lettered BISCUIT, three-inches tall, slapped my back again, then departed.

I returned my attention to the animated rooster. Thoughts drifted to the live-action model. I missed the cocky bastard. Too long since...

"Too long, brother, too long." His voice echoed my thoughts.

"Hey, Rooster," I said without turning. "There's a four-foot cock on your door."

"Your point, Tails?"

"Overcompensating." Now I turned, taking him in. Expecting and receiving the smile that illuminated the 60-foot billboard outside.

"Think what you need to sleep at night, brother."

His words melted away ten years' absence.

"Just finished soundcheck. Come in, brother."

I walked into Rooster's dressing room, and four preselected jean/shirt combinations covered his couch.

Rooster spotted my cast, nodded the Rooster nod, snagged a Sharpie, then strutted over. He drew his cartoon rooster on the upper right of Biscuit, where the cast ended, above my elbow.

He beamed. "No one'll be closer to your heart, brother, I'm right there." He pointed to the cast but emoted more.

"No one, Rooster."

"You're the closest thing I got to a brother."

"Yeah."

"So, baseball?" Rooster asked, looking at my cast.

"Over...I think."

"Just the arm?"

"And the drinking."

"Sorry, Tails, you picked a job with an expiration date."

"Fitting, don't you think?"

We sat, glad to occupy the other's orbit. So tight, for so long, we fell into rhythm. But the discomfort of the present proved daunting. I witnessed the start of Rooster's career. This new and improved version seemed slightly unfamiliar—bigger, badder, better—and that seemed impossible.

Most people don't know the hottest star is the rare blue star. For the geeks, the blue star burns at over 10,000 Kelvin, or 17,530 Fahrenheit. Despite the stats, I don't grasp how bright a blue star shines, but I promise Rooster offered a similar radiance.

"Get the passes I sent ya?"

I shook my head.

"But I gave them to Charla to send to..."

Watching him come to the moment of realization proved entertaining.

"She still hates you, brother."

"You're sleeping with her, that's your problem."

"If you call sleeping with Charla a problem, then you haven't…"

I raised my eyebrows.

"Screw you, Tails."

"She already did. Remember, she harpooned me first."

Rooster laughed, the electric inviting laugh that welcomed everyone to his party. "I hate your ass right now, brother, and remember all the reasons we don't do this anymore."

"Well, not all of 'em."

"Don't go there, brother, don't go dark. Don't dive into those thoughts. Dark waters there, let's not go backstroking in 'em."

"Only a few days now."

"Damnit, Tails. Cut that shit loose. You're not your dad, and you never met your grandfather. Ain't how it ends for you, brother."

"Hope you're right, Rooster."

"I am right. Hell, I'm always right. Just ask my staff."

"'Cuz they're not biased at all, cashing them checks."

"Exactly. So why are you here?"

"You sent passes."

"You didn't get 'em and crashed the party."

"Charla doesn't want me around. She's your tour manager, and a…more. I love you, Rooster. Didn't wanna make your life tougher than necessary."

"So, again, why today, brother? You haven't been to one of my shows in a decade. Must be a powerful need."

"Some idiot plastered your ugly face on billboards all over Houston."

"Someone committed to beautifying the city."

After all the chatter and barbs, we forgot to hug. I stepped up, he pulled me into a Rooster hug. Same smell, same lean muscled body, the same Rooster. We held longer than needed, regretting the years without each other. Stress dropped from me like rain in a Southeast Texas thunderstorm. I felt lighter when we parted.

"So, you decided, huh?" asked Rooster.

"Decided what?"

"You're going back there. That's why you're here. You want me to go with you."

"Today's your last tour stop."

"So."

"You can see your mom."

"I see Mom all the time. She flies to me. That's what planes are for, brother. People fly to the stars, Tails. Stars don't travel to the people."

"It's your mom, Rooster."

"Chic flies in all the damn time. Let me repeat it, so you can read my lips. *I ain't going back there, Tails.* Not for you, Two Bucks, or Chic. Not if Jesus himself stepped down from Heaven..."

"Okay, I got it."

"But you feel you gotta go?"

"Gotta face that place, face her. See the demons again, know if they're real..."

"They're real, brother. If you're searching for demons, the Old Place sits in the right zip code."

"True."

"You met a girl?"

"What?"

"You got pluck. I can tell."

"Maybe." I answered, unsure of what else to say.

"Details?"

"You know my agent?"

"Sure, Stanley."

"His daughter."

"You slept with your agent's daughter. You tapped both of Charla's sisters, both of 'em. You need boundary training, brother."

"Anyway, his daughter came into town, or I thought she did."

"What?"

"Perfect, gorgeous, funny, educated, and she had a crush on me. Hell, she even loves baseball."

"Sounds like a fantasy."

"That's the problem. She might be a figment of my imagination. I flew into Houston with her, had dinner coupla times, then…"

"Ah. Brother, your agent's daughter."

I shrugged.

"Look, who am I to judge? But damnit, Tails, for once pick a woman who's inbounds. Try it. For shits 'n giggles."

"What can I say? I like train wrecks."

"No shit. Then what happened?"

"She disappeared."

"Possible commentary on your lovemaking."

"Screw you, Rooster. Anyway, no record of her at the hotel, none. The only staff member who saw her with me left for vacation."

"Wow."

"There's more."

"No. You didn't."

"I called Stanley's office…"

"You dumbass."

"And thanked him for sending Elora down to help me transition to Houston. He scoffed, then told me he wouldn't let his daughter within ninety feet of me."

"Smart man."

"Such a dick."

"That's what they say. So, this woman…"

"Elora."

"May or may not be a figment of your imagination."

"Nailed it."

"That's messed up, brother."

"Yes."

We sat stewing in thought. Rooster stood, then walked to the ensembles on his couch. He selected the black-and-red outfit. We did not talk as he dressed. Rooster slid into one of the twenty pairs of custom-made boots racked on the back wall, then stared in his dressing mirror.

"Now that's what perfection looks like, Tails." He winked at my reflection in the mirror before strutting to his fridge and removing cold

Shiner Bocks. He popped the tops. Cool smoke rose as condensation formed on the outside of the bottles. Rooster strutted over and extended his arm.

"Your choice. You don't have to drink 'cuz I am."

"The bottle's open, Rooster, hand the damn thing to me."

He complied. We sat and sipped for a few minutes.

"So, you're determined to go back home."

The gloom that poured off me earlier resettled on my shoulder.

"I have to. I'm asking again, will you come?" My request resembled begging.

"No, I won't, brother."

The door swung open and in she walked. Charla James, the rock and the hard place. A femme fatale worthy of Raymond Chandler novels. The atom bomb of exes.

But damnit, she looked hot. Curvier than memory. Betty Boop-esque.

Her head volleyed from Rooster to me. "Hey, asshole."

I raised my Shiner Bock in acknowledgement.

She eyed Rooster. "I told you...him or me. I couldn't be clearer."

Rooster chuckled, then said, "Well...ahh, I need to check with Biscuit and the crew." He commenced his retreat. "Make sure everything's ready to go. The opening act'll eat an hour, but..."

"Him or me, you stupid son of a bitch."

"Charla, we got a good thing going, but don't threaten me, girl."

"In case you need a translator, that's exactly what I'm doing."

Rooster smiled, serenely almost. "Gotta new song stuck in my head. Need to work it through. You two play nice."

"Him or me, Rooster." Charla's words chased Rooster out of the room.

The door swung closed, and I occupied a room with Poison Ivy.

"Thanks for the passes, Charla," I mocked.

"Tails, don't screw this up for me."

"Always 'bout you, Charla."

"Rooster told me you're out for the season."

"Bet you been praying for me."

"Oh, I prayed all right. My prayers got answered." Charla tapped her right arm. "God is good." The words hung in the air.

Bitter, but to be fair, even more toxically intoxicating than my memory. "And Rooster's a better lay than you."

"He may be. But you left me after he signed his big RCA contract. Coincidence."

Charla glared.

"You're fucking him for money. Probably fucking him out of money?"

"Maybe he thinks it's worth it."

"It's not, not close." She launched the bottle Rooster emptied at me. I snatched it from the air left-handed, happy she tossed it glove side.

"Want to sign my cast?"

"You're an idiot."

"If that's the case, why'd both of your sisters...?"

"F.U., Tails." She turned and stormed out. The slamming exit was almost as dramatic as her entrance.

"We tried that...It didn't go so well," I said to the empty dressing room.

The Astrodome

Sunday, July 25, 1999, 11:48 PM

Rooster's opening act, Cradle to Grave, surrendered the stage around 9:00. Applause erupted at 9:30 as Rooster strutted to the mic and said, "God did bless Texas. Whew. We're all so pretty."

I stood beside Biscuit, enjoying every riff, lyric, and antic. Energy never waned. Rooster and the Curs conducted a ninety-plus minute clinic in rocking an audience.

Finally, sweat pouring off his face, Rooster bowed, waved, thanked Houston, and strutted off the stage. Rooster high-fived us on exit. Once clear of the stage, Rooster mini-jogged past the entourage.

"Boss man's gotta piss."

I laughed.

The original members of the Curs greeted me as they passed.

The chanting pulled my attention back to the Dome's floor.

Thousands of fans held lighters chanting...

"Rooster!"

"Rooster!"

"Rooster!"

I discovered I chanted with them. Rhythmic clapping reached deafening intervals.

Biscuit answered the question before I asked. "Like this every night. Miami to Minneapolis, Moscow to Melbourne. Rooster's worldwide, bro."

As a kid, when Little League season ended, occasionally coaches brought us to see an Astros game here in the Dome. The games' details are long lost to memory. Running concourses, racing up the steps, buying an Astros' piggybank, gorging hot dogs, cotton candy, and caramel corn, remain with me forever.

After high school, but before Charla-gate, Rooster and I attempted to see each other often. Rooster hustled the bar circuit, singing to two or two hundred. Crowds got bigger each month. But witnessing Rooster here in the Astrodome, transformational.

I experienced joy words could not express. Life without that joy now seemed unfathomable. Certain moments define us, define everything.

This moment did.

Rooster went missing from my life ten years ago. Not one meeting or call in a decade. Still, I know he watched my games on TV. Of course, I bought every Rooster album. I knew every song, word for word, chord for chord.

Rooster and the Curs failed to leave one hit song for an encore. They performed every Top 40 release. Nothing in reserve, they bled out on the stage.

So, when I felt Rooster's hand on my shoulder, I wondered what came next.

The chant continued, non-relenting.

"Rooster!"

"Rooster!"

"Rooster!"

"Goin' back out?" I asked.

"Yeah, brother."

He listened to the roar, holding his arms out like a condor warming in the sun. Absorbing the energy. Rooster received it, an antenna, collecting the signal.

He stood worshipping in his church. The Curs bumped past him and back to the stage, familiar with Rooster's ritual. His eyes remained closed, still in the depths of channeling the energy.

Once his drummer sat down, the lead guitar player began strumming. A full sixty count later, my best friend opened his eyes.

"You got anything left in the tank?" I asked.

"Watch and see, brother," Rooster answered. He winked at Biscuit.

"Oh, damn," Biscuit said. "Shit's 'bout to get crazy."

"What do you mean?"

"Be ready to take cover, bro. That's all I'm saying."

Lights rose in the Dome, Rooster bowed to the Curs. Turning back to the audience, he announced, "Houston, how about the rockingest, hell, the cockingest band in country music. The Curs." The crowd rumbled past tolerable octave levels.

"Well, you got me out here."

More screaming.

"But I sang everything I got. There's nothing else," Rooster toyed.

Boos enraptured the Astrodome.

"I get it. You want another song."

Applause trickled through.

"I mean, I would too. We're pretty great."

Rooster laughed; his face projected on multiple stadium screens. Forty-foot Rooster heads everywhere, just what the world needed.

"Well..."

Cheering started.

"If the boys are willing..." Rooster looked back to the Curs, they nodded. "...and I guess if you demanded..." The electricity in the Dome rose. "...we could test a new song...you guys'll be the first to hear it..."

Octave levels exploded.

"I mean, only if you want..." Rooster spread his arms, closed his eyes, and looked to the heavens, again channeling the crowd's energy.

"*Rooster!*"

"*Rooster!*"

"*Rooster!*"

Rooster dropped his arms as the guitar tech draped Chicken Little, Rooster's signature guitar, over his shoulder.

"So, you guys grew up in the county, like me." Whistles and clapping encouraged Rooster. The drum started first, pumping up the audience.

"Where I grew up, we didn't have a garbage man."

The bass guitar ripped in with the drum.

"We didn't need a garbage man. Everything got tossed into the burn pile, or trash fire, depending on what part of Texas you're from."

The lead guitar trickled in next, engaging the bass guitar at first, flirting almost.

"Thing about a trash fire, it looks innocent, but you gotta pay attention. Keep your eye on it. Or it can burn your whole damn house down."

Now the lead guitar took charge, inviting the drums and bass guitar to step back and enjoy the show.

Boom, everything stopped cold.

Dead...nothing.

"Oh, hell, bro..." I heard Biscuit beside me.

"I's like to dedicate my new song to my new ex-girlfriend, Charla James. I call this diddy 'Trash Fire'."

"Holy crap."

"There ain't nothing holy about this, bro."

And the Curs were rolling.

I feed you every evening, I always follow through.
And when I fire you up, girl, you have a job to do
I look away a moment, just to carry on
And by the time I look back, girl, my whole damn house is gone
You just inflame...
You don't inspire
Girl, you're Trash Fire
You burned my friends and family, what they do to you
But you got your talons in me, as devils tend to do
You're not fireworks, baby, lighting up the night
You're not a homecoming bonfire, warming me, so nice
You just inflame...
You don't inspire
Girl, you're Trash Fire

Just as Rooster ripped into an epic guitar solo, 109 lbs. of leather pants and pure fury blew between Biscuit and me and torpedoed my best friend. Rooster never felt the impending Charla-cane. She body-speared him.

Rooster ended up on his back, guitar pinned by Charla's knees to his torso. Mine, and now Rooster's ex-girlfriend, attacked. Claws out, Charla ripped into Rooster's face.

The stadium erupted in screams and shock as Charla's attack crescendoed.

Biscuit sprinted, as much as a 350-lb. man can sprint, to the tussle. I followed right behind him. The shock of the moment dulled my senses.

Biscuit, with considerable effort, redacted the whirling dervish of Charla James from Rooster, claws flying.

"Rooster, I'll kill you. I swear on my life, you stupid redneck, I'll kill you." Additional members of Biscuit's crew appeared and wrangled Charla away.

Rooster sat up as the stage lights extinguished. Mumbles and whispers filtered through the crowd. No one grasped what to do next. I kneeled beside where I last saw Rooster, trying to find my bearings in the blackness.

"Hey, Tails."

"Hey, Rooster, you okay?"

"I'm f'ing great."

"What'd you mean?"

"You just witnessed the greatest ending of a country music concert of all time."

Two Days 'Til I Die

July 26, 1999, The House of Pies on Kirby, 4:44 a.m.
"Arrr," I mumbled, admitting to hangover's unrelenting assault. My aching, tainted body explained its opinion to me—pissed off. I sat, unsure of how or why I lived, despite the 80-proof pollutant poisoning my damaged body.

Well, you probably guessed by now, I like lists. Lists soothe me when I'm stressed. Apologies, I'll try to make it fun for you. A quick science lesson in layman's terms. Here we go.

You may ask yourself, *"Why do hangovers hurt so much?"*

1) Alcohol makes you piss—a lot. You can't stop pissing. So, your body dehydrates. Basically, your brain gets too dry. No matter how much alcohol you drink, you piss it out, you drink more, but you get increasingly dehydrated. Meet the mother of headaches.
2) Alcohol causes dry mouth and the rankest of breath, especially mixed with 2:00 a.m. two-fer-tacos, which seemed mandatory...at the time.
3) Alcohol creates flu-like symptoms, called "bottle flu," or flop sweats.
4) Alcohol irritates your stomach lining, increasing the release of acid. Cue stomach pain and nausea. Add the above-referenced tacos, guess where that one leads.
5) For entertainment value, alcohol messes with brain chemistry, causing "hangxiety." While drinking, a calming buzz warms you. I won't bore you with science, but when you stop drinking, anxiety and paranoia invite themselves to your mental mosh pit.

The paranoia subsided as I glanced across the table at Rooster.

I upchucked standing beside my best friend's Lincoln Navigator an hour earlier. One hand on the hood, one dangling by my side. Rooster's hand on my back, looking away, repeating, "It'll be okay, brother. It'll be okay." Occasionally adding, "Try not to splatter on the Lincoln, brother."

Biscuit babysat us all night, remaining in the background, allowing us to exercise our poor decision-making muscles. The hulk now occupied the next booth, our ever-present protector.

Rooster puked hours earlier, outside the Velvet Elvis, or Ale House. Hell, I don't remember. He stopped drinking, sobering from partner-in-crime to protector. Once I redecorated the asphalt in front of his Lincoln, we stood, or staggered, on equal footing.

Now sitting at a booth at the House of Pies, Rooster looked fried. Deep scratches marked his face.

"How'd we let her come between us?" Rooster studied his menu.

"It happens, Rooster."

"But you and I...we're family."

"We are family. I forgave you long ago. You need to forgive yourself."

"Yeah, I guess."

"Look, Charla James stalked the lead horse. She only showed interest in me after scouts from the Cardinals, Astros, and Cubs showed up at my games. Coincidence?"

"She did take a sudden interest."

"I can blame her. But I knew better."

"Knowing and resisting, two different horses."

"Tough to resist. We started dating after the Cardinals drafted me. She moved in when I hit the majors and informed me of our engagement after the Cardinals won the World Series in '82."

"Even though you barely got off the bench," Rooster ribbed.

"Thanks for that."

"You're welcome," he said.

"When I got traded and became a starter for the Padres, Charla pushed for a wedding date."

"I bet. But you didn't want to marry her?"

"No, I didn't want to marry anyone."

"To be fair, maybe you were the one using her."

"Fair."

"But?"

"Next, whispers started back in Silsbee about a trust fund Larry set up for me before he died. And like a bloodhound to a scent..."

"Charla followed the money."

"Even though I maintained no relationship with Brandy."

"You're a grown man. You still can't call Brandy Detals your mother."

"I am thinking of two words. The first word rhymes with duck. The second is *no*."

Rooster laughed.

"Anyway, Charla traveled to Houston to suck up to Brandy, kiss the Winthrop family ring, make sure there would be money left for me...translate *her*."

"Somehow Charla discovered, when I played in Houston, I got twenty tickets to each game."

"Sweet."

"Stanley negotiated into my contracts. Anyway, after returning home from a ten-game road trip dead tired, Charla greeted me at the apartment in knock-out mode."

"What'd she want?"

"Exactly. Her interest in me ran well behind her interest in my contract and trust fund. Anyway, back to that night. Charla said she made dinner. I never witnessed Charla microwave quesadillas, much less a full meal. She sensed my befuddlement."

• • •

"Ordered dinner. I had it delivered."

"Sit down. I'll take your bag back and start some music," she said.

"She dropped my bag on the bed and then started Cole Porter's 'I've Got You Under My Skin.' I sensed high-level manipulation in my future. But there are worse things than being used by Charla James."

"Your mom had the best idea," Charla said, *returning to the room.*

Ahh, there it is.

"You guys are buddies," I said, concerned.

"I'm looking out for your birthright."

I bet. Despite my thoughts, I said nothing.

Charla continued, "I told your mom you get twenty tickets when your team plays in the Astrodome."

Here we go.

"Your mom offered to auction the tickets off to raise money for her favorite charities."

"Usually, I just give those tickets directly to a kids' charity."

She continued, unperturbed. "Your mom's plan's better. After the game, you stop by the seats, bring teammates, shake hands, sign some baseballs, create an experience. Businesses will pay thousands of dollars for that type of client experience."

"I don't know."

"Your mom promised it would go to a worthy cause."

Brandy Detals' plastic surgery support fund, I thought, even then.

"And the charity will pay me a 10% fee for the money it raises."

Ahh.

Charla's charm dialed to ten. "Please do it for me. It's a chance to partner with your mom."

"Don't call her that."

"Your mom?"

"Never call her my mom, she's Brandy."

"Not for her then, for me," she cajoled.

And that's how it started.

• • •

The sound of an earthquaking sneeze brought me back to present. "Sorry, bro," Biscuit said.

I no longer sat in the apartment, admiring Charla, dressed for persuasion. I now resided in the restaurant with Rooster. Biscuit guarded our six.

"Over time, Charla and Brandy became tight. But Charla learned fast. She watched Brandy blow through my dad's estate like a blowtorch to papier mâché. I made good money, she liked that, but *boom*, you happened. Everyone understood you were the next big thing. You signed a three-album deal with RCA. Charla followed the money. Inevitable."

"Shocking, she only loved me for my money." He smiled, showing me he long ago understood the truth.

"Maybe she loved you," I offered.

"*And* my money," Rooster said, then laughed.

"The money's usually the answer in the Charla calculation."

"I should've said no, brother."

"But saying no to Charla...not easy."

"No." Rooster resembled a scolded child.

"I'd bet Charla came at you when your defenses were down."

"No excuses, brother. I screwed up. I..."

"Cut it loose, Rooster. The worst part wasn't you sleeping with my fiancée."

"Or the photos in every tabloid," he offered.

"The headlines sucked. 'Rooster cock-a-doodle-does best friend's fiancée.' That one was funny at least."

"I hated myself."

"The press frenzy paled compared to losing you. But here you sit."

Rooster contemplated. He opened his mouth, then closed it again.

"Spit it out, Rooster."

"Charla still visits Brandy. They're tight."

"The same species."

"Yeah," he said. "I still can't believe you nailed Charla's sisters."

Biscuit's lumbering laugh echoed from the next booth. "Cold-blooded, bro."

"An appropriate response. She dropped me and slept with my best friend. Worse, she manipulated you. You were afraid to call me."

"You knew."

"Of course...so, I banged her sisters. Seemed mandatory. Not my best decision...nor my worst."

"No...telegraphed what part of you did the deciding," added Rooster.

While the server refilled our coffee, my stomach signaled for food, but my brain recognized the need for discrimination. "Soup?" I said to the server.

"Me too," followed Rooster.

"Chicken fried steak for me," said Biscuit from the next booth. Rooster exhaled disgust. "Sorry, boss, I'm hungry"

"Funny, Charla hated me more than any man on the planet..."

"Until last night, bro," Biscuit added.

Rooster glared.

"I'll shut up. Give you two some space." Biscuit pretended to look out the window.

Rooster and I sat a long time. I cannot speak for him, but for me, I enjoyed warming in his glow. I forgot the white heat of his presence. The gas generator-esque hum. As if plugging into Rooster would power shopping malls.

Last night's Rooster, the Rooster for the masses, intrigued everyone. Not me. I remember the real enchilada with chili gravy, extra cheese, and onions. Rooster without cameras, microphones, and an entourage. That Rooster sat in front of me now, the Rooster of my childhood.

We said nothing until soup arrived. Chicken noodle today, thank God something light. Brightly colored carrots and peas swam in a bath of rich yellow broth. Fat bubbles signaled butter's addition, making the soup richer, more filling. The smell beckoned me.

As I blew on my first spoonful, aroma wafting through my senses, Rooster said, "I'll go."

I continued blowing, not talking too fast. I enjoyed the first spoonful, then more, celebrating his words. Relief washed over me.

"You sure?"

"No, but I'll go anyway."

"Was it as bad as I remember?"

"Parts of it."

"The other parts?"

"The greatest time of my life, you forget that part, Tails. Always do."

"I need you to go, to remind me."

"Well, the best parts start with Chic, you, and, well...Braelyn Ryan."

Rooster Tails Reunited

6:22 p.m.

Rooster and I sipped soup in silence. Two words, **Braelyn Ryan**, pushed us into reflection. Biscuit allowed a few autograph hounds through, most for Rooster, one straggler for me.

After we ate, we stood in the House of Pie's parking lot. "Biscuit's team'll get you home. I gotta say good-bye to the guys. It's tradition when we wrap a tour."

I returned to my elegant apartment, still haunted by the decorating ghost of Elora Banks. To redirect my thoughts, I packed my clothes quickly. Then I spent ten minutes wrapping two bottles of Tennessee's finest, padding the elixir with towels and duct tape. I may not care about my wardrobe, mental health, body, or emotional well-being, but damnit, I'll protect my booze.

Biscuit picked me up at Lamar Tower and dropped me at Rooster's building. The front desk manager greeted me. "Hello, Mr. Detals. Rooster's waiting for you."

Before I took a step, the manager said, "Let me keep your bag." After securing my duffle, he followed me to the elevator, inserted a card, and selected the top floor.

Upon arrival, I realized Rooster's suite occupied the entire floor. A hall led to one door, wide open. I walked into opulence. As a baseball player, I witnessed my share of toney pads, but Rooster's pen outpaced them all.

"Hey, Tails."

"No Charla? You live here alone?"

"No Charla. Could you imagine?"

I shook my head.

"Bought her a place five years ago."

Rooster took me on a home tour. Neither of us hurried to start our journey. When he left to grab his suitcases, I stood overlooking Houston's skyline.

"Hey, before we leave, wanna see something cool?"

"Who'd say no to that question?"

"Been dying to show somebody. Honestly, besides Mom and Two Bucks, you're the only person I trust. Follow me."

"What's going on?"

"Couple of bones of songs I worked on showed up on other people's albums."

"Could be a coincidence."

"Once, twice maybe. But it's happened four times in five years. So, I decided to stop that shit."

We stepped into his recording studio. "Watch this." He mumbled the date of my birthday, to be fair also his birthday, then two more numbers—three and nine—as he typed them into the panel.

"Not funny?"

"That's why I said it out loud, to give you shit. Needed something no one else would consider."

A hidden panel slid open from under the sound mixer.

"Wow..."

"Yeah."

I studied the keypad on the door. "If you planned to keep this private, why's the pad in an obvious place?"

"That's the genius. Same keypad locks the room, with a different code of course. Perfect disguise."

"Oh."

"It's the most advanced whole-home audio system in the world. All digital. It plays and records."

"Shit."

"Records everything. If I have a song idea in bed, or in the kitchen, I belt it out. The system records and dates the audio file. Absolute proof I created a song."

"No one else knows about this?"

"Not Biscuit, not Charla, no one. Just you."

Rooster wanted to show someone his new toy. He flipped open the laptop and showed off the software, playing back a tune he started while packing. Incredible.

A few minutes later, he re-engaged the system, hiding his new toy. He checked the apartment, grabbed his bag, and then locked up.

We said little for an hour, as he navigated to I-10 and started the trek through Baytown and Beaumont to Silsbee. As we passed by the San Jacinto Monument, I decided to re-address the name-bomb he volleyed during our meal together.

"Braelyn Ryan, huh. I haven't thought 'bout her in years," I started.

"Liar."

"Okay, sure, I think about her. But I haven't spoken her name in years."

"Yeah, brother. Saying her name's like discovering a new tune or finding an answer to a prayer..."

"Never got over her, huh?"

"Hell, have you?"

"No. But she probably coughed out a dozen kids and looks like shit."

"Incorrect," Rooster said with supreme confidence.

"Seen her?"

"Yeah." Rooster gazed into the distance. Rooster shook his head and smiled, saying nothing. He was there with Braelyn, wherever there was.

"She came to my New Orleans gig, few years back. She's got five kids but looks great...better. She and Cam visited backstage. Cam was dying then, dead now."

"Cam died." Braelyn and Cam, the anointed ones. Cream of a small-town crop. The champion stallion and prize mare at the smallest of ranches. Cam's and Braelyn's parents were best friends, as their parents before. Good people, the bedrocks of our town. I admired their families, still do.

Their parents, the town, even the school district, understood Braelyn and Cam would be married. An inevitable union, even when I met her in first grade. Despite the montage of novels about couples rebelling, fighting their families' goals, Braelyn and Cam seemed content with their preordained marriage.

The perfect couple.

Before her marriage, Braelyn became our school's dream girl. Popular but inclusive, cheerleader and drama nerd, nominated for the homecoming court but campaigning for Charla James to win Homecoming Queen.

According to Charla, her mother withered away, deathly sick. Bedridden. After Charla won Homecoming Queen on the strength of Braelyn's endorsement and the sympathy vote, her mom miraculously recovered.

Cam started school two years ahead of me. But Braelyn was my classmate. Over my elementary, junior high, and high school career, most male classmates fell in love with Braelyn. She dodged the suitors' awkward advances, then shepherded the failed Romeo into her cadre of friends. The poor boy's phases of rejection: head spinning, confusion, admission of failure, acceptance of fate.

Braelyn only had eyes for Cam, with a few months' exceptions.

Rooster filled in blanks for me. "Cam had a stroke. Few years ago. Braelyn took care of him, treated him like a king. According to Chic, Braelyn tried to grant Cam's dying wishes before he passed."

"They watched you play in Chicago a few nights before they saw me."

"What?"

"Cam wanted to see you play. And see Wrigley Field before he died. You were with the Padres still, slaughtered the Cubs that night."

"But they didn't call or visit the clubhouse after..."

Rooster's eyebrows raised.

"Yeah," I said, agreeing begrudgingly, remembering Larry's floating body.

"Never the same after that day. After we found your dad."

"No, not for any of us."

"Best summer of my life before that."

"I saw Larry more that summer than the rest of my life combined."

My thoughts drifted; Rooster's did too. Because Rooster lived in a different school district, we survived our freshman year of high school separately, he at Warren High School and me at Silsbee.

Rooster, who forever abandoned baseball after the failed no-hitter, led the life of the most popular kid in school. He starred in every other sport at Warren High School, while he worked at the Old Place under Two Bucks' direction. He saved every penny. By his freshman year, Rooster scratched together enough to buy a used Gibson Les Paul. The guitar he uses to this day, the rebuilt but never abandoned Chicken Little.

I worked the Old Place too, but never got paid. Never minded not getting paid. I earned my keep, and for better or worse, that place built me. Still, one thing always bothered me.

"When you formed your band, you guys played shitty gigs at the bars on the outskirts of Silsbee and Beaumont."

"That was the best, brother."

"That's just it. We were like brothers. But you never asked."

"Asked what, brother?"

"You never asked me to play...in your band."

"No, no, no, no...and again no," said Rooster.

"Wow, I could've picked up the drum better than Chester."

"I could offer up bullshit, but you know the answer."

"Did I suck that bad?"

"Yes, but that's not the reason."

"Cut to it, asshole."

"I didn't want Rose Petal in another part of my life. If you were in the band, Rose Petal controls another part of me. Or worse, shuts me down."

His explanation hurt but made sense.

While Rooster flourished, I survived freshman year by avoiding trouble. Elementary school and junior high years proved easy. Most of the kids and families knew my family.

Like most boys, I longed for Charla and Braelyn, but had zero chance at either. Still, my group of friends, male and female, insulated me from bullying. But your freshman year is different. You find yourself dropped into a new environment, a newly pressed teenager.

Men share the halls with you. Physical adults grown into their man bodies. Four years older, light years ahead physically but still maturing mentally. Testosterone and insecurity, an unstable concoction.

These man-children haven't met you but understand they can intimidate you. Newly formed, still unstable, these testosta-monsters torture you and desire the most beautiful girls in your class. Why wouldn't they?

The fairer sex, your classmates since kindergarten, face expanded opportunities. The previous year, in eighth grade, you were the alpha male. Now your female classmates witness the more "matured" samples of manhood, the juniors and seniors, new to them, never before sharing a campus.

My status plummeted from alpha to beta male at best, and omega male at worst. I did not play football, the sport that launched American high school's social seasons. My sport, baseball, started in spring. So, in my new campus mates' eyes, I possessed no value.

I hit my growth spurt the summer after freshman year. I did not master scholastics, dress stylishly, or own a cutting wit. Like fellow freshman, I endured the bumps in the hall, the verbal jabs, and outright insults.

Being Rooster's best friend changed you. He projected invincibility. Even though he did not physically protect my backside, his mentality rubbed off.

My freshman adventures started with Braelyn Ryan, got resolved by Rose Petal's reputation, and ended with a floating carcass.

Ninth Grade

I turned the corner of mid-hall and there she stood, Braelyn Ryan. For the first time, Braelyn occupied campus with her older, preselected boyfriend, Cam. When we arrived at Silsbee High, the cult of Cam Perryman blossomed throughout the community. The city's finest football player, athletic scholarship offers already in pocket. The brightest student, with more academic opportunities than athletic. Damnit, a nice guy too. Shit, I liked him and hated myself for liking him.

Being Cam's girlfriend granted Braelyn the freedom most freshmen did not possess—to walk the halls undisturbed. No single student would tussle with Cam. However, one family tested the waters—the Mauler clan. Silsbee's largest, meanest, most colorful, and oldest clan.

The Mauler's pioneering members arrived in what became Silsbee in the 1890s and acquired hundreds of acres of farm and forest land in Hardin, Jasper, and Tyler counties. No recent Mauler progeny reached their forefathers' financial success. The last three generations succeeded in two areas:

1) Propagating—hundreds of Maulers scattered over three counties
2) Sticking together—the younger Maulers ran wild and in a pack.

The Maulers, buoyed by numbers and reputation, feared no one.

Teachers guarded the doors outside their classrooms, but mid-hall, near the library, existed outside educators' sight line. The upperclassman ruled the mid-hall, so avoiding time there became freshmen priority. But, each day, after fifth period, my class schedule demanded a quick pass through the mid-hall gauntlet. Most days I hustled through before upperclassmen could notice my intrusion. But not this day.

Rounding the corner, I crossed into the mid-hall danger zone. Braelyn and Charla stood frozen, surrounded by three twelfth-grade Mauler cousins.

The comely cream of the freshman crop proved irresistible to the Maulers. Unlike most of us, the Maulers were unafraid to launch an assault. Terry and Tal blocked the girls' next step. Tig Mauler, who stood behind them, slapped both girls' bottoms. Charla turned to slap him, but Tig caught her arm in mid-air.

For no reason, other than hormones and stupidity, I counterattacked. I dove into Tig's backside. Cowardly, but when it's three on one, you leverage opportunities, even shitty ones. Tig's noggin, full of nothing but Skoal dreams and bad intentions, slammed into the locker. He dropped to the floor, out cold. My victories ended there. Terry and Tal tossed me floorward, then punched and kicked the innards outta me.

I felt like a piñata at a broomstick convention, battered, wondering when hard candy would shoot out my ass. But instead of peppermint twist, blood poured from my mouth.

Charla attacked, getting pushed to her backside. Braelyn screamed, summoning the most able guardian. I'm positive teachers headed out of the way, but not before Cam tackled Terry and Tal.

Just as I thanked God for a fair fight, Tig rose from locker-induced slumber and called "Yip, yip, yip, yip." The Maulers' call to arms rang through the hall.

Within seconds, three younger Maulers dove into the fracas. Now six Maulers attacked Cam and me, with no other hallmates or teachers stepping in.

Cam struggled, country strong, but not fast enough, to fight off six Maulers with limited help from a 135-lb. freshman. Then, in the middle of the fray, one of the younger Maulers recognized me. I knew him, Tick Mauler, a sophomore. One grade above me. More importantly, Tick knew something about me.

He whispered three words to his Mauler brethren. "Rose Petal's grandson."

Those words ended the fight.

I guessed wrong. The Maulers feared one person.

• • •

Charla hurled insults in Tig's direction, as teachers, coaches, and one vice-principal escorted the Maulers away. Tangled between two coaches, Tal spat in my direction. "Real tough, protected by your grandmother..."

"Shut up," Tig ordered, the clicking of their boots the only sound.

Mrs. Mack, my history teacher, waited to escort Cam and me to the principal's office. I remained on the floor bloodied and battered.

"Well, now I know why rednecks call boots shitkickers."

She raised her eyebrows.

"'Cuz they kicked the shit out of me." Mrs. Mack fought a smile.

Despite being in classes with Charla and Braelyn for years, and despite my crush on both, we shared little interaction. I said maybe forty words to the tantalizing twosome over the years. Deep, engaging elementary school conversations like "Tag, you're it." At ten I worked up to, "Wanna play kickball with us?" In eighth grade I mustered the Shakespearean by comparison, "Can I eat your Snack-pack pudding if you're not?"

Watching Braelyn fawn over Cam, I understood her boyfriend reigned as Hardin County's luckiest man. No room for debate. I climbed to my elbows, spat blood to the hard linoleum floor, coughed, then sat up. Mrs. Mack extended her hand. I waved her off, then with the confidence of a fawn, taking her maiden steps, fumbled forward.

My unsteady rise to vertical and wobbly steps toward Cam were my first moments of manhood.

I offered my hand. He took it and I helped him up, his weight almost capsizing me. Cam slapped my back, communicating everything one man could to another. The best moment of my life. For the next three seconds.

Then Braelyn Ryan kissed me on the cheek and said, "Thanks, Tails."

Cam's backslap nosedived to a distant second.

Despite my suspension from school, I received no ass-whoopin' from Two Bucks or Rose Petal. A visit from Braelyn's mom, before I arrived home, saved my butt. In this case, literally.

The fight's details traveled to Warren High School. Upon arrival, Rooster demanded an overview. My best friend accepted my exaggerated role in the tussle.

Chic doctored me, as Rose Petal huffed from the kitchen.

Next, I entered a strange Texas Twilight Zone. My favorite foods adorned the kitchen table that night: chicken fried steak fingers, cream-and-pepper gravy, green beans doctored with bacon, jalapeno cornbread casserole, and Rose Petal's famous Texas Sheet Cake. Never before, or since, were my favorites laid in front of me concurrently.

In my years at Rose Petal's, my grandmother never organized a birthday party. Of course, Rooster and I shared a birthday, and Chic orchestrated grand affairs for her son. In the early years, she tried to make me feel just as important as Rooster. Still, I accepted my position as the bash's back-up banana. Birthdays marked another opportunity to accent my father's and mother's absences in my life.

That night, Rose Petal's food offering became the closest thing I experienced to a celebration of my existence. My grandmother never acknowledged such. Her food spoke volumes.

Furthering the celebration, Two Bucks hugged me, double-slapping my shoulders while in his grip. He performed his greeting upon arriving home, before opening a beer, the utmost compliment.

After serving my suspension, everything changed. Everyone, even the Maulers, understood I lived under Cam's protection and Rose Petal's. Despite my previous loner status, I now occupied the outskirts of Charla and Braelyn's crowd.

The suspension granted me a short-lived bad boy persona, attracting my first limited interest from female classmates. When baseball season arrived, the one area I excelled, my status improved. Life changed on multiple fronts.

One day in May, I arrived home to spot a new Mercedes parked near Two Bucks' truck. I heard Chic singing once I stepped closer to the Old Place. Then I knew my wayward co-creator, Larry Details, graced us all with his presence.

I walked in to find Larry sitting on the sofa, mucking it up with my best friend. Rooster arrived at the Old Place before me most days. Larry's mood changed from jovial to judicial when he said, "Hey, son." He rose to shake my hand.

"Where's Brandy?"

"Your *mom*," he emphasized, "stayed in Houston. She's organizing the 75th birthday party for your grandfather."

"Wow, wonder if she'll ever bother to plan a..." I mumbled.

"What, son?"

"Nothing."

"Anyway, I needed time away from...ahh....." Larry looked at Two Bucks, who tipped his beer in response. "From...ahh...Houston. I needed time away from Houston." He seemed to reassure himself. "My investment firm runs itself now...so I came to help around here."

"Good thing," said Two Bucks. "'Cuz, we barely survived the last five seasons without ya. Can't believe anythin' got done without Larry Details in town. Miracle."

"Shut up, Two Bucks," bellowed Rose Petal from the kitchen. "Extra set of hands'll be nice."

So, for the first time in memory, Larry planned to occupy my periphery. Strange. Larry attended my last baseball game, which seemed like hitting the lotto.

The last day of school, my life changed even more. I trudged down the hall, staring at the hall clocks every few minutes, aching for summer's start.

A hearty backslap knocked me from lethargy. I turned to see my hero. "Hey, Cam."

"Tails, I need a favor."

"Sure, anything."

"I'm working at a camp again this summer, in Wyoming."

"Okay..."

"I'm teaching kids rock climbing."

I stood, not understanding my role in the discussion.

"Anyway, most years, I ask Jimbo or Tate to watch out for Braelyn, but they're coming with me this year."

I nodded.

"So anyway, can you look out for Braelyn this summer?"

"Sure," I answered, too excitedly.

"Not the toughest of duties, huh?"

I shook my head.

"But I'm trusting you, Tails."

And just like that, the summer between my freshman and sophomore year offered more promise than a trip to Astroworld with an Andrew Jackson stuffed in my jean pocket.

Summer After My Freshman Year

I wasted no time in fulfilling Cam's request. Darting from bed, I snatched my morning chore list from Rose Petal and knocked them out before 9:45. Per my hopes, Rooster and Chic had not arrived at the Old Place yet. Rooster, unaware of my new responsibility because I did not mention it, slept in on summer's first day.

I picked up the Silsbee phone book and thumbed through to the Rs. Crap, four Ryan families listed in the white pages. Cam could have provided more help, maybe sharing Braelyn's phone number. Cam guessed I possessed enough incentives to power through the challenge.

I met Braelyn's parents but never knew their first names. They were Mr. and Mrs. Ryan. Two Bucks knew them, from his time tipping flask with Mr. Ryan during the game and inappropriately flirting with Mrs. Ryan, a favorite Silsbee sport. Still, asking Two Bucks presented itself as a last resort.

I eliminated one of the four Ryans, Patrick Ryan, a grumpy curmudgeon who shared a pew with me at church. Leaving three candidates for Braelyn's parents. My first call was a failure, no answer. My second proved more fruitful. I dialed the Richard Ryan residence. An old woman answered.

"Hello..."

"Yes, ma'am, I'm ah...well, I was wondering..."

"Betcha your callin' for Braelyn."

"A...yes."

"I'm afraid you got the wrong number..."

"Okay..." I started to hang up.

"Don't hang up, son," she said in a comforting voice.

"Sure."

"Whose are ya?"

"I'm...a...Stephen or ahh...Tails Detals..."

"Rose Petal's grandson?"

"Uh-huh."

"And..."

"Cam...well he asked me to, ah, well, look out for Braelyn. This summer."

"It's the first day of summer vacation. Guess you wanted to get straight to it?"

"Didn't wanna let Cam down," I fumbled.

"I bet. What a responsible young man."

"Well, I'm...ah...going now..."

"Wait, I'm her grandmother. You won't find her number in the phone book sitting in front of ya."

I looked down at the phone book in my lap.

She continued, "It's unlisted. Would you like it?"

I nodded, then pulled myself together mumbling "Yeah...I mean yes, ma'am."

She shared the magic digits. I scribbled them happily. After looking around to ensure my privacy, I dialed. Crap, greeted by the most annoying sound in the world, the busy tone. Four tries later, success.

Sunshine greeted me when I heard, "Hello, Tails."

"Ahh, hey, Braelyn."

"Grandma guessed you'd be calling. She doubted you'd waste time."

I blushed, happy miles of phone line separated us.

"Mom's taking me swimming at the sandbar 'bout noon. Anyhow, since according to Cam, you're my protector and all..."

More blushing.

"Want to join us?"

"Sure."

"Just warning ya'...my brother's coming too."

Ehh, I thought, but remained silent.

She continued, "Mom can pick you up."

"Okay, my address…"

"Tails, everyone knows where the Devil's Oak is."

I asked Rose Petal for my afternoon chores and completed several before noon. Ten minutes before twelve, I stood on the patio in cutoff jeans, gripping a towel, praying to depart before Rooster arrived. Hormones, and thoughts of Braelyn, even with her mother as chaperone, overruled lifelong friendship.

Then Chic and Rooster stepped into the clearing. As Rooster approached, he examined me, spotting my redneck swim trunks and towel. A quizzical look overtook him.

Seconds later, crushed shell and gravel under car tires signaled the approach of Mrs. Ryan's station wagon. Braelyn waved out the window.

Rooster and I played Little League with Braelyn's older brother Earl, a serious incompetent. I took biology, but remained baffled Braelyn and Earl shared DNA. Braelyn's turn as Little League sweetheart made baseball an afterthought for the team.

My best friend's head volleyed from me to the Ryan's car, then back. Rooster's glare convicted me of betrayal. Driven by the same hormones as me, Rooster darted to the car. Before I could stop him, he raced to the Ryans. I heard him start. "Hey, Braelyn. Hello, Mrs. Ryan."

"Hey, Rooster," said Braelyn and Earl in unison.

"Hello, Rooster," said Mrs. Ryan.

"Tails tells me you're going swimming," Rooster lied. "Got room for one more?"

Rooster, no towel, no shoes, just a T-shirt and cutoff jeans, climbed into the car. Before I could object, Rooster squeezed next to Braelyn and grinned.

"There's room next to me," said Earl.

Tossing river mud at Rooster and Earl, diving into the creek, and racing shore to shore filled the afternoon. But make no mistake, the day's peak was peeking while Braelyn and Mrs. Ryan, the reigning town beauty, stripped to new summer swimsuits and laid out on the river's sandy shores.

I smiled to myself, remembering Earl begging, "Guys, stop staring at my sister." The day ended early when Earl tackled Rooster from behind during a river scrum. A loud pop proceeded Earl rolling in the shallows, collarbone snapped. Idiot.

And so, summer started. Mrs. Ryan never took us swimming again, but our summer got better.

Days later, Braelyn's brother, broken collarbone and all, was bussed to summer camp, proving beyond a doubt God's existence. An incredible summer ritual began. Rooster arrived early. He and I pressed through morning chores with Dad and Two Bucks.

When noon arrived, too hot to survive in the fields, Mrs. Ryan dropped Braelyn off. She, Rooster, and I spent the summer exploring the creek, woods, and ponds. Within days, Rooster and I struggled to remember a time without her.

She picked up bullfrogs we cornered, got peed on by the tortoises she lifted, and climbed every tree. We were simpatico. Yes, we ached for her in ways fourteen-year-olds don't understand. Braelyn's beauty and Rooster's and my summer growth spurts promised a hormone forest fire. Especially with the addition of an accelerant.

One day, Mrs. Ryan dropped off Braelyn and Charla, the abovementioned accelerant. Both girls wore cutoffs and T-shirts. The towels they toted and peeking bikini strings left stupid grins on Rooster's and my faces.

Charla showed no interest in traipsing through the woods. Within seconds, she asked, "Where's the closest sandbar?"

Rooster said, "If we take our bikes, we can be there in 20 minutes."

Rooster and I rolled bikes from the barn as Charla announced, "I'll ride with Tails." Since I seldom spoke to Charla, I was surprised. She and Braelyn, our class socialites, attended baseball games, but still, many classmates did, so nothing special there.

Then logic took over. She selected me because I represented the more familiar option. Charla never met Rooster before today.

Rooster's bike boasted a banana seat with plenty of room for two riders. So Braelyn sat behind him and wrapped her arms around him. Just as my envy climbed, I realized my seat only had room for one.

"Hold the bike steady, Tails," said Charla. I enjoyed every motion as she climbed on my handlebars. Instead of turning her back toward me, she faced me and rested her feet on my legs. "Don't let me fall, okay?"

Her bright pink bathing suit top shimmered through her worn white T-shirt.

"Pay attention..."

"Okay."

"To the road, Tails."

Unwelcome honesty stumbled from my mouth, "...yeah...I'll...ah, do my best."

Rooster and I shared unbelieving glances during the journey. My eyes navigated past Charla's petite form, paying attention to obstacles. I dodged the worst potholes, but my passenger's body quaked in response to the road's uneven surface. The visual buffet assaulted my...ah, midsection...in ways my brain remained unequipped to hide. Charla's left foot on my thigh and the adjustments each bump forced, pushed me to tilt. I prayed my body's indiscretion remained unnoticed.

The bike ride plays often in my memories and stood as the highlight of adolescence, for a few more minutes at least.

We reached my favorite spot on the Neches. Soft white sandbanks, chocolate waters, and rich green pines dotted our views. However, the most tantalizing views began stripping to their bathing suits. Charla and Braelyn rolled out their towels as Rooster and I ogled.

The girls started sunny-side up. Rooster and I stared, jaws inches lower than usual. We both breathed heavily, in full teenage lust, Charla's pink and Braelyn's white bikinis covering just enough to keep us from drooling like rabid dogs.

For distraction, Rooster and I dove into the Neches, or skipped stones. We walked up and down the bank talking, eyes locked on the sunbathing beauties. The girls seemed content to bake in the sun and unintentionally...or intentionally...torture us. Both girls so perfect, I doubted the sun's ability to improve one detail.

A half-hour later, the two turned in unison, bottoms now facing the sun. Charla reached back and unhitched her top, rotated, pulled the top from under her, and placed it to her left. No tan lines. She rose to her elbows, snowy white breast contrasting the rest of her body; only Charla's nipples remained unexposed, pressed to the sand.

Part of me, barely under control before, vaulted to attention.

"Braelyn, stop being a wimp. Your mom's not here." Charla reached over and untied Braelyn's bikini string, ripping the white top from under her sunbathing partner. Unlike Charla, Braelyn's back had a pure white stripe.

Embarrassed, Braelyn said nothing. Unlike Charla, Braelyn pressed herself to the earth. Understanding Braelyn's predicament, Charla upped the stakes. She leaned over, showing enough of herself to drive me insane, and pulled Braelyn's bottoms clean off too.

"Charla, give those back," Braelyn beseeched.

Instead, Charla raised her hips, sliding down her pink bikini bottom.

Rooster and I stood like statues abandoned centuries ago in a deserted garden, still unmoving, feet cemented in place for eternity.

Braelyn's bright white bottom, compared to her long tan legs, reminded me why teenagers called it "getting mooned" when a passenger flashed their buttocks from a car window.

Braelyn remained facedown, her heart-stopping backside exposed. Charla turned to face us, one hand covering her lap, the other holding her breast. "Okay, boys, only fair."

"Charla!" Braelyn said.

"I've never seen one. I want to," said Charla. "You're only gonna see Cam's the rest of your life. Let's peek at a few."

Charla raised her eyebrows, asking if we possessed the stomach to play poker at her level.

Braelyn propped up on her elbows and peeked around. "I didn't ask for this, but Tails, Rooster, it's only fair."

Charla pushed us all in, dropping her arm, exposing her breast. My first pair.

Rooster and I unbuttoned our jean shorts, letting them drop to the sand. Charla nodded approvingly, taking in both. Even Braelyn smiled...guiltily.

Rooster pushed back. "Braelyn, you're next. Like you said, it's only fair." She turned, granting my first, second, and third wish. Braelyn sat for mere seconds, long enough to view Rooster and my...well. Then she jumped to her feet and sprinted toward the water. A moment I replayed hundreds of times. Charla stood and walked past us, glancing down. "You two going to stand at...full attention, or are we skinny-dipping?"

We joined in. After a few minutes of bumping, tussling, and grab-ass, Braelyn exited the water as quickly as she entered. She dressed, then said, "Time to get going." Palpable guilt played in every word.

She studied me to see if I felt similar remorse. Cam selected me as Braelyn's protector. I looked down; failure engulfed me. I mouthed, *Sorry*.

Despite my guilt, hormones demanded I admire Charla exiting the river. She whistled when Rooster and I followed.

And just like that, summer ended.

Around 4:00, Mrs. Ryan picked Braelyn and Charla up. I mourned their departure, understanding the day's imprint on my brain. However, I failed to grasp the events' inevitable consequences.

Rose Petal expected me to return to the field that day. I started drinking coffee the year before but found myself caffeinated without an afternoon cup. Working beside Two Bucks and Larry, I aspired to hold my own. That afternoon, for the first time, I proved capable.

That summer, watching Larry work, I understood Rose Petal's gold standard. Efficient, strong, and smart; the task seemed simpler working by his side. Larry slapped me on the back after we finished in the field. To be fair, Larry seemed to consider me with respect at the dinner table, after our toughest of days.

Labor Day approached. Summer's swan song. Happily, at the time, marking mere days to Larry's birthday.

I slopped the hogs when Rose Petal called to Larry, "Brandy's on the phone."

Rooster and I finished our respective tasks, hosing off hands and face, before starting to the house. Manning the porch swing, Two Bucks swigged his longneck before saying, "Wouldn't go in there."

I noticed Chic, now sitting on Two Bucks' pickup's tailgate, twenty or thirty yards from the house. Seemed strange. I never saw Chic sitting outside doing nothing. Then I heard it.

"No, I'm not coming home yet." Then chirping from the phone. I looked at Two Bucks. He shrugged.

"Yes, I know it's your dad's birthday." The phone chirping transitioned to squawking. I tried not to focus on it and looked to Rooster.

The porch creaked as Rooster stood and jogged to Chic's side. She seemed to be crying. An onslaught of squawking continued. Slowly, night sounds of a Texas evening offered relief. I focused on them.

"No, she's not here..." Larry peered out the window, staring at Rooster and Chic. I sat across from Two Bucks. He finished his beer, popping the empty on the table. Unlike most evenings, he did not rise to gather another longneck.

The tortured phone call drug on. Other sounds intermingled—pots lowered to the stove, a kettle whistling, a wooden spoon tapping the side of a cast-iron pan—sounds of Rose Petal. My grandmother would not surrender her position in the kitchen to approaching armies.

Minutes later, Two Bucks rose and plopped down beside me and took my hand, something he never did before. I smelled field grit, homemade cow manure fertilizer, and beer intermingled into his perspiration. The scent strangely comforted me.

For reasons I don't understand, my head dropped to Two Bucks' shoulder. I would have rested my head there forever, relishing the comfort he offered. Filing through memories, I knew Larry never offered me his shoulder.

Thirty minutes later, the phone slammed down. Within seconds, Rose Petal bellowed, "Dinner."

Everyone trudged inside, each approach step more careful than the step before. Larry opened the screen door and attempted a smile.

Braelyn didn't come over the next week. Rooster and I waited each day. Each day we dined on disappointment as Braelyn stayed away.

Rooster and I were best friends, are best friends, but after discovering girls...well. Each baseball toss possessed less pop, trees seemed less in need of climbing, trails that beckoned us the week before remained silent.

Even Rose Petal noticed. "You two pout like a preacher who misplaced his collection plate."

A week without Braelyn ended on Larry's birthday. I worked up the courage to call. Mrs. Ryan answered, announcing my name.

Then the sound of Braelyn lifting the phone. No "hello," no "I missed you." Silence.

"Hey, Braelyn."

"Hey, Braelyn, that's all you got."

"I'm sorry 'bout…"

"You know Cam can't hit a girl."

"Oh…okay."

"So Charla'll get off with dirty looks. But Cam's going to beat you to a bloody pulp."

"I'll take every punch. I deserve it."

"Not sure you do, but it'll happen anyhow. I gotta tell him."

"Okay."

We both remained silent. I treasured each Braelyn breath. "So…"

"Tomorrow's your dad's birthday, Rooster told me. I'm coming over to help if that's okay."

"Oh…yeah. So, Rooster told you?"

"He called yesterday?" Braelyn answered.

I thought I connected Rooster and Braelyn. Direct communication between the two troubled me. "Oh, good."

"See you two tomorrow."

I said nothing.

"I missed you two idiots," she said before hanging up the phone.

• • • •

As Larry's birthday approached, I wondered if Brandy would travel to town. Chic, Rooster, and I refused to let Larry's, and of course his twin brother, Two Bucks' 39th birthdays, go by without celebration. That morning, Rooster and Chic arrived early carrying gifts wrapped in newspaper.

Rooster and I attacked our chores with fervor. We had little money; we did Larry's and Two Bucks' chores as our gift to them. The brothers seemed appreciative. Both started drinking early. Rose Petal cooked enough food for a few more months.

Braelyn arrived around noon.

Mrs. Ryan demanded a picture of the three of us leaning against her station wagon. "Get closer, you three." Rooster and I complied happily. "Braelyn, put your arms around them." Mrs. Ryan snapped her picture, forever capturing my stupid grin. Smiling, she hugged her daughter and said, "Just call me when you're ready, angel."

Braelyn reported to Chic for assignments.

Rooster and I worked through the hottest part of the day and finished all chores assigned and volunteered. At 4:00 p.m., iced Lone Star and Frostie root beers filled Two Bucks' beat-up Igloo cooler.

Rooster and I, coated in sweat, raced to the shower. As usual, he beat me. Minutes later, still damp from quick showers, we changed into Sunday jeans and shirts, both striving to look our best.

I walked to the porch and pulled a Frostie, nodding to Two Bucks and Larry, already several beers into celebration. The condensation coating the root beer bottle beckoned me. I popped the lid, then held the bottle to my forehead, enjoying the cool, and downed a long gulp. I burped as the patio swung open. Braelyn held a plate of deviled eggs.

"Elegant, Tails," she smiled. She delivered deviled eggs to Two Bucks and Larry. Each man rested their beer between their legs and collected as many eggs as they could hold. I seldom saw Larry and Two Bucks beside each other, and just for a moment, I noticed their shared traits, twins yes, identical no. Different and eerily similar.

A few neighbors brought presents, like Chic's wrapped in newsprint or brown butcher paper. No frills. Larry and Two Bucks dutifully opened their presents. The fading night sky persuaded Chic to flip on the yellow porch light.

The brothers seemed grateful for each gift, thanking all guests. Strangely, Two Bucks decided to pace himself. Yes, he was snockered but less so than an average Wednesday. Larry matched Two Bucks beer for beer. Two Bucks could not surpass Larry's business success. But Larry, or possibly no living man, could out-drink Two Bucks.

Around 10:00 p.m., the party faded. Mrs. Ryan arrived to collect Braelyn. Guests shared good-byes. Rose Petal long ago cleaned the kitchen and headed to bed. Rooster, Chic, and I cleaned the porch and living room. As Chic straightened the sofa, Larry stumbled from the bathroom.

"I'm going walking."

"Now?" said Chic.

Larry stumbled onto the porch, not answering. Two Bucks held out another Lone Star; Larry waved it away, stumbling past. Then, for reasons I still fail to fathom, he wobble-ran toward the Devil's Oak. I followed.

When I caught him, I stood under the Devil's Oak arbor for the first time. "Wish you'd met 'em." Larry looked to where Buddy Detals would have swung.

"Me too," I said, thinking of my grandfather for the first time in months.

"Don't follow me, Tails."

"What?"

Larry pushed me down, and my head banged against the rusted tractor. Fading in and out of consciousness, my eyes opening and shutting, head swirling, somewhere between dream and awake, nightmare and nighttime. My eyes proved unreliable. But my ears told me he headed through the cornfield. My thoughts ran to Edgar Allan Poe's *The Raven*... Nevermore.

The Devil's Oak

Planting one hand on the ground, I rose to a knee. Swirling greeted my rise. My thoughts ran to battered Hanna-Barbera villains—after losing their battle, tweeting bluebirds circling their noggin. I shook my head clear, remembering where I stood. Not on hallowed ground...the opposite of hallowed ground.

I absorbed my environment. Familiar facets of the Old Place warped back and forth to an inner soundtrack. Techno-colored rainbows lit my surroundings. Terror gripped me. My body remained under the Devil's Oak, but mind occupied nightmare. Understanding my proximity to the Oak heightened my connection...but connection to what?

The creaking of a taut rope, swinging in the wind, passed through me. Calls of the night escalated. My senses ran raw, goose bumps covered my body. Then something brushed my head. At first, I only saw work boots and dirt-stained jeans. I understood, my grandfather's specter, visited me.

Curiosity forced my eyes to dissect the scene. Buddy Detals' neck remained intact. Unbroken. Strange to note, even in nightmare. I forced myself to stare into his eyes, an inner courage I embraced, if only for seconds.

His dead eyes begged me to understand. Unfortunately, my courage failed to hold ground long enough to translate his message. I ran.

Not looking back, grasping, I was never there, and of course...always there. I held my terror inside. Screams offered no resolution in dreams. After reaching the amber light of the Old Place, I turned back.

Buddy Detals, nor his son Larry, nor any ghost of East Texas legend, swung from the Devil's Oak. Hands on knees, I breathed in and out, never losing sight of the Oak. Ensuring no dream army birthed from the Oak's branches galloped my direction.

Something far more terrifying occurred. The Devil's Oak waved, daring—no, inviting—my return.

Then the shaking. "Wake up, Tails," Rooster begged.

"What..." I mumbled, confused, flailing for my bearings, but happy for Rooster's presence.

"Where's your dad?" asked Two Bucks, standing above Rooster, surveying the surroundings.

"Don't know. I, ah, lost him..."

"Why're you here under the ahh...?" Rooster asked.

"I followed him here."

Two Bucks shook his head. "Well, I guess no day dodging chores goes unpunished."

"You'd be punished every day," Rose Petal said, stepping from the shadows.

I watched a thousand smart-ass responses process through Two Bucks' brain. He ignored each. "I'll go get 'em."

I tried to stand but failed. Two Bucks asked, "Did ya sneak beers from the Igloo? You look drunk."

"You'd know that look," Rose Petal said.

"No, I hit my head," I said, not mentioning Larry Detals' push or visions of my dangling grandfather.

"Rooster, you and Chic head home, search for Larry on the way. I'll search for 'em after I get Tails settled. The only person who knows these woods better than Larry is me."

Or Rooster and me.

Two Bucks reached down and lifted me as easily as a case of longnecks. He started walking to the house. "I'm okay, Two Bucks, put me down."

"That's okay, Tails...for once, let someone carry you."

I found the experience strange, comforting, and unfamiliar.

After being dropped on the porch, I wobble-walked to my room, Larry's old room, a room I shared with him that summer. Earlier, Chic turned on lamps, positioned the box fan, and pulled back both beds. I opened the window, peeking out.

Two Bucks followed his brother's path toward the Devil's Oak. Unlike Larry, Two Bucks veered, offering the Devil's Oak ample separation. I wondered if Buddy Details' hanging ghost visited Two Bucks. If so, did those visions haunt my uncle, shape his decisions, contribute to his...?

My eyes drifted to the gently swaying Devil's Oak. The evil puppeteer who guided the tree's actions earlier no longer controlled the strings. The tree offered no haunting messages or wicked invitations.

More a force of habit than decision, I crawled into bed, leaving the light on. For Larry, of course. Not because I feared the darkness. Breathing to control my panic at first, watching the box fan for distraction, comforted by the sound and rhythm of the blades, assuming incorrectly a sleepless night awaited. The purr of cool air circulating, whispering...then.

Rooster shook me awake. Shocked, he sat in my room. Rooster and Chic never arrived before I rolled out of bed. Battling disorientation, my eyes rolled to Larry's bed, sheets still folded back, undisturbed.

Rooster translated my confusion. "He never came back. Two Bucks looked all night. He picked up Chic earlier. I walked over."

"Okay. Ahh..."

"Mom's worried sick. Even Rose Petal seems concerned."

I raised my eyebrows.

"In her own way."

"Strange.

"Yeah, Rose Petal keeps repeating...shoulda known. We're searching for 'em in groups. Two Bucks and Chic are together. I called Braelyn. She'll go with you and me."

•   •   •

"Brother, you okay?"

Rooster's voice jerked me back to the present.

"Yeah, Rooster, I'm fine." Letting myself complete the journey back to the now, I considered my surroundings. I sat beside Rooster in his Navigator's polished leather seats. New car smell adulating my nose, bulleting toward my finale, accepting I would reside in Silsbee, Texas, for my 39th birthday.

I wondered how long I lived in memories. Staring out the Navigator's windshield, I recognized Beaumont, Texas. Rooster and I had not talked since the San Jacinto Monument. The exit for 96 North, the Lumberton/Silsbee exit, loomed ahead. We looked at each other, accepting that a force demanded our return, like salmon pulled back to their spawning area. Of course, many salmon die on their return journey. Not the most comforting thought. Rooster answered my unasked question.

"You been living in your brain a while, brother. Didn't want to disturb you."

"Thinking about Charla and Braelyn, the time we..."

"I replay that day often," admitted Rooster. "Those pink and white bikinis, then the lack of 'em. I have ah...let's say enjoyed the benefits of my lifestyle. I've met a beautiful woman or two, but..."

"Yeah, me too. I get it."

"Brother, I'll never ever forget that day. That's not where you were, though. Not the whole time."

"Not the whole time. Larry's birthday..."

"Rough day."

"Yeah."

"Spill it, brother."

"In my memories, I remember you clearly."

"Course ya do, everyone remembers the Rooster."

"I remember Two Bucks, the beers he drank, the aroma of him, the way his pants hung low enough to spot butt-crack. He shaved once a week when Rose Petal made him. His dark, kind eyes offered more than his actions delivered. I remember your mom, my first crush, and..."

"That's sick, brother."

I did what friends do; I pushed into his discomfort. "Yeah, ahh...the way Chic walked, an art class could be dedicated to it."

"Brother, again...my mom."

"When I was 10, I got excited for her hugs, the perfect height for a face full of..."

"One more word, brother, and I'm pulling over."

"I just thought of something."

"What?"

"She stopped giving me hugs when I was about..."

"Probably 'cuz she spotted you sportin' wood, you pervert."

I laughed for a full sixty count. Relief flooded me, comforted me. Rooster's answer, although plausible, rang false.

"Possibly..." I answered. "But I don't think so. At some point, the hugs just stopped. Sad, she was the only person who hugged me."

"Sorry, Tails."

"Anyway, not the point. I remember every migrant worker Two Bucks hired. Every one. I remember my teachers, preachers, and the people in the bleachers."

"But..." led Rooster.

"But I don't see her face."

"Rose Petal."

"I don't, won't, or can't remember."

"Brother, I do."

"That's the point. Rose Petal has an unforgettable face, but I forgot it somehow. Since I got traded to Houston, the nightmares started. About the Old Place and the Devil's Oak. In those nightmares I see my grandfather swinging from the Oak. I've only seen Buddy in pictures, but there he is, haunting me."

"I see Larry's face, from working beside me in the fields, and his terrified death face. But the point is I remember him. The faces, they're all right here." My finger thudded against my noggin. "But not her, ever."

"I see her clear as a punch to the nose."

"In my memories and nightmares, her back's turned, or she's in the next room, in the shadows, or out of my sight line."

We contemplated, then I continued.

"There's more, though. The Old Place, how do you remember it?"

"As my second home."

"Have you ever gone back?"

"No...no...no, no, no."

"Me neither. Do you remember the Old Place as good or evil?"

When asked a question you do not want to answer, multiple strategies present themselves. Please note, I am ashamed and not proud to admit I have used each option:

1) Rebound, ask a question in return. Examples: *Well, Tails, the important question is how do you remember it? What are you looking to achieve by asking that question?*

2) Stall, pretend you did not hear or understand the question: Example: *I am so sorry because of the road noise, I don't feel I got the full scope of your question, can you explain it in detail?*

3) Silence, underutilized but effective. Just shut the hell up.

4) Exit, say good-bye, run, leave for an important "meeting." Example: *I would love to answer that question, but the mandatory staff meeting starts in five minutes.*

5) Distraction, change the dynamic. Example: *Hey, the next round of tequila's on me.*

6) Change the subject, old faithful, the favorite of the male of our species. Rooster chose this one.

"After we found your dad, Braelyn never seemed the same, with you, me, either of us."

"Yeah."

Then silence took over, #3 on the list above. Feel free to mix and match all six. A special dysfunctional bonus for you.

Rooster's avoidance tactics answered my question more clearly than a Stephen King novella. I stared out the window as we crossed Village Creek, a blackwater tributary of the Neches. The entryway path to my destruction. A reminder of all that happened, all who passed, and all who are slated to pass.

Nightmares and tainted memories may disagree, but the woods did not seem more or less threatening the morning after Larry's disappearance.

When the search began, the crunch of pine needles under my feet mimicked every day before. The Piney Wood's smell entwined with rain, welcoming me back, a familiar playmate. Crawdad castles built brick by muddy brick decorated the lower landscapes. Light trickled through the trees, shimmering in and out, changing complexion with each forward step.

I considered the search for Larry a lark, not treating my responsibilities with the gravity they deserved in retrospect. Believing Larry Detals stumbled out drunk and slept it off, Rooster and I shot the shit and stole glances at Braelyn's backside.

Impossible as it seemed, or probable based on her passing from childhood to womanhood, Braelyn looked more striking each time we saw her. The fairer member of our search team took her role more seriously than her hormone-charged companions. She turned frustrated, catching our eyes where she suspected they would rest.

"You guys...would prefer if I led the way? Because you're immature twits. But if we're going to find him, don't you think one of you dipshits should lead? Oh, and try thinking with your brains."

Hands on her hips, she awaited a response.

"Rooster found Larry and Two Bucks' old tree houses a few months back. He coulda went there," I offered.

Rooster shrugged; Braelyn rolled out her arm in grand fashion. Rooster led. "Where's Chic and Two Bucks searching?" asked Braelyn.

"Not sure. Two Bucks started west, before him and Mom started fighting," added Rooster.

"Hmm."

We continued our path, roughly northeast from the Old Place to the tree house.

A scream, clear, concise, and cringeworthy, cut through the forest. A half-second later, Chic's cry echoed again. Rooster power-shifted into full sprint toward Chic's distress call.

Before I could turn, Braelyn followed closely behind him. Like my nickname, I tailed them both. I spent my life following Rooster.

But in memory, Rooster never flew faster through the forest or with more intent. My best friend hurdled fallen logs and crashed through crisscrossed branches toward Chic's cry.

Moments later, I pulled even with Braelyn, instincts deciding to keep pace with my classmate, instead of passing, in case she needed protection.

Then the thought hit. Some creature caused Chic to scream. A woman who walked these woods thousands of times without a peep. Mid-sprint I imagined the beast causing her reaction.

Chic offered no second scream to triangulate her position. Instead, her deep, heavy sobs guided us. As we got closer, I guessed our destination: the swimming hole.

The swimming hole did not feature sandbars for picnics. Sun could not fight through the tree arbors to tan bathing beauties. But on scalding Texas afternoons, no place cooled the body or refreshed the soul quicker than the swimming hole.

Ten yards from the hole, after catching his foot on a knotty cypress knee, Rooster went airborne. He crashed, then grunted. Chic screamed again, as Braelyn and I burst through gangly wild privet bushes. I paused, fighting sensory overload. The surroundings offered thousands of triggers.

Rooster lay unconscious. Chic now cradled him in her lap, as tears stained with mascara dripped from her cheeks. She seemed unconcerned with the danger that initiated her scream. At first glance, I did not spot Two Bucks.

Why would he leave Chic alone? Unless she was not terrified for herself. I spent a moment worrying about Two Bucks' safety, then reaffirmed what I decided years ago. My uncle was unbreakable. Not like a superhero or God. Two Bucks survived every day, despite immeasurable poor decisions, unscathed, unaffected, unchanged, often inebriated. Protected by a nonjudgmental guardian with immeasurable tolerance for drunken missteps.

I heard it first, the cascading of a goliath cutting through water, not the sound of side-winding water moccasins or dog-paddling nutrias. Something massive. Before I turned, Braelyn's scream splintered the woods.

Unsure if I turned fast or slow, I don't recall turning at all. I pushed Braelyn back, protecting her from whatever threat approached. In retrospect, I needed protection.

"Get in here, Tails," Two Bucks said. "Need your help, this is...ah..."

Two Bucks failed to finish his sentence. The least emotional man I knew—correct that, *know*—choked up, his only emotional surrender to dragging his dead brother to shore. I stood near the swimming hole's deep drop, so I dove in. My head emerged quickly, choosing not to spend extra time under the haunted water that claimed a life.

Hours of questions sprouted in the milliseconds underwater. Why here? Why yesterday? Why did he come home? Why did Brandy not attend her husband's birthday? Why did my grandfather, Buddy Detals, and his son Larry kill themselves on their birthdays? Is that my fate too? Do I possess a deadly family chromosome?

Two strokes and then I arrived at Two Bucks' side. Maybe it's not Larry, I hoped.

My last thought evaporated, like partygoers when booze runs out. Even though his face pointed toward the swimming hole's bottom, there was no mistake. Two Bucks and I steered the corpse to the shallows.

Yards away, Rooster moaned into consciousness. Chic cooed. "It's okay, baby. Thanks for coming so fast. Come back to Momma, Rooster."

I envied Rooster and hurt for him. He awoke from nightmare to cruel truth, a tough double-header. As an addict, or because of my past, I frequently visit nightmare-ville.

Consider your most recent nightmare. When awakening from a dreamscape, terror dissipates as you stretch, yawn, and note your surroundings. When your toes touch the floor, your daily tasks bull rush your conscience. The nightmare is demoted as your brain's priority becomes less important. Then, no matter how bone-jarring the nightmare, the lessons and warning presented find themselves forgotten as coffee percolates, bacon sizzles, and eggs fry, sunny-side up.

No matter how cruel Rooster's nightmare, that dream would fall to the wayside. Coddled in Chic's loving arms, staring into her eyes, the nightmare would hold no sway. I understood one truth, a truth Rooster now faced: reality's cruelty trumps nightmares.

Rooster, now awake, turned as Two Bucks and I pushed Larry Detals, or the husk of him, to shore. Rooster rose, stepped toward the swimming hole, waded into the water, grabbed Larry Detals' hands, and pulled him to dry ground. Only Larry's toes remained in the killing water. Two Bucks and I stepped out of the water.

Rooster, me, and Two Bucks stood over his dead brother.

A quick inspection followed. No missing appendages or digits, no chunks of meat ripped from Larry's backside or trunk. He simply drowned. Based on limited but persuasive evidence, he was not attacked.

Chic's voice pulled me from my thoughts.

"Damnit, Two Bucks, I told you he'd be here, you drunken fool...I told you...but did you listen...we could have saved him." I never heard Chic attack before, but this moment, venom poured from her, then tears. "We could have saved him."

Two Bucks said nothing, not defending himself, nothing. He just studied me.

I watched Braelyn drop to her knees, embracing, comforting Rooster's mom, letting Chic's tears flow. Sobbing, the forest's only noise. The wood's residents remained silent, honoring the dead.

"Should we turn him?" asked Rooster.

"I'm not doing it," I answered.

Despite the question, Rooster remained stuck in neutral. Two Bucks bent down to flip his twin brother, the brother born just two minutes and thirty-seven seconds before him, according to Rose Petal's oft-repeated tale.

After the summer of my ninth-grade year, the summer of Braelyn, or the summer of my dead birth father, drowning emerged as my new point of study. I read articles, scoured scientific notations, and viewed every morbid picture at the school and public library. Most materials implied drowning was the most peaceful way to die. According to experts, drowning offered a serenity not found in other forms of death.

Despite numerous sources, I cannot believe that thesis. When Two Bucks flipped Larry Detals, pure terror decorated the dead man's face.

Navigating the Lincoln

Almost Home

Daydreams and memories bull rush your reality at the strangest of times. Memories might overwhelm you while waiting in the grocery express lane, sparked by tabloid covers. Daydreams have short-circuited my brain at unproductive team meetings. Today, the past hijacked my thoughts while riding in a country music star's Lincoln Navigator.

I analyzed my last few moments. Did I experience a memory or dream of finding Larry Detals? Possibly a combo of both? Everything seemed on point, factual, little or no fantasy intertwined. I chalked up the specific incident to memory.

I considered death in a small town. From my experience, big cities know little about death. Sure, city deaths occur at the same rate as small-town deaths. In metroplexes, funerals remain an afterthought, friends finding excuses not to attend. Smaller communities lend themselves to tighter bonds.

In small towns, death hovers close by, his visits often celebrated. Wakes and funerals remain one of the most common excuses for small-town assembly. Rich spreads of fried chicken, deviled eggs, potato salad, fried catfish, and sheet cake greet funeral-goers and wake attendees. Rooster joked that the funeral food spread consistently proved superior to birthday buffets. My experience proved his theory true. Country folks celebrate death more enthusiastically than the banality of another birthday.

I attended dozens of Silsbee wakes and funerals. The open caskets. The dead resting in beds of satin or velvet, in my thoughts, threatening to rise and attend their party. I never became desensitized to the departed laying inches away from where the host expected me to eat chicken fried steak fingers and gravy. Despite the glorious food, I never possessed an appetite.

Rooster's Lincoln continued to eat up the road. Rooster hit the windshield wipers. Now only two miles separated me from Rose Petal. "Phew..." Rooster said. "I still remember his face when Two Bucks turned 'im."

Surprised Rooster resided in the same mental space as me, I answered, "What?"

"You were mumbling about finding him in the swimming hole."

"Was I?"

"It's weird. Your dad was a multimillionaire and physical freak. He outworked the hired help."

"In the Texas heat," I added.

"He married into one of the most storied families in Texas. Tall, handsome, smart, the perfect son."

"Shitty father," I added.

"Bullshit in a Brooks Brothers suit," Rooster continued. "But he was always nice to me."

"A fucking saint compared to Brandy."

"Amen, brother."

On the amen, my thoughts ran to Elora and the mystery of her disappearance. I struggled with the possibility that she never existed. Which meant the insanity that killed Larry and Buddy crept closer to me.

"Brother, before we face Rose Petal..."

"I need a drink."

"Maybe more than one."

"The maybe seems superfluous."

• • •

We pulled into the bar's parking lot, where farm-battered Ford F150s, field-dented Chevy step-sides, and dirty Dodge Power Wagons littered the parking lot. Rooster waited for me to assemble the pieces. I looked at the blinking pink neon sign twenty feet in the sky.

Braelyn's, the sign announced.

"What the hell?" I asked. "How does a woman like Braelyn...?"

"Smart move if you asked me. Braelyn's idiot brother took over the family business and drove it into bankruptcy. Cam's parents love Braelyn and try to take care of her and their grandkids. But Cam had eight brothers and sisters. That spreads the butter pretty thin."

"I'm sure Cam made a good living..."

"But he never bought life insurance. He was just so young. Never thought to. Cam's money got eaten up by years of disability after his stroke. Braelyn opened the bar after Cam died. Braelyn used her own money and a loan from Chic and Two Bucks."

"Two Bucks lent money?"

"He invested in his favorite asset, alcohol."

"Free beer for life."

"Safe bet. Braelyn's an excellent businesswoman, smart move when you think 'bout it."

"Drunk men don't mind looking at beautiful women."

"They do not. But according to Mom, it's more than that. Braelyn worked to ensure women felt welcome too. Mom works there sometimes, to help Braelyn. Mom said the bar struggled the first few months, but Braelyn's printing money now."

We stepped inside. Rolling smoke, pink neon, and the smile of an angel greeted us. She spotted us right away and came running. I caught myself watching her move, cowboy hat lilting back to show off her face, low-riding cutoff jeans, big silver buckle, and a rodeo shirt tied just above her peeking belly button. She jumped into my arms, wrapped her legs around me, and kissed me on the cheek.

"My one-time protector."

She smiled, before letting her boots drop to the floor. Jealously, I watched as she offered Rooster the same greeting. "How lucky am I? A baseball all-star and the biggest name in country music stops by my little bar? We need a picture; I'll put it next'a the old one." She thumbed for us to walk toward the bar. Braelyn nodded to a similarly dressed bartender. "Leslie, grab the camera and snap a picture of me with two old friends."

Braelyn stepped to the middle, wrapped her arms around the two of us, and smiled as Leslie took three quick pictures.

Braelyn beamed at us both. "Follow me, boys." She led us to the bar, and I found myself in a familiar position, staring at Braelyn's backside.

She patted two barstools before sashaying around to the bar. Pictures of Cam and Braelyn's kids (I counted five) decorated the bar. Right next to the Jack Daniels, a familiar picture from summers ago held a place of honor. Braelyn, in the middle, our threesome posing in front of Mrs. Ryan's station wagon. A warm glow passed through me, knowing she kept the photo.

Before we ordered, three highball glasses clapped down in front of me. Southern Comfort flowed into them. Braelyn winked and the three of us tipped glasses. The warm amber liquid easily, too easily, glided down my throat. Rooster's empty glass hit the bar first, milliseconds before mine and several seconds before Braelyn's.

She set her glass down and shrugged. "I have nothing to prove, unlike two boys I remember."

Then I mustered. "Sorry about Cam."

"Did you knuckleheads think a girl could stand a visit from her best friends after her husband died?"

The word echoed around my head. *Best friends*. She did not talk to me once after that summer.

"I am so..."

"Don't start, Rooster."

I tried next. "Braelyn, I didn't know."

"Bullshit, Tails."

Rooster took the horns for me. "You're right, no excuse for me, Braelyn. Tails didn't know 'til yesterday. Today he's here."

"But Two Bucks and Rose Petal..."

"He hasn't talked to Rose Petal in 20 years, and Two Bucks hasn't been to see either of us since..."

"But you musta..."

"We caught up for the first time in a decade, coupla nights ago."

"But you're best friends, why the hell haven't...?"

"Charla," we answered in unison.

"She took you both away from me."

"That's not how I remember it," I mumbled.

Braelyn looked down, called out, as she called us out seconds earlier. Then, the hordes closed on Rooster. Old friends, including the Mauler clan, and every woman populating the bar surrounded the Piney Woods' most famous export. The mob tugged him away from us, leaving Braelyn and me alone at the bar.

Braelyn studied my battered arm and the cast that protected it. "I watched it when it happened."

"On TV?"

"Yes, we had it on here. When Cam was alive, he and I watched as many as we could. He hated you for a while. But having a real-life major leaguer from town wore him down. We watched every game we could, but it was hard because you were playing all over the country."

"I bet."

"I got excited when you got traded to the Astros. Then, well..." She looked at the cast. "Looks like my turn to sign it."

She lifted my arm, kissing the cast, leaving a glossy lipstick imprint. I found myself jealous of the plaster. I watched her sign: *To my protector and best friend. Love, Braelyn.*

"You keep saying we were best friends."

"I did, we were."

"Were we?" I asked. "You didn't talk to me after Larry's funeral. Not at school or Tiger Drive-In. Not on the phone, not once. Speaking of a 'I could have used you' moment. That was it, Braelyn."

"There's a lot you don't know, Tails."

"How 'bout you explain it?"

"Cam came back days after your dad died, I told him about the...ahh...the skinny-dipping. He planned to beat you to a pulp. After I told Cam about your dad, he backed down. But only after I promised. Promised not to see you two ever again."

"Cam graduated two years ahead of us, you coulda..."

"A promise is a promise, Tails. I broke his heart. Hell, he hadn't seen me naked at that point, but thanks to Charla, you, and Rooster, well. Anyway, with Cam dead, you and Rooster are the only two living men to see my birthday suit..."

My thoughts wandered back to that day. She slapped me. "Stop thinking about it, Tails."

"I won't lie, Braelyn. Today's not the first time."

She blushed.

I looked her up and down, taking her in. "You look…"

"Ridiculous," she finished.

"Not a word I'd use."

"Tip-flirting's important when you have five college tuitions in your future, so…" She spun so I could admire the ensemble.

I clapped.

"Tails, it wasn't just Cam."

Rooster battled back to the bar, parting the crowd, hugging, high-fiving, and backslapping.

Braelyn read the disappointment on my face and reacted. She reached behind the bar and pulled out an acoustic guitar. "Show the locals you're not washed up, Rooster."

My best friend looked from Braelyn to me, picked up her signal, and strutted away. The crowd followed him to the bar's stage.

"It was more than Cam. He told me I couldn't talk to you, I accepted. But I shoulda fought to be there for you when your dad died. Later, shame kept me away, kept building, getting bigger. If it means anything, I never forgave myself for letting you down. The second biggest disappointment of my life, after losing Cam."

I plunged into the thought itching my brain since Rooster mentioned it. "You and Cam came to my game?"

"Cam's last trip. He wanted to see you two, and there was zero chance of you idiots visiting us. You lit it up that night, two for four. I think you had a triple."

"I remember. Wrigley Field, I bounced one into the ivy. Why didn't you guys come down after the game?"

In the background, Rooster started playing. Even on a battered bar acoustic guitar, his singular style dominated the room. No singing yet, only picking.

"Cam was so proud; he loved you like a little brother, before…"

I hung my head.

"Stop it, Tails. You were forgiven by that point. Cam admitted later he'd have been there beside you, eyes popping out his noggin, jeans in the sand. But I hadn't forgiven myself for deserting you after your dad died."

She held out her bent pinky. "How about we forgive each other?"

I looked at the extended pinky, took it, and nodded.

Indecision rippled through me. In front of me stood the love of my childhood. Perfect in every way. But Elora Banks haunted me. Unfortunately, Elora may or may not be an invention of my imagination. I looked to Braelyn and smiled, thinking that maybe, just maybe, beautifully packaged salvation stood in front of me.

One minute later, Rooster solved my conundrum, informing me I never stood a chance with Braelyn.

Rooster started singing. Not the brash country rock that defined him onstage, but a ballad. His next guitar lick enraptured his audience. Time slowed as "Always on My Mind" flowed from Rooster's lips through the microphone. Rooster stared past every other woman, singing to Braelyn.

A decade before, I watched Rooster rock the honky-tonks, perfecting his craft. During performances, his eyes bounced woman to woman, flirting with each. Not tonight.

Tonight, Rooster performed for an audience of one.

The summer the three of us spent together washed over me. I accessed the drawer of Braelyn memories. Mentally opening all file folders. I allowed my coloring of each event to evaporate, acknowledging the truth.

That summer we were the three amigos. But Braelyn rode with Rooster the day we biked to the sandbar. She always chased him first in tag. He led our adventures. I tailed behind.

I admitted to myself, Braelyn looked at Rooster in ways she never looked at me. For Cam's sake, her seeds of attraction for Rooster never grew, but they were planted. I tailed Rooster most of my life and now I tailed him for her. Or worse, I never competed for Braelyn. What an imbecile. A blind fool. I never saw the light. Until now.

Braelyn moved up the bar for a better view of Rooster. Moments later, she drifted toward the stage, surrendering to the electric pull of one of the world's most charismatic performers.

I pounded the bar twice and looked at the pretty barback. She dropped two shots of Southern Comfort in front of me.

As Braelyn inched closer to Rooster, I pounded the bar twice more. Shots arrived. Drunken oblivion whispered seductively, reminding me we were lovers. My ever-present sweetheart, right around the corner, waiting with open arms. Another few drinks promised our reintroduction. Ahh, there she is. Hello, gorgeous. Good to see you...again.

One Day 'Til I Die

July 27, 1999

Addicts often enjoy or suffer rich imaginations. Dreams appear real, feel real, fear real (not a misquote), and operate in a world so similar to yours that only the slightest hints allow the dreamer to confirm residence in nightmare.

Knowing you reside in dream offers comfort but less than you imagine. After all, you occupy a world without reality's rules. A fact offering horrific options to your dream-weaver.

So, I found myself standing at the swimming hole, staring at the bloated body of Larry Detals. The corpse, like in memory, faced the swimming hole's bottom. In this demented concoction, the corpse slowly motored to shore, feet first.

Just a dream, just a dream, I repeated.

Jus...serrr...ream...bubbled up from the drowned man. Jus...serrr...ream.

Sploosh. Awkwardly, horrifyingly, the corpse flopped over.

Still, despite being belly-up, the face remained obscured by his bloated stomach and the dark water. The man who abandoned me in Silsbee drifted toward shore. With a soft *thud* and water waking around him, Larry Detals' corpse arrived.

Trapped in place, witness, not participant. My eyes returned to Larry Detals.

Water gushed from his mouth, more and more and more, before the waterlogged wraith wrestled to a sitting position. Terror, mirroring the day we found him, colored his face...but dead eyes beseeched me to understand.

The corpse's head turned, raising his hand. A red, white, and blue ribbon dangled from one decaying finger, and a coin?

Wanting me to comprehend, the drowned man scraped closer, fingernails in soil, dragging himself, offering the...

I screamed.

A familiar voice sliced through the dream, coaxing me home. "Hey, sleeping beauty."

The voice's owner slapped me. My first thought, Braelyn or Rooster. Farm-carved callouses scraped across my cheek disproving my assumption. Thick hands, with crooked aged fingers, slammed into my other cheek. Then back to the other side. I recognized those hands.

His slap carried intention. Not hard, but aggressive enough to wake a drunken screaming fool from nightmare.

My crusted eyes remained fused shut. Alcohol-induced salt, sweat, or sugar shards coated my lids and lashes. An alcoholic's eye-goo superglue.

Poor life choices prepared my rescuer to assess and solve the situation. Strong wrinkled thumbs jammed into my eye canals and forced the shards away. Blinking, I stared into the aged face of my uncle.

Shaking his head, Two Bucks Detals took a long draw of his longneck before standing. My bed du jour felt uncomfortable. Rotating my aching head right then left, I assessed my location: Braelyn's stage. My brain motored to life, sputtering and spitting at first through pain and mental fog, sorting facts from fancy. Two fact turds floated to the surface: Rooster played here, Braelyn and Rooster began coupling.

I sat up, assaulted by a flip-flopping stomach. The bar stood empty. Braelyn and her bar staff cleaned the place. More accurately they cleaned to the level any bar ever really achieves.

Two Bucks held out his beer. "Hair of the dog?"

"Yeah, no, thanks." I looked at my watch. 8:37 a.m.. "You're drinking before 9:00 a.m. now?".

"Seemed appropriate. Braelyn called. Asked me to scrape a drunken fool off her stage."

"How'd you get in?"

He dangled keys. "I'm an investor. Braelyn bought back most'a my shares. I kept hold'a enough..."

"To drink for free. Braelyn's taking a bath on that deal."

"Allows Two Bucks to keep his bucks in his pocket."

"Where's Rooster and Braelyn?"

Two Bucks' raised eyebrows served as my unwanted answer.

Once again, second to Rooster. Not important enough. Not selected first, or at all.

The one person, or one woman who selected me first, my erstwhile decorator, my favorite travel companion, may or may not be a figment of imagination. Still, if Elora Banks proved to be real, if...

Heavy thought for a waking drunk.

The dead weight of my arm locked in a cast greeted me. Turning, I checked a box. I occupied the real world, cast and all. Not the world of floating corpses.

Taking a moment to study, I noted names, crude drawings, dirty jokes, and one...limerick (I think) now covered my cast. Some doodles occurred when I stood upright. Others happened after consciousness and I had a falling out. I propped up on my elbows. Rooster left my leather duffle bag by my left boot—classy. A more appetizing priority overtook his need to deliver me to the Old Place. Who'd blame him?

Two Bucks downed his longneck before turning bar-ward to further slice into Braelyn's profits. Two Bucks' uniform remained unchanged— worn but clean jeans, pressed, field-stained shirt, scarred but somehow perfect work boots. Over his shoulder, he said, "Sit there stewin' if ya want. Chores'll be there when we get home."

"I don't have chores; I don't live there."

"Where ya sleeping tonight?" His answer implied inevitability.

Ahh...the clank of an empty beer bottle tossed to the trash, next to an open fridge, then the crisp sound of a popped longneck, followed by the discarded cap spinning on the floor. There may be a million alternative universes, but none exist where Two Bucks bends over to retrieve the cap.

He walked to me, no stumble or swerve, two morning beers, nothing to his oft-polluted system. He plopped in the chair closest to the stage before downing half of his second longneck in one tilt.

I considered the one woman who selected me first. Saying her name in my head, an internal prayer. *Elora Banks, Elora Banks, Elora Banks*. Making her real, proving entrée and exit in my life, served as my connection to sanity.

Failure to prove Elora's existence punched my crazy train ticket. A train ride my grandfather and sperm donor (okay, you can call him my father, I can't) failed to survive. Elora Banks, a woman I barely knew, or possibly did not know, held the skeleton key to my fate.

Even trapped in thought, my senses performed dutifully. My ears registered beer rushing down Two Bucks' throat, the distinct swish of a final gulp, then the empty bottle hitting the table. Senses flagged me, announcing the inevitability of the burp, promised in advance, and delivered in style by my uncle.

"Damn, Two Bucks, cover your mouth. My nose hairs singed, for gosh sake."

"Funny, you think my burp's the worst stank in this bar?"

I lifted my arm and sniffed. Stale alcohol and poor decisions greeted my nostrils.

"Let's hit the road. She's ready for you..."

Rose Petal Detals awaits.

• • • • •

Magnetism overwhelmed me as Two Bucks' truck propelled us closer. Considering my nightmares, patterns seemed important. For decades, I shoved this place's memories into a mental filing cabinet marked, *DO NOT OPEN—DUMBASS*.

The Devil's Oak, then the Old Place, seeped into my dreams days before my trade to the Houston Astros. Upon arrival in Houston, dreams intensified. Last night, my first night back in Silsbee, Larry Detals' corpse invited me to his swim party. Was *geography* jiggering the lock to my mental filing cabinets, opening the drawer to mental collapse?

Was it *timing*? My 39th birthday freight-trained into the station tomorrow.

Or both, mixed into a toxic brain bisque?

Two Bucks' truck navigated the winding road to the Old Place. He turned off the ignition a hundred yards out and glided into his spot. A nice trick, when arriving home late, to avoid waking the house's matriarch.

"Old dog, old trick."

Two Bucks laughed. "New tricks don't play well here."

I heard an ear-shattering squeal, understanding the task Rose Petal Detals saved for me.

"You've guessed your *first* chore."

"First chore," I said. "She can't expect me to show up and..."

"That's exactly what she expects."

"But I have a broken arm."

"Then it'll take you twice as long. Longer if you bitch 'bout it."

I walked to the porch, betting a wardrobe change awaited. Correct, my old jeans, work shirt, and work boots.

These artifacts rested in my closet, predicting my return. Nothing wasted on the farm. Newish cotton socks were the only recent addition to the wardrobe. The new socks, not a surrender to Rose Petal's "nothing wasted" mantra, but a testament. She used my old socks to dust the house or wrap pipes for winter.

I stripped my noxious Southern Comfort, sweat-scented clothes. The morning air enlivened my naked frame. After stretching, yawning, and touching my toes, I dressed for the task ahead, snapping buttons by rote. Worn work boots welcomed my feet, as if I occupied them days before, comforting and frightening.

I chose not to look to the pigpen while dressing. Procrastinating...you bet. Striving to keep my memories of her face blank as long as possible. The task Rose Petal selected for my return to farm chores did not encourage expediency.

Disturbingly, I recognized each piglet's vocalization. Whines of impending doom from waiting piglets, not sure of the day's agenda. Wails of the captured piglet, closer to pain, but still not processing the oncoming procedure. The high-pitched squill of the piglet during the lightning-quick operation. Then, the haunting sob of the aftermath.

After dressing, I trudged to the pigpens. I spotted Rose Petal's back first. Strong and thick, not an ounce of fat, despite her age. Aware of my presence but unconcerned, she focused on her task.

Castrating piglets sounds cruel, *is* cruel. The justification for castration, simple. People don't buy bacon or eat ham that smells like dark murky boar piss.

Non-castrated hogs develop a rancid smell, an overpowering BO, similar to a Mount Everest of game-used socks and jockstraps. Hunters kill mature wild boars to protect environments or mount the beast above their fireplace. No sane person without a powerful need would eat their kill. Even far-flung, Indigenous tribes avoid eating a mature boar's meat unless on the brink of starvation.

Castrating male piglets, no matter how small, is a two-man job. One man to snatch the piglet and hold them, legs splayed open while the second performs the task. A young man or powerful man's task on most farms. Not at the Old Place.

Back still to me, Rose Petal snatched the smallest piglet by the back legs, dropped it in her lap. Her back obscured me, but I knew the task from memory. The piglet screamed, then bellowed in pain, before Rose Petal dropped him to the ground. Blue iodine mix dripped from the area formerly occupied by the piglet's balls.

Rose Petal dropped the severed piglet parts into a bucket positioned next to her. Disturbed and impressed by her efficiency, I watched a beat too long.

"Don't remember you, lazy. Did city living make you useless, like what I dropped in the bucket?"

I looked at my cast.

"Not a man, if ya can't muster to ya chores." *Note to self: her verbal castration skills intact.*

I opened the pen's gate and stepped inside; the piglets offered a wide berth. She rose from the wooden castrating stool Buddy Detals built for her decades ago, put her hands on her hips, and turned toward me. No hug or handshake was offered.

I forgot the crystal-blue strength her eyes wielded. Rose Petal stared through you, past you, and dissected you, concurrently. I forgot. Hell, 20 years passed since I stood near her.

Two decades of Southeast Texas sun further wrinkled her face. But Rose Petal yielded not one ounce to Father Time in posture or countenance. Not nearly as scary as in my dreams and more terrifying concurrently.

Rose Petal nodded in my direction, then resumed her position on the castrating stool. I counted seventeen piglets in this pin. Mature hogs and this crop's female members occupied the other three pens.

"Got the runts myself. Grab the fat boy there," Rose Petal said and pointed with her elbow. Muscle memory captained my actions. Even with decades away and a broken arm, this task offered no challenge for me.

Blocking the pigs' cries from my mind resembled batting in big games. Stepping into my private mental space, my quiet place, I rallied. Snatching the target piglet by the back legs, I spun the animal while moving toward Rose Petal, pig's legs splayed open, piglet balls displayed. Rose Petal sliced, squeezed, amputated, and swabbed iodine in seconds.

One down. I dropped the piglet, he hobbled to the far corner of the pen. His world ended at pen's edge. My mental emasculation mirrored the pig's physical state. However, the pig proved smarter than me. The castrated animal understood he could only run so far.

For twenty years, I failed to understand. My journey led back here, trapped in this place, damaged, in pain, mentally castrated. Not exactly like the piglet, but maybe close enough for Rose Petal.

Meet the Maulers

With two of us working in unison, even with my busted arm, we completed the task in minutes. Rose Petal stood. "You missed breakfast, but there's a skillet'a jalapeño cornbread casserole."

"Sure, okay."

"It's my job to feed ya'. I'll do my job if you do yours."

"Always about the chores with you, nothing more."

"Go see what Two Bucks lined up. The work'll give you time to rid yourself of the whiskey sweats. Not learnt a damn thing, have ya?"

I fought a chuckle.

"Didn't think I'd recognize that smell? Smelt its markings for generations. Did ya bathe in Jack Daniels or Evan Williams?"

My nose validated her claim.

"I'll wash your city clothes."

"Okay."

"So they don't stink up my house."

"Thanks, Grandmother."

"Ehh..." She waved me off before walking away.

Only when I thought she stepped out of earshot, I mumbled, "Good to see ya, Tails, missed ya, Tails. I love ya, Tails."

"I heard that. Stop your whinin', it's unbecomin' a grown man."

I laughed despite myself. Rose Petal continued, "Go see Two Bucks. Man's 'llergic to work, he'll pass off chores faster 'en a politician'll screw constituents."

Rose Petal found her wit endlessly amusing. The rest of us populated the less appreciative.

"We drank Southern Comfort," I mumbled, answering her earlier question. "Ironic, because I'm in the South and you don't offer any."

She did not turn.

Years spent on the farm train your ears for hundreds of sounds, many unidentifiable to city folk. The sound of snapped peas clinking into a tin bowl, the music of dried corn filling deer feeders, the oozing of slop emptied into the pig trough, the rhythmic chortling of a trash fire. Drawn by the sharpening of field blades, I located Two Bucks. High-pitched grinding, as enchanting as any siren's call, tapped into the best days of childhood.

The workshop's shade offered respite from Southeast Texas' pounding summer heat. Add inappropriately entertaining stories, a dozen Snap-on Tool Girl posters, a beat-up radio tuned to my favorite stations, and Two Bucks' ever-present Igloo cooler stocked with beer for him, Coca-Cola, Frostie, or Nehi for Rooster and me, and you understand the charm.

A smile curled onto my face as I opened the workshop door. The scent of sparks filled my nose. "Hey, Two Bucks."

Rose Petal labeled blade sharpening a Two Bucks task. Less taxing than fieldwork, in the shade, and near a cooler.

"Hey, Tails. 'Bout sixty bales need to be delivered to Tig Mauler. He's running Pop's place. Load up the trailer, take my truck." Two Bucks' truck keys zipped through the air before I objected. I snatched them left-handed, glove side in my old life.

I held up my cast-encased right arm.

"Want me to sign the damn thing or d'ya rather get to loadin'? Snatch the bale with your good hand, guide with your broken wing."

Grumbling silently because enunciation offered no friendly ears, I walked around front. Hundreds of bales filled the barn. Bales of hay vary in weight depending on each farm's bailing equipment.

The Old Place's half-century-old baler produced traditional two-string hay bales. Two- string bales weigh between 40 and 70 lbs. Not challenging, decades earlier, after I grew into my teenage body. Problematic now, with one functional arm.

I engaged my inner Two Bucks, asking, *How can I complete this task with minimum effort?*

First, I pulled Two Bucks' truck around. Attaching an empty trailer to a truck hitch is easier than attaching one stacked with sixty hay bales. Getting the trailer attached one-armed took creativity. I managed.

Next, I backed the trailer until I bumped hay bales. No wasted steps.

Finally, time to load. After embracing scents that unlocked doors to childhood memories, I lifted the first bale. Lifting with legs and back, using my arm as a guide, I managed the first ten bales. The second ten bales offered pain, not to my damaged arm but in muscles unused for decades. Twenty bales stacked on the front third of the trailer, not an appetizer for the younger me, now seemed an incredible accomplishment. Accepting how much age, addictive habits, and time robbed me, I walked outside to stretch. While pulling my knee to my chest, my senses fired.

First, the birds stopped chirping, announcing a new presence. I inhaled, knowing my day improved. Next, mother and son, harmonizing, "Go Tell it on the Mountain," soothed me. All worry fell away as Chic and Rooster stepped from the forest into the clearing while finishing their final verse.

Chic approached tentatively. "Long time, Tails." No "Hello, my sweet honey child," from my youth. No hugs or smiles. She examined me, like a diner perusing the Red Lobster holding tank, finger ready to point to their entrée. I imagined my lobster-self, pinchers rubber-banded shut, hiding behind my brethren, waiting but knowing the inevitable finger-point loomed, sealing my boiled and buttered fate. The three of us felt the discomfort.

Did Rooster recount my...ah...affinity for her hugs? No, that theory did not ring true. Hmm...

Chic checked herself, ending her analysis, knowing I translated pieces of her thoughts. Guilt overtook her as she took two steps back. Clues clinked into place. Like an archaeologist dusting exposed fossil, I swept away topsoil. Too early to label my finding: tortoise, tarpon, T. rex, or pterodactyl. But dark secrets lay deep beneath Chic's veneer.

Despite the warm greetings Chic offered in my youth, I never considered her my mother. My brain leafed through the Sears Roebuck catalog of memories. Chic loved Rooster with all of her heart. She'd kill for him. In my youth, before high school, I felt her love but understood my position—distant second to Rooster. I understood and accepted that fact.

Then the world changed, and I fell from second to...

"See you inside." Chic turned, looked over her shoulder, and walked toward the front porch, ending the awkward stalemate. I turned to my best friend.

Rooster's broad, stupid smile broadcast his evening's pleasures. Jealousy sucker-punched me first. Hate rose as I considered the wonders of Braelyn.

How...why did I always lose to him? Second again in a two-man race.

Hate evaporated when he uttered, "Need help, brother?" Rooster stared over my shoulder at the hay bales. My misgivings floated downstream.

Buoyed by Rooster's two functional arms, we finished loading, stacking, and strapping in short order. I tried to convince myself, sans cast, that I would keep pace with Rooster. Load secured, he hopped into the passenger side as I one-arm wedged into the driver's seat.

"Where to?"

"Pop Mauler's. Tig's place now, according to Two Bucks."

"Tig may work it, but it's still Pop's. Chic says the old man rules from his rocker. Spewed man-seed all over town into his sixties. More kids than ditches got tadpoles. Must be 85 by now."

Being back in Silsbee, driving familiar streets, instincts and memories controlled every turn. We drove in silence, me refusing to ask about last night after he and Braelyn abandoned me. Rooster not offering detail. His stupid, serene smile translated enough.

Rooster spoke, changing the subject, even though we were not talking. "So, this girl you met?"

"Elora."

"Any news?"

"No," I answered curtly. If he avoided talking about Braelyn, I could avoid talking about imaginary girlfriends.

"So, it's like that."

We turned onto a pothole-infested asphalt road and bumped our way to Pop Mauler's. Once we reached his place, I steered toward their barn. Just before I started backing in, I spotted legs sticking out from under a red '74 GTO.

I backed the truck into position by memory as Tig popped from under his prize possession to greet us. The hallway fight over Braelyn and Charla was decades in our past. Tig stepped to us and shook hands with a firmness necessitated within the Mauler clan. "Two Bucks said you two were coming. Didn't believe him."

"The smell'd usually keep me away," Rooster started.

"Good thing we don't screen for shitty music. You wouldn'ta passed the gate."

I laughed.

"Don't need lip from a washed-up, one-armed ballplayer either." Tig smiled.

Greeting behind us, the three of us hugged and backslapped. "Good to see you boys."

"You too, Tig," I said.

"Yip, yip, yip" he called. Teenagers poured from house, barn, and field toward us. Tig looked to the assembled Mauler clan, nodded to the hay bales, then to the barn. "Come on. Pop asked for you two." He waved, we followed.

I turned back to watch the mayhem. Tig's crew unloaded half the trailer before we reached the porch. The tin-roofed home, once a small cottage, now featured multiple wings added by carpenters of varying skill levels over decades. The Frankenstein-ed home stood as a salute to function and Mauler breeding, long ago surrendering any nod to beauty or symmetry.

As we stepped onto the porch, Tig repeated the family call, softer this time. A gangly eight-year-old emerged through the screen. "Lexi May, bring Pop out. Then wrangle lemonade."

The mop-topped beauty pushed ill-fitted glasses up on her nose, mush-mouthed, "Yessir," then disappeared.

Spending time with the Maulers did not rate high on my to-dos, but it soared compared to Two Bucks' chore-list or prolonged interaction with Rose Petal. I dodged my demons for decades, putting them off, her off, appealed to my black belt in procrastination.

Tig motioned for us to sit. The rusted metal chair I selected offered outspoken disagreement, creaking and croaking. My seat lilted groundward, then recovered, adjusting to my weight, begrudgingly deciding not to collapse. The oft-repaired wooden chair Rooster selected seemed sturdier but bemoaned being inconvenienced. Tig smiled. My guess was we passed some demented test he enjoyed. Our host took refuge on the cushioned porch swing. He rocked slowly, smiling.

Moments later, the bespeckled ragamuffin returned with Pop Mauler, trying but failing to assist his entrance. He slapped her hands, huffing in her direction. Despite Pop's discouragement, Lexi May followed Tig's orders and shepherded the octogenarian to the porch's sole well-maintained chair.

Pop Mauler now occupied his throne, the seat of Mauler clan power. Not just here, throughout the Piney Woods. A small table rested beside his throne. Every country boy grasped the table's purpose.

A brown stream dribbled from Pop's mouth toward his chin. Lexi May reappeared with a spit cup. Not noticing the girl, Pop grabbed the cup and launched a brown steam of spittle and tobacco into it. Next, the spit cup took its place of honor.

I was aware of Pop Mauler, most locals were. Like the long-dead Buddy Details, Silsbee residents spoke the name of Pop Mauler with a mix of awe, fear, and curiosity. Still, I never sat in the old man's presence before today. So, Pop's summons surprised me.

"Been seein' you boys on da' TV."

He lifted the cup and spit again, not expecting answers. "Made somethin' of yourself. Not like my useless waste'a sperm." Pop turned to Tig, who rolled his eyes.

"More kids 'an six months after a goat orgy. Not a damn one of'm worth what I left behind in da' shitter this morning. Shoulda made it tougher on d'ese soft dicks. D'ey may'a left'n found 'dere own way in da' world. Stead's hangin' round here, livin' oft da' tittie."

"Heaven on earth here, Pop," Tig countered.

"Shut your hole, Tig, if I wuz wantin' you 'pinion I'd bitch-slapped it outta'ya," Pop cackled.

Tig displayed immunity to Pop's insults. After pausing to spit and dribble into his cup, Pop upped the stakes. "Least people don't end up pushing daisies 'round here."

Pop stared directly into me when pronouncing the last sentence.

Lexi May returned with three glasses of lemonade, all she could carry, and served her dictator first. He scraped Red Man tobacco from his cheek into the spit cup, swigged the lemonade, and used it as mouthwash before spitting the yellow-brown mix into the cup, cleansing his palate.

The girl served Tig next. I remained unclear if Tig was the child's father, grandfather, or uncle. The distinction, though perplexing, remained unimportant while Pop held court.

Recognizing Rooster, the child served him the last glass in her possession. Only after receiving a smile and nod did she return to the kitchen to fetch my lemonade. "Et tu, Lexi May?"

Pop downed his remaining lemonade in one draw.

Tig led, "Wife's back in our bedroom. Convalescing."

"Ain't convalescing. She's watching her programs, dat's all she does. Almost as pretty as lazy...but not quite. If I listen to da'damn intro to *Days of our Lives* again, I'll shoot myself."

"I'll turn the volume to 10 tomorrow. Be doing this world a favor."

"Leavin' you high on d'a hog," Pop waved him off. "You sit in d'is chair, hell no, a fool wid'out da tools."

Tig continued, "Anyway, she just watched your live show on the HBO. If I don't walk you back, I'll get an ear chewing."

Tig opened the screen for Lexi May as she returned with my lemonade. Rooster and Tig disappeared into the house.

Only after they departed did I say, "Tig's your favorite, huh?"

"Don't I make it clear 'nuff?" Pop half-grinned. "All da' time I spend training 'em. Leaders hav'da deal wit da most shit. Makin' certain Tig's like my dick, always up for the job."

Pop pulled the Red Man packet from his pocket, then two-finger reloaded his chew before lamenting, "Buddy Detals 'wuz my best friend."

"I thought you guys hated each other."

"Dat's da' small-town gossip in your ear. Oh, Buddy and I fought plenty. Specially after he won your farm from my idiot brother in da' damn poker game."

Ah, the infamous poker game.

"But came'ta an understandin'. Over time, Buddy paid us back in a sense. He worked da' land better d'an my lazy brother woulda."

"How'd he pay you back for a farm?"

"Little at a time. When one of da' clan wuz hurtin', Buddy Details showed up wit' a pickup full of corn or bushels of peas."

"Hardly settles the bill."

"Not if he did it once, but he did a bunch'a times. Lot'a Maulers. Round Christmas, he'd drop a few hogs off."

"Wow."

"Once, when my fool nephew wuz in da hospital, bill got paid. Never proved it, but it wuz Buddy. My daughter, da only one da make somethin' of herself, wanted a college education. Girl won a mysterious one-time scholarship for future nurses. No one heard dat scholarship 'fore or sense. When Buddy's car need'a repair, he took it'da Tig's daddy's garage. Buddy Details did more for me d'an my own people."

Before today, this piece of local history remained unclaimed to me.

"Course, da' biggest favor he did was marrying your grandma."

"What?" I asked.

"Oh, Rose Petal was da belle of d'a county. I can still see her, so beautiful. Tall and wid'a hip. Fine lookin' baby factory. Still get rumblins' when I dink 'bout her spiffied up for da dance. Boobs thrust skyward like 'dem honing beacons, bait for da unsuspectin'.'"

I cringed. Someone describing Rose Petal that way flip-flopped my stomach.

"Don't give d'at look, boy. She wuz fine-looking. Course, retrospectin', her crazy outpaced her pretty. But no one know'd dat then. We all made a run. But t'ank God I missed out on d'at booby prize." He laughed at his own joke, dribbling spit signaling time for his next spit.

"Buddy smartly stopped spittin' out kids after Larry and Two Bucks."

I raised my eyebrow, telegraphing interest.

Pop continued, "Case he could plot d'a getaway," he said. Then Pop shut down, a statue, stuck on pause. He stared over my shoulder, communicating telepathically with a harbinger out of my line of sight.

Despite my chair's vocal complaint, I turned to spot the inciter of Pop's stasis. An old oak, similar in age, if not in shape to the Devil's Oak, hijacked Pop's thoughts.

I waited for Pop's return; brown spittle dribbling toward his chin pulled him back, he spit. Pop considered me, obviously forgetting I co-occupied his porch. Like an Evinrude purring to life, Pop's brain reengaged.

"Then, Buddy ended up at rope's end. Not d'a getaway I suspected. Til da' end...happiest man in Texas...bout most d'ings at least." Pop paused, heartbroken. "Heard legends Buddy wuz tippin' heifers...or tippin' other d'ings late at night. Know wha'd I mean?"

Was Pop saying what I thought? His nod confirmed his accusation.

"Had to do somethin' to keep d'a smile on his face. Wit d'a public beatdowns Rose Petal's mouth inflicted on 'em. 'Magine the ass-whoopins he took at home."

I studied Pop. Foul-mouthed sure, senile possibly, but far from stupid.

"Her mouth 'id cut ya 'nta scrap. I swallared my fair share of her bile when she pulled Buddy out'n da bars. But despite everything' 'til da end..."

Then Pop sat silently.

No one claimed the Mauler's mayhem could be held in check. Still, locals understood Pop Mauler owned the most sway over the clan. Residents begged Pop to arbitrate squabbles between the Maulers and the townsfolk. Pop long ago ascended to small-town demigod status. Stories of his backwoods wisdom passed from one gossip circle to the next.

Few questioned his words of wisdom, even when delivered with the subtlety of battery acid to flesh. Pop possessed no filter, no governor. His wit, delivered quickly, but with no consideration for aftermath. Words flamethower-ed from his mouth, singeing everyone in his periphery.

So, when Pop paused, considering his next syllable, I understood the situation's gravity. The man who controlled the rowdiest clan in Silsbee appeared tentative. Watching him sort syllables, calculate word order, and even clip his speech to perfection, terrified me.

Stalling, he again pulled out his packet of Red Man, supplementing his chaw. Time stopped as I watched Pop ponder on his throne.

"I...*can't*...believe Buddy Detals killed himself."

Can't an interesting selection. If Pop said, "I don't believe your grandfather killed himself," he pointed to murder. Can't could be translated two ways.

"I was so surprised he killed himself."

"I believe someone murdered him."

Time for clarification. "Pop..."

The swinging screen door announced Pop and I were no longer alone.

"Thanks, Rooster, that'll be the highlight of her year."

"You're welcome, brother. But tell your wife not to pinch my ass next time."

"Calm down. If you don't want women pinching your ass, don't spray-paint the Wranglers on."

"Your wife pinched *my* ass, and you're tellin' me to calm down."

"When you're gone, my wife'll still be thinkin' 'bout that ass. You won't be here, so she'll...ah, redirect."

"Tig, you are one son of a..."

"Remember..." Pop said, popping his noggin with his wrinkled knuckle.

"What'd you say to him, Pop?" asked Tig.

"If I wanted ya to know, I'd a jotted it down in one-syllable words," Pop cackled before spitting in his cup. The old man's attention returned to me. "You look mighty comfortable in d'at chair. Betch'ur in no hurry to return to d'at hell now."

Tig said, "Pop, leave him alone."

As I processed the revelation about my grandfather, Pop Mauler opened a fresh can of shit-which.

"Always wondered where Rose Petal buried d'a pastor's body."

"Pop," Tig huffed.

Wow, Pops loaded both barrels of his sawed-off shotgun today.

"Aw, shud'up. D'ese two probably helped her ditch d'a pastor's body."

Not the two of us, I mumbled internally. Rooster looked confused. I never told him about the maggot-infested corpse of our missing pastor or what happened.

Mentally, I sailed from the Mauler's porch into memory. The Piney Woods soared around me. That chocolate night returned all at once. The ache of my arms from carrying dead weight, more specifically a dead man, for twenty minutes.

Rose Petal ordered, "Grab his boots again, or come up here and help me drag 'em."

I considered my options. My arms hung to my side, useless. In reality, I doubted I could lift them. I did not want to be in proximity of the pastor's maggot-ridden face, but the promise of using different muscles outweighed fear. I rationalized that darkness would mask the pastor's face.

I walked next to Rose Petal. "Can we flip 'em over at least?" I begged.

Rose Petal spun the corpse with disturbing ease. I grabbed one shoulder and she took the other. I looked to her but darkness mercifully shrouded my view.

The shuffle of our steps and the corpse's boots dragging through pine needles the only night sounds.

"You'd a skipped this chore if you stayed out from under the house like I told ya. Or kept your trap shut." Her words rang in my ears.

We trudged 10 minutes in silence. Finally, happy with our location, she said, "Make your way back. Fetch shovels."

The screen door's creaking brought me back to Pop's domain. Lexi May breezed by and beelined to her clan by Two Bucks' trailer.

"We didn't help Rose Petal bury anyone," Rooster assured.

Pop cackled, head volleying from Rooster to me, then back to Rooster. "Well...*you* didn't."

Well, That's Awkward

Rooster's head ticked from Pop to Tig and then to me.

I remained silent, masking the truth from Tig, but not from Pop, or now Rooster. I steered the conversation to Tig's GTO. Jackpot. Tig blathered for ten minutes. Long enough for me to get up and leave without confirming Pop's accusation.

I focused only on Tig, but Pop's and Rooster's eyes fed on me. After saying good-byes, Rooster and I returned to Two Bucks' truck.

Once the door slammed, Rooster said, "What the fuck, Tails?"

I shrugged.

"You didn't tell me?"

I turned the ignition. The truck bumped down the pine tree corridor of the Mauler's property, the first link to our trip home. I waited until we reached the yellow striped asphalt to answer my friend. "Didn't need you living with nightmares too."

"Why didn't you tell the cops? That old woman could be a monster."

"I guess."

"But..."

"It's complicated."

"Okay, but still..."

"I told someone."

"And."

"Didn't work out."

"Who'd you tell?"

"Brandy Detals."

"Your mom, why? What the hell?"

"Brandy was…"

"A piece of shit."

"Yeah, but at that age, you believe the Tooth Fairy leaves quarters under your pillow and that the woman who birthed you isn't a money-guzzling psychopath."

"What happened?"

"Brandy hung on every detail. After that, I think she…ah…took something."

"What?"

"A finger or something, to blackmail Rose Petal."

"Why the hell would Brandy blackmail Rose Petal? Brandy's family's loaded. Your dad became more loaded. Brandy didn't need anything from Rose Petal."

"Brandy wanted something."

Rooster looked perplexed.

"Brandy wanted Rose Petal to take an inconvenience…off her hands." Saying nothing, I allowed Rooster to piece the puzzle.

He did not want to verbalize the horror but needed resolution. "Brandy forced Rose Petal to take you. That's the year you moved to Silsbee full time."

"Bingo."

"Wow. Screwed up."

"Want more screwed up?"

"Not really."

Two Bucks' truck motored on as asphalt turned to concrete, concrete to bridges, bridges back to concrete, concrete back to asphalt, all surrounded by soaring pines.

Asphalt surrendered to the crushed shell and gravel, then the Old Place. The place I would die…tomorrow?

"Okay, tell me," Rooster surrendered. I slowed the truck to a crawl.

"The night Brandy and Larry abandoned me here."

"Yeah."

"I used to sleep in my underwear."

"Yep, tightie-whities."

"My first night back, after the..."

"Blackmailing."

"Yeah, Two Bucks pulled out to get drunk while Rose Petal whooped my ass. Hour later, I woke up. Strange 'cuz I slept hard. So, I felt out of sorts. Rose Petal sat on the bed near my lap."

"Creepy."

"Seconds later, I realized I was naked. Sheets pulled back, underwear around my knees."

"What the hell."

"Then...the ahh...razor blade was against my penis."

"The straight razor she shaved Two Bucks with."

"I think she sharpened it...right before."

"Shit."

"When a blade's against your dick, you know things. She said, 'If you tell another soul, you'll answer to Talia, not Tails. Understand?' I said nothing.

'Want to keep your Vienna sausage?' she asked. I nodded. She said, 'Say somethin' if we gotta understandin'.' I said, 'Yes, ma'am, yes...we do. Then she stood, folded the razor, and walked away, shutting the door. The next night we buried the body."

Rooster gulped.

"Started sleeping in my blue jeans, buttoned-up, with a belt on."

"Really? Wait, I remember now. We didn't have sleepovers anymore. I thought you grew out of it."

"Didn't want to explain to you..."

"Woulda been weird. Shit, when we got older, you slept at my place once, you wore your jeans. Said you forgot pajamas."

"Sounds like a lie I'd tell."

"Wow."

"I sleep in blue jeans to this day."

"Shiiitttt." Rooster reached down and grabbed his package, checking in with his fellows after the nightmare I recounted. Rooster whistled after the inspection. "Can't blame you."

We pulled up, and the truck stopped in Two Bucks' parking place.

Before I opened the truck door, Rooster reached out and held my shoulder. "Tails."

"What?"

"When I was a kid, you had everything. Rich dad, beautiful mother. A cool if drunken uncle. A grandmother, that despite her...quirks...put food in front of ya. Clean house. Your own room."

"Your point."

"I bunked with Mom in a one-bedroom, one bath, asbestos-siding shack with no air-conditioning."

"I remember."

"Even before ya told me this, I would'na traded places for a truck bed of Grammy's."

"I'd have given up everything for a mother like Chic."

"True, brother, true."

"How about a highlight reel?"

"Hit me."

"I am a 38-year-old MLB baseball player at the end of my career. Due to my injury, I'll never play again."

"Probably."

"Showed up drunk and Butz kicked me out of the Astrodome."

"Dumbass."

"I'm in love with my agent's daughter who may be a figment of my imagination."

"Shit."

"Or she blew me off."

"No double-dipping."

"My grandmother's a murderer."

"This one's on me. Your mom's a narcissistic bitch."

"Who used a murdered preacher to blackmail Rose Petal into raising me."

"You found your groove, brother."

"My grandfather killed himself."

"And."

"My birth father killed himself."

"You're shifting gears, not even at top speed, brother."

"I'm an alcoholic."

"We covered that earlier, but I'll allow it."

"My best friend didn't talk to me for ten years because of a girl."

"Sorry, disallowed."

"Excuse me?"

"What's your best friend's name?"

"Cole Michael Brewster."

"You mean the Rooster."

"Yeah, sure."

"Having Rooster as your best friend outweighs the negatives. Hell, you get to say, 'I'm best friends with the Rooster'."

"My former girlfriend left me for the Rooster."

"The Rooster favored you up there. You're welcome."

"Fair. Oh, last night the Rooster slept with Braelyn Ryan, the woman I've wanted since first grade."

"If you're best friends with the Rooster, shit's gonna happen, disallowed. You got anything left?"

"Oh, let's not forget, my 39th birthday's tomorrow. Based on family history, I'll kill myself."

Rooster rubbed my shoulder. "Tails, you ain't killing yourself. I'll be here, brother. By your side."

"Okay," I answered.

Somehow, releasing that venom soothed me.

My stomach rumbled to life, and I remembered Rose Petal's promise from earlier. "Rose Petal made a skillet of cornbread casserole. She left it out. My grandmother may be..."

"But the woman can cook."

"Rooster?"

"Yeah, Tails."

"I love you." I had not uttered those words since my parents ditched me here decades earlier.

"Yeah, brother, me too."

Rooster told me he loved me before, but I never followed suit. I meant it too. Voicing those words notched a victory, small but important.

I would find Two Bucks and Chic and tell them. Saying I love you before I departed this earth seemed important. I might offer an "I love you" to Rose Petal, despite everything.

Brandy Details, that was another story. The Devil waited for that woman to enter Hell. Hopefully, he reserved a prickly pear cactus to shove up her ass.

. . .

Sitting in the kitchen, my best friend's eyes fused on Rose Petal. Knowing she disposed of Pastor Talemore fascinated him. Rose Petal remained unaware of additional inspection. Rooster started his third slice of jalapeno cornbread casserole, soaked in Louisiana hot sauce. I stopped at two, finishing first.

Two Bucks returned from a trip to town, dropping a grocery store tabloid in front of Rooster. "Looks like Charla sold her story to the gossipmongers. Got off some good ones. She said you always wore a big belt buckle, 'cuz it wuz tombstones for a dead dick."

"Not bad," I said.

Rose Petal continued cleaning. Rooster laughed and began scanning the article, not his first time in this tabloid's pages. I, however, had no interest in the details of Charla and Rooster's split, I was only glad it happened.

I walked to the garbage, scraping all crumbs from my plate into the trash. Next, I rinsed my plate on the sink's right side, before dropping it into Rose Petal's premade soap and Clorox water to the left. Upon the plate's submersion, bleach scents tickled my nostrils. Dropping non-scraped, non-rinsed plates into Rose Petal's Clorox water bordered on mutiny. Even Two Bucks obeyed the proper steps of dirty dish distribution.

While Rooster finished his third pie-shaped slice of cornbread, I wandered into the living room for research. Pictures of Buddy Details littered the house. Still, I never studied them before.

Three framed photos rested on the sofa's side table. I started there, acknowledging the resemblance: stance, height, facial structure. Buddy's shoulders filled up his shirt, but the ill-fitted garments hung like a potato sack on his narrow torso. No mistaking the bloodline.

I reviewed every framed picture in the house. Buddy Details sported ear-to-ear grins. Next, the old scrapbook under the coffee table, once again, same shit-eating grin. There were clipped articles about him from the *Silsbee Bee* winning various accolades or supporting charities. Same damn smile every time.

Was Buddy's grin real or practiced? Honestly, each smile seemed damn sincere. I pressed my face almost to the images' surface. Begging each picture to share secrets.

Chic entered the room, her steps' rhythm unmistakable. The floor groaned under Two Bucks, complained under Rose Petal, and popped under me, but not Chic. The floor reacted differently to her frame—light, almost musical creaking marked her entrance.

"Chic?"

"Yes, Tails," she said, turning to me.

"You knew Buddy pretty well, right?"

"Sure. Buddy was like an uncle to me. Happiest man I ever met." She turned to her work.

"If he was so happy, why'd he...ahh...hang himself?"

"Never thought about it." Chic, despite her coolness, now looked nervous, upset even. In my mind, a pink neon sign flashed one word: *Liar.*

"Never?"

"Never," she answered, doubling down on her lie.

I wallowed in her lie, analyzed it. Why would Chic lie? Of course, she thought about Buddy's suicide. Buddy Details' rope swing served as the county's biggest story for decades.

I breathed, accepting I could not force Chic to tell the truth. Remembering the lightness of telling Rooster I loved him, I blurted, "Chic, thanks for everything you did for me."

"Welcome, Tails."

"Chic, I never said this before, but I love you."

"Thank you," she answered.

"You're the closest thing I had to..."

"Don't say that, Tails. I ain't your mother."

"I'm sorry..."

"Never was. I have a son. One. Rooster's my son."

"Oh...okay."

Thoughts of the dinosaur fossils returned. Chic's words brushed more dirt away. This newly exposed memory fossil, hinted, asked, no, *begged* for me to solve its secrets.

As a young boy, I was Chic's second son, her 'sweet honey child'. Then I wasn't. Finally, the timing hit me. Her affections ceased at the swimming hole.

Before we found Larry's floating corpse, Chic radiated warmth. After his drowning, she managed our relationship, kept me at arm's length.

In her mind, showing me affection somehow betrayed Rooster. I felt her discomfort before but did not understand until this moment. Chic was the warmest person in my periphery. So, I pushed, trying to stay close. But as if by duty, she only allowed herself to be my best friend's mother, our housekeeper, and a farm employee. Nothing more.

I stared, seeking explanation. Instead, Chic returned to chores, ignoring me. My "I love you experiment," offered dark answers, but the key word there is *answers*.

Pushing harder into darkness, facing terrible truths, offered a path to salvation...doubtful, but to understanding...maybe. I might die tomorrow, on my 39th birthday, but not without spitting in the face of my monsters—all of 'em.

The Road

Step one: locate my old Astros piggy bank. After ransacking my closet, I found it, weighted down with decades of dimes, nickels, and quarters. Seconds later, a cracked piggy bank and change cover my comforter. After separating five dollars in quarters and stuffing them in my pocket, I turned attention to step two: walking thirty minutes to town.

I donned an old ball cap and stepped out the front door, jingling from pocket quarter overload. Passing from yard to driveway started the most important journey of my life. Knowing sun-softened asphalt roads came next allowed my brain to shift into neutral. Embracing the sounds of the Piney Woods, I dove inward.

I recognized the first monster I must face, but the other ghouls needed definition. Breathing, allowing my monsters to raise their hand, announce their presence, and take their place in line seemed logical. The order surprised me, might surprise you.

Monster #1: The *end* of my baseball career.
Monster #2: The Devil's Oak
Monster #3: Rose Petal Detals
Monster #4: Brandy Detals
The Big Kahuna Monster #5: My Addiction

Pulling myself from monster ranking, stepping out of my brain, I looked up, surprised by my proximity to town. I selected the pay phone near J&M

Supermarket. Yes, I would pass ten pay phones on the way, walking by Beall's, TSO, the Fire Station, the backside of Farmer Funeral Home. Experiencing my hometown one last time seemed important.

Old acquaintances pulled over, offering rides, but I refused, because of or despite the sweat pouring off me. Some drivers feigned disappointment, but most seemed relieved I would not drip odorous sweat stains on their car seats. Sweat, an important ingredient to the process, a culling of toxins I inflicted upon my body. One walk would not correct decades of liver and kidney damage.

Still, I demanded one thing of myself: no drink today. Just this one day. I need sobriety as an ally today. "One day at a time, one day at a time, one day at a time," I repeated. Passersby gawked at me like a crazy homeless man. Fair enough, they spotted me, arms akimbo, muttering to myself.

The thought smacked me; I am a homeless man, never purchased a home, lived apartment to apartment, team to team. I laughed at the irony, acknowledged laughing at yourself, also a sign of insanity. Shaking it off, I approached the grocery store of my youth, Rose Petal's favorite J&M.

I stepped into the shade of the covered front entry, lifted the pay phone, and dialed the number by heart. The operator said, "Please deposit two dollars and fifty cents."

I loaded quarters enjoying the clinking sound each time. Then the ringtone. On the fourth ring, she picked up.

"Top Talent, Inc., 'ow may I 'elp?" answered Stanley's assistant.

"Hi, Pilar."

"'ello again, Tails. We 'ave talked more this week than we 'ave for years."

"Yes, Pilar, can I talk to Stanley?"

"Un momento."

"But Pilar, I don't have time to hold. I'm on a pay phone," I said, before realizing I talked to "hold" music.

I waited, knowing the next words I would hear. "Please deposit seventy-five cents for one minute." Again, the clinking sound as coins clicking through. I remained on hold, only one dollar and seventy-five cents in my pocket.

Thank God he picked up. But it wasn't him. "Un momento, Tails." Again, hold music before I screamed, "I'm on a pay phone, damnit."

An exiting shopper directed a withering stare as she carted by, three kids in tow.

I paced within the limits of the pay-phone cord.

"Please deposit seventy-five cents for one minute." Three more quarters clinked. Four quarters remained in my pocket. The infernal hold music droned on. I railed internally when the operator announced, "Please deposit seventy-five cents for one minute."

I fed three of my last four quarters into the phone. Each clink upped my agitation level.

Pilar picked up after the deposit. "I'll transfer."

The distinct sound of a phone transfer, then, "Hello, Tails."

Brevity seemed my only option. "Call the Astros. Tell 'im, I'm done. Cut me. They don't owe me another penny. I don't want their money."

"Your mouth's costing you money. Tails, stop the oral diarrhea."

"Not a cent. I'm retiring." I added with a flourish, "I'm taking my baseball glove and going home."

"Sure, Tails, but..."

"I need your word. Swear on your beloved New York Yankees."

The recorded operator returned. "Please deposit seventy-five cents for one minute."

"You're at a pay phone, you should have called collect."

"Promise on the soul of Yogi Berra..."

"Please deposit seventy-five cents for one minute."

"I promise, Tails...on Yogi..."

Then...disconnection.

No job, no money, no pressure.

I mentioned my walk to the pay phone was the most therapeutic of my life. The return rallied ahead, because I remembered Trusty, our trashman.

Because Rose Petal, and by extension Two Bucks, owned and operated a farm, people considered the Detals successful. Still, we lived off our land, seldom spent money. Rose Petal saved money to buy more land and create more income to deposit more money.

We were country folk and cheap. We burned our garbage, but occasionally Trusty, the freelance trashman, stopped by to pick up an item my grandmother or Two Bucks decided not to torch.

Trusty collected the garbage of people in unincorporated Hardin County, areas not supported by city services on the outskirts of town. His truck featured various shades of rust. Trusty's truck tires were as bald as the before picture in a Hair Club for Men commercial. Every time Trusty's truck died, the engine huffed, spittled, and croaked, debating the pluses and minuses of ever starting again.

Our garbage man's home became legend, cobbled together with the county's trash. Still, every time I saw Trusty, he sported the biggest smile in the county, always whistling, laughing, and backslapping. Happy to stop for drinks with Two Bucks or laugh as Rose Petal shooed him off the porch.

Trusty never learned to read, but each of his four children graduated college with no financial aid, based on money the trashman earned recycling garbage into something useful. The children's most important asset, their father's wisdom. In time, Trusty's witticisms rose to legendary status, repeated throughout the county.

Once when a country shopkeeper disrespected Trusty's wife for her handmade clothes, the trashman marched into the business. Local lore recounts the interaction.

"If'n ya treat m'wife like trash 'gain…"

"Who do you think you are, Trusty, marching in here?"

"I'm de' guy who picked up everythin' you done throwed out. If'n you want, I can share what ya'stuff in de'garbage wiffin the minister…de' stuff you been hidin from your wife."

The shopkeeper drove to Trusty's house that night and begged Trusty's wife for forgiveness.

I should know better than to shoot my mouth off to the town's foremost purveyor of wit. Unfortunately, that afternoon, my *know better* malfunctioned. Rooster and Chic went to Beaumont on Chic's day off. Two Bucks avoided his share of the chores and sat on the porch tipping longnecks with Trusty. I fumed past the tipsy twosome a dozen times, performing various duties, most of them Two Bucks'. Each pass, my ire blossomed.

Something about Trusty's laugh. His ease bothered me. My insolence bubbled over. "Trusty, you pick up trash for a living. Why are you always so happy?"

He sat there, not taking my question as the insult I intended. Instead, the garbage man deep-dove inside himself. Trusty appeared frozen, befuddled. Then the Trusty smile blossomed. An inner peace most will never experience flowed from him.

"Tails...people gots all deez tings to pay fer. Bills, bills, 'n more bills, keeps 'em up nights. Worry stuck on'em likes de'smell of dog shit on der' shoes. Den, one day' dat stuff dey worry bouts...ends up on the corner, waitin' fer me in de'trash. All d'stuff dey worry 'bout dey' throw wayz in a year 'er twos."

He sipped his beer, reveling in his words. Even then, I understood my trashman's wisdom. Still, Trusty shared one more lesson.

"But nots me, Tails. I gots nuthin, so I gots nuthin da worry 'bout."

That's right, Trusty, I said to myself, *f#$king A right*.

Camp with Gramps

"What the hell you doin'?" asked Two Bucks, seeing my old sleeping bag fly from the closet to my bed.

"Sleeping outside."

"It's late summer, in Texas, stupid, you're gonna sweat like a strawberry doused in sugar."

"Like a hog when Rose Petal's short on pork chops," I answered.

Two Bucks chuckled.

I continued rifling through camping supplies not touched in twenty years. "Where is it? Where is it?" I mumbled, searching for Texas' most essential camping tool.

Thank God, orange lid, my twenty-year-old can of Off! Bug repellent. I prayed my can of Off! aged like fine wine. If not, twenty-year-old bug repellent beat the crap out of no bug repellent.

"You're an idiot," said Two Bucks. "Take my Igloo at least."

"Planning on it."

"Where's Rooster? Why ain't you two hangin' out?"

"Where'd you be if you were him?"

"Butterin' up Braelyn…"

"That'd be my guess," I said, smiling after locating my childhood flashlight. Marching to the pantry, I nabbed fresh Duracell D-batteries. Rose Petal stocked her home with unmatched precision. Trailing floor creaks told me Two Bucks tagged behind.

"Where you campin'?"

I raised my eyebrows.

"You ain't takin no rope with ya?"

"No, and I ain't dipping in the swimming hole like your brother."

"Better not, or I leave your bloated ass floatin.' Not planning no dirt nap tonight?"

I shook my head.

"As for me..." started Two Bucks.

"Headed for a beer?"

"You didn't pluralize the last word of that sentence, shoulda."

He paused, like he wanted me to change my mind.

"Okay," Two Bucks said. Then the strangest thing happened. He hugged me.

Moisture passed from his cheek to mine. Before I could process the tear, my uncle power-slapped my back, distracting from the rare show of emotion. "Stay safe, Tails." Two Bucks released me seconds before it became awkward.

First, I heard his creaking steps, then the swing of the screen. Minutes later, his pickup rumbled to life. Now just Rose Petal, me, and the Devil's Oak remained. Quite the threesome.

As Two Bucks promised, when I stepped out the screen door, humidity slapped me, promising pearls of perspiration even on my short walk. The yellow porch light choked out the night, but only for the glow's 12-ft. radius. Embracing the glow, I stood, staring down the night.

Blackness awaited steps away. Croaking, buzzing, creaking, and the mating sounds of night welcomed me, as I girded myself for the battle.

I left my sleeping bag and Two Bucks' cooler, filled with Coca-Cola and ice, on the deck. Stepping yards from the porch, I coated myself with Off!, leaving the aerosol can to collect in the morning, assuming I survived the night. A touch-and-go proposition.

Inviting Monster #2, dunt-dunt-duuhhhh, the Devil's Oak, to the battle, I stepped toward my tormentor, sleeping bag and Igloo cooler in hand.

The Old Place contained a half-dozen walking paths. Hard dirt trails beaten down by repeated work boot trips to and from a point. No path existed between the Old Place and the Devil's Oak, the grass approaching Devil's Oak vibrant and virgin. Few footsteps intruded on the Oak's dominion.

I approached, making my path, tentatively stepping under the arbor for the first time in decades. Scattered grass patches struggled for survival under the tree's shaded arbor. Broken sunlight, limited photosynthesis, and the tree undercarriage created a dead zone for grass...and grandfathers.

Based on lack of acorns, refuse, and fallen limbs, I assumed Two Bucks instructed seasonal workers, unfamiliar with the tree's legend, to clear the Oak's undercarriage. Kneeling, I brushed away twigs and pebbles before rolling out my sleeping bag. The bag greeted my nostrils with smells of abandoned bedding, coated in years of dust, stored for decades in my dark closet, sealed from the light and air-conditioning. Distasteful but mild, the odor offered nothing to stop my battle with the Oak.

Moving the cooler next to me, a symbol of Two Bucks, a redneck familiar or talisman, offered a modicum of comfort. I kicked off my boots, removed my shirt, then climbed into the sleeping bag. The bag, more accustomed to the body of my youth, begrudgingly adjusted to my adult frame. Moments of wiggling forced my body and the sleeping bag to an uneasy but mildly comfortable agreement. Most of us remember sleeping bags as gateways to adventure in our youth.

But my older body felt every ground abnormality. Realizing I forgot a pillow, I put my arms under my head, staring through the Oak's arbor at the stars. The view, beautiful and terrifying, offered herself to me in whole. I accepted all of her.

"I'm here. You've been waiting. Let's see what you got."

I considered the stars, wondering if they observed me as I observed them, hoping they caught the good stuff, praying they turned away from my mishaps. My thoughts recounted the times I hoped the celestials looked away.

Horror movies or scary books contribute to nightmares or sleep deprivation. Not for me; I do not watch the first or read the second. No need to examine someone else's nightmares. I'm stocked up.

Finding a dead body under your home, dragging said dead body into the woods, burying it before your tenth birthday provides plenty of kindling for dreams' bonfires.

Dragging a floating carcass to shore fills the tank of dark thought. Add the gasoline of Grandfather and birth father offing themselves on their 39th birthday. Plenty of mental trash fire material.

Honestly, I accept blame for some nightmares. If you watch haunted house movies, your dreams will drop you inside a creepy Victorian mansion. If you read graveyard tales, your unconscious will meet you between the tombstones. I studied hangings and drownings.

After collecting whispers of Buddy Detals' death, hangings served as my dark fascination. In Silsbee Junior High's library, I easily accessed pictures of death in the gallows.

Most people know John Wilkes Booth killed Abraham Lincoln at the Ford Theatre. Booth died from a gunshot wound after lawmen tracked him. Most Americans do not remember eight others were tried as coconspirators in Lincoln's assassination. Four were hanged. The terrifying image of the four hanging corpses occupied the pages of my textbooks.

The four doomed conspirators wore black or gray, hard to translate in the grainy black-and-white photo. Union soldiers and soaring brick walls surround the gallows. Observers occupied the photo's left side, some dressed for the moment's morbidity, others regaled in "late for a picnic" garb.

George Atzerodt, David Herold, the movie-star-handsome Lewis Powell, and ill-fated Mary Surratt, dangled yards above the ground. Mary, the first female executed by the US government, died quickly, as did Atzerodt. Their necks snapped, offering quick death as a reward, the sound resonating through the crowd. I imagined that snap, not crisp like a dried oak branch, but sappy and wet, like a thriving pine's limb.

Death welcomed Mary and George without complication.

Not Powell or Herold.

If muscled men fight the rope, their necks may win round one. Herold and Powell battled, kicking violently, tensing their neck muscles, railing against death. Powell swung his body wildly and once brought his legs to sitting position.

But strangulation waited in the wings, slower but persistent in mission, waiting for the condemned men to concede...death remains undefeated.

Lying under the Devil's Oak, drifting between thoughts of Lewis Powell, Mary Surratt, and sleep, my grandfather shed the shackles of death, time, and worlds to join me, like he had years ago on the night of Larry's death, and in nightmares since.

Wondering if I dreamed or remained conscious? Did my eyes close for hours or seconds, sure of another presence under the Oak's arbor?

First, I heard him.

Rope creaking, weight tensing, testing the Oak's limb. Sound alone delivering the promise of terror. There were more ear clues to collect. Kicking, battling and, yes...cursing. My last date with Buddy Detals under the Devil's Oak lasted mere seconds.

Now, I found myself bound by my sleeping bag. I kicked out and sat under the oak, not turning to Buddy's struggle, knowing the wraith would wait for me. Instead, I studied the dreamscape.

The ground below me differed from the ground I spread my sleeping bag on. Acorns littered the ground. One of my hands rested on the soil. The dark dirt felt cool and safe, despite my surroundings. My other hand rested on cracked acorn shells. No cast protected my arm. Despite evidence of my dream residence, the pain of a hand pressed against the jagged acorn shell felt real...was real.

As a country boy, I remembered oak trees drop acorns in September and October. Colored memories of bike rides, my tires crackling acorns, such a specific and beautiful sound. My grandfather died on Halloween, his birthday, during the oak's acorn-orama.

Grandfather first visited me the night of his son's suicide. Was that visit a warning, a haunting? Mere coincidence seemed unlikely.

Now, in this dream, the acorns proved telling. Buddy Detals, the hanging man, chose the dream's place and timing. Specific for a dead man. My eyes darted to the deciduous trees dotting the Old Place, each dressed in orange and red regalia. Critics say talented authors possess a distinctive voice. Was my grandfather known for showmanship communicating in his?

Behind me, the kicking and battling continued. I waited, hoping the specter would lose his battle with the noose. But Buddy Detals refused to surrender. He needed me to watch. Understanding his demand, I turned.

Buddy whipsawed the rope with his neck, battling the Devil's Oak, country strong, refusing to concede. Neck muscles tightened, firing like pistons. Buddy's arm stretched for the ropes with each kick. His hands landed inches short of their goal.

Sweat poured from his face, rope bruises colored his neck. Tonight's communication not dream, but chronicle. I stood witness to Buddy Detals' death. Then it hit me. Why stand there? I must help him.

My feet remained concreted, telegraphing my role as observer, not participant. Buddy Detals suffocated at rope's end. His will and his neck remained unbroken. He fought death, never accepting defeat, to the end.

I screamed.

0 Days 'Til I Die

I bolted upright, confused.

After watching noon matinees enrobed in the theater's cool darkness, your body experiences day shock when stepping into early afternoon sunshine. I experienced that sensation now, expecting to awake in darkness, surrounded by specters and stars. Instead, crowing rooster, the gurgle of hungry hogs, and daybreak greeted me.

As a child, the halls of elementary school seem huge, the size of banquet rooms. Returning adults find the halls ten or fifteen feet wide, smaller than memory. Observing the Oak, it seemed less menacing, no longer my dream villain, vanquished by one night under the branches. Just a tree.

An important fact registered in the dream, new information, a key cog to lifelong questions. I gripped the dream's essence, but the images escaped like sand through my fingers. The more I focused, the faster the clues drag-raced away.

Hoping the cog presented again when needed, I rolled my sleeping bag and opened Two Bucks' Igloo. I swigged a Coca-Cola, burped, and collected my supplies for the return walk.

I considered the mental checklist of my monsters. Two check marks for me. I faced the end of my baseball career and slept under the Devil's Oak.

More monsters ahead.

Celebrating minor victories seemed important. In elementary school, students collected gold stars for their accomplishments. Fleeting memories of my youthful second-grade teacher peeling golden star stickers from a roll and handing them out danced through my head.

Why stop handing out gold stars in adulthood? We still crave them. To be fair, raises, bonuses, all-star selections, and slaps on the ass replace gold stickers in the baseball world. I assume other professions offer similar replacements. *Note: I do not recommend ass-slapping in the non-baseball world...for obvious reasons.*

I placed my sleeping bag and Two Bucks' Igloo next to the ancient can of Off! before tackling pre-breakfast chores. Crushing them, thanks to the boost of confidence and the lack of alcohol pollutants in my system. Two Bucks collected me near the pen.

"Breakfast," his only word.

I sorted the legendary tales of my grandfather's death. I spliced the mini versions into one conglomerate. He ate a full breakfast, stuffed himself. Wait...that's it. The cog dropped into place. The life-changer.

I walked to the front porch as the ghost-memory of Larry Detals thrust out the screen door, across the porch running toward his date with drowning. I let him pass, refocusing my thoughts. *Don't distract me, Larry Detals, let's solve your father's death first. You're next.*

My first steps into the Old Place announced my arrival from the dark fog I endured for decades. I heard Two Bucks and Rose Petal putter around the kitchen. Then the distinctive pop of a longneck.

"It's 7:30 in the morning, Two Bucks."

"One-thirty in Scotland."

"You've got a busy day in front of you..."

"It's Sunday."

"It's a farm, Two Bucks. Never Sunday on a farm. Pigs don't take the weekend off, still need feedin'..."

"I spent every Sunday of my life here. Ya don't think I know?"

I entered the kitchen. Now a man, today, maybe for the first time. Sober for all of twenty-four hours, not a record, but noted in the win column, gold star for me.

I sat at the breakfast table soaking them in. My mother and father, not actually, but in reality. I considered their flaws for so long, blamed them for everything.

Now I considered their strengths.

Playing professional sports colored my opinions. My favorite players showed up, shut up, and suited up. My best teammates played through pain when more talented players nursed calf tweaks or sore ribs.

Two Bucks' gift during my childhood—presence. Always there. Uneven, irresponsible, drunk, sure—a triple crown of bad parenting. But kind. So kind. A grin spread across my face when Two Bucks plopped down for breakfast.

"Stop starin', Tails. You're creepin' me out."

I studied the spread in front of me—breakfast displayed unassumingly. No garnish or floral arrangement to distract from countrified perfection. Fluffy biscuits exploded from the pan, crispy crusted tops and soft moist centers awaited counter-softened butter and homemade strawberry jam.

Frying ham sizzled on Rose Petal's stove top. I recognized the sound from memory, different from bacon's or sausage's crackles. Rhythmic if you listened. Rose Petal removed the ham and sat it on a platter with an old dish towel to drain grease.

The roar of a half-dozen eggs poured into ham grease overtook the kitchen, comforting. A cloud of steam wafted from the pan. The smell of a country breakfast filled the room. I embraced all five senses.

Two Bucks watched, confused by the new, present me. A me unconcerned about baseball, my place in the world, another drink, or a woman. Present, right here, right now.

I seldom live moment to moment or enjoy the people in front of me. When you are present, people notice.

"You okay, Tails?"

"Never better, Two Bucks." I considered the cast encasing my arm, thankful for the injury that forced me home. I thought I came home to face my demons. Incorrect. I'm here to thank my saviors and find myself.

"I love you, Two Bucks."

"Need a beer, Tails?"

"No, I don't need a friggin' beer. When someone says they love you, proper etiquette dictates you return the sentiment."

"What's etiquette mean?"

"Etiquette means..."

"Screwin with ya. I'm a hick, not an idiot. Love ya too, dumbass."

Rose Petal pulled the fried eggs from the stove, then dropped the ham and eggs in front of us on pre-placed pot holders. The unindoctrinated might guess Rose Petal ignored the conversation between Two Bucks and me. Anyone growing up at the Old Place understood she processed every syllable.

She sat and held out her hands. Two Bucks took one, I took the other.

"Father, forgive our sins, thanks for your bounty, and bless this food to the nourishment of our bodies. In your son, Jesus Christ's name. Amen."

"Grandmother," I started.

"Get it over with," she said.

"I love you."

She cut a piece of ham and guided it to her mouth. As she chewed, Rose Petal looked toward the kitchen's one window, over the sink. At first, I assumed, to avoid the conversation.

Then I witnessed the impossible. A tear trickling down her face.

One tear, no more. Her body battled additional waterworks, after failing to halt the one rogue tear. Only a drop of moisture escaped before her body's defenses rallied.

Rose Petal focused on the window. Rays of sunshine that cut through the window exposed her emotions. The tear glistened in the sun.

I counted Rose Petal's strengths. Yes, Brandy Detals extorted Rose Petal into taking me. Still, Rose Petal could have shirked her duties. My grandmother did not.

Rose Petal led with dependability, teaching work ethic, attending occasional baseball games, although she considered sports a waste of time. I dissected the table, everything in front of me. Grandmother said she loved you through food. Her love dialect was homemade jam, biscuits, cream gravy, fried eggs, and ham.

The words "I love you" seemed unimportant. I took a biscuit, buttered it, spooned on jam, and took a bite of love. Just when I gave up on any return of my words, Rose Petal took my hand. She squeezed it three times to represent three syllables.

Squeeze one, I
Squeeze two, love
Squeeze three, you

I savored each squeeze, realizing they were more important than words any family member, teacher, coach, or teammate shared. Three squeezes, all she offered, more than I assumed her capable of.

We ate in silence, unusual for a family that used breakfast to map out the day's tasks. Reveling in this meal, these two people, this moment, before I faced their role in Grandfather's death. Two Bucks finished first. He scraped his plate, rinsed it, then dropped it in the bleach water. I waited, wanting to catch them off guard.

Once Rose Petal buttered her biscuit, I asked. "How'd you kill him?"

"I didn't kill Pastor Talemore, or at least I didn't mean to," she answered without emotion.

Not the killing I meant. What the hell, let's explore it.

"Didn't mean to?"

"Huhh, do we have'ta discuss this?"

"Today's my birthday. I'm betting no presents await me, no cake's in the oven. This is what I want. My present."

"If I go to jail, you go to jail too. You helped me bury the body. Then Two Bucks moved it. We'd all go." Ah, self-preservation, not the most attractive of qualities.

Wait, it hit me. Finally, the most important leap in logic of my life. Years of counseling finally paying dividends. Fear gestates in your gut, but it often presents to the public as anger. When people are afraid, their natural inclination is to show anger, bitterness, and venom.

Did Rose Petal live her life in fear?

To solve my life's riddles, I needed to address her fear. "I have no desire to send you to prison. I love you. Just want to know what happened."

My words seemed to calm her. "Well, Two Bucks was off drinking. You and Rooster were in school. Chic shopped for groceries in my truck. I was cleaning up the kitchen after breakfast. Didn't hear the pastor's car pull up."

"The farm told me something was up. Pigs sound different when strangers are walkin' 'bout."

"So, I pulled the shotgun down." Rose Petal's eyes traced to the shotgun mounted above the buffet. "Then there was pounding on the door."

"In the country, before you pound someone's door, you call out so you don't get shot. You announce who you are and your intentions. Pastor Talemore lived in town, not a country boy. Moved here from the big city. Guess he didn't know. I'd a thought all his time in Silsbee he'd of learnt. Either he didn't learn, or he came to intimidate me. So he was an ignoramus or stupid."

Despite the situation's gravity, Two Bucks chuckled. I shot him a *what the hell* glance.

"Come on, that was funny," he offered.

Rose Petal continued. "Since I didn't know who did the banging, I carted the shotgun with me. I stepped quietly, avoiding the creaky spots in the floor. His back'us turned to me, distracted by the pigs 'er something.

"I recognized him, even from his backside. He and I'd had words before, and I wasn't in a talkin' mood. So, I raised the shotgun before I opened the screen. I was 'bout to say, 'Off my property 'fore you get an ass-full of buckshot.' He turned at the creakin' of the screen. I raised the shotgun to shoo him. His eyes got big as saucers, scared, real scared. He stepped back, but his foot caught on the porch edge, tumbled backward and sideward at the same time. Head cracked open like a pecan when he hit the cement step. Sickening sound. Remember it every night when I sleep."

She sat there a long time; Two Bucks sipped his breakfast beer. Despite the story laid out in front of me, I noted he had not finished the bottle, apparently pacing himself.

"I knew everyone'd assume I kill't 'em on purpose. So, I drug the body under the house. Found his car parked up the driveway, keys in it. I parked it back at his church and hiked through the woods back here. I didn't tell anyone. Until you climbed under there and mouthed off to your mother."

"Don't call her that. Brandy Detals was never a mother to me, but you were."

"Ehhh."

She stared at her worn house shoes, tamping her emotions. "I'm so sorry about threatening your...manhood that night with the razor."

"That sucked," I added, happy my penis remained attached.

"I ain't never forgiven myself. I was scared, so scared, I'd go to jail. Or worse, lose my home. This place was everything to me..."

She stopped herself.

I paused, trying to translate her incomplete sentence. When it became obvious she would not continue, I said, "I'm so sorry, Grandmother."

"But every time I see you sleep in your jeans, I cry. Don't let no one see it, though. Anyway, couldn't figure what to do. I'd never kill't anyone before."

Those words bounced around in my head. *I'd never kill't anyone before.*

The Old Place Kitchen

"You killed someone before," I said.

Rose Petal stared, confused.

"Think I'd know if I did."

"You killed Grandfather."

"Buddy Detals kilt himself," she answered.

"No, he didn't. Pop Mauler swears Grandfather was the happiest man in Silsbee."

"Pop 'id know, those two…" Disgust, disappointment, or both crossed Rose Petal's face. "Always drinking, chasing skirt," she answered.

"You knew?"

"Yep," she answered. "You'd smile too. If you dipped your pen in everyone else's ink bottle."

"He ate a big breakfast. Every story about that morning says he did."

"Stuffed himself," she continued.

"Why'd he stuff himself if he planned on hanging? Full stomach and hanging don't mix." The mental picture returned of Buddy Detals fighting for life, battling and losing against the rope.

"'Cuz he didn't plan to die that day," she said.

"But you said he hung himself."

"No, I didn't. I said he kilt himself."

"What the hell's the difference?"

"He kilt himself by diddling his way through town."

I asked, "What…who…?"

"Someone with a rope, I reckon," said Two Bucks.

"Someone tired of my husband's pecker betwixt their wife's thighs." Only after Rose Petal chewed and swallowed her next bite did she continue. "Probably a couple of 'em. May'a been a line of menfolk."

"But the cops investigated, right?"

"The sheriff acted like he investigated. But the sheriff's and deputy's wives...whew, fine-looking women. Women who had a habit of hanging around the bars when their husbands were working."

"Why didn't you do something?"

"Couldn't prove nothing. The law was against me. And why would I?" said Rose Petal. "Buddy cheated on me. Threatened to sell the farm, my home. Then there were the rumors."

"Rumors?"

"He mouthed off 'bout divorcing me."

Now I saw it. The hurt, the bitterness. More importantly the fear. Rose Petal Detals loved the Old Place, she poured her sweat, love, heart, and soul into the land under us. But she lived in fear her philandering husband would rip *her home* away via divorce courts, local politics, or small-town backslapping.

Her home.

Fear expresses as anger, I repeated to myself.

"I loved that man, God help me, but someone did me a favor."

"Seriously, you had no clue?" I glared at Two Bucks.

"No, but I didn't worry 'bout it much. Man treated Larry like a god, me like a spare."

"Did Larry...?"

"Never told him. He was off at school. Less he got involved, the better," said Rose Petal. "Or so I thought," Rose Petal mumbled, staring at her shoes. For the first time, Rose Petal wilted into a sympathetic figure. "When my son kilt himself..."

"For God's sake, someone could've told me. I spent my life assuming Larry and Buddy killed themselves on their 39th birthdays. I felt doomed to the same fate."

"What a stupid idea," said Grandmother.

"You just said Larry killed himself on his 39th birthday. How could you have missed that?"

Grandmother processed her next words. "I tried to keep Buddy's death from you, never talked about..."

"You didn't, but the whole damn town did. You had to guess I'd hear about it. Really. Everyone in town's afraid of you, everyone. They tell stories about you," I said, looking at Rose Petal. "You too." I looked to Two Bucks. "And this damn place."

Rose Petal said nothing.

"We..." I paused to ensure understanding, "...are the Big Thicket's *Friday the 13th*, *Halloween*, and *Nightmare on Elm Street* combined. Here they consider us their personal horror franchise. And this place, this place...is the *Poltergeist* house to them. Everyone's waiting for the Devil to suck this place back to hell."

"Now you're exaggeratin'," said Rose Petal.

"They think you killed your husband and a pastor. They're convinced the Devil's Oak is immortal, protected by evil. Oh, and this place is cursed."

"Now I understand something they don't. You're not scary. You were just scared."

She squeezed my hand again, three times.

I...love...you.

"I love you too," I said. "For God's sake, did it occur to you maybe...maybe I needed to know? We're family. You can't just toss memories in filing cabinets and lock them away!"

But I did exactly that my entire life. Rose Petal and Two Bucks seemed to understand and accept my arrival at the crossroads. All the file cabinets in my head bolted open at once. Every single one. Memories now stood in front of me, to face, all of them.

"For the record, I'm pretty sure Larry didn't kill himself either."

Rose Petal begged, "He's dead. For once, out of respect, can you call him your father?"

"I know for a fact, Tails' father didn't kill himself," said Two Bucks.

Now Rose Petal looked stunned.

The Old Place Kitchen (Continued)

"Okay, who should go first? Seems like we're both sitting on something."

"Well, you're busy blatherin'. Mouth's warmed up," said Two Bucks.

"Okay, my theory's going to sound like bull."

"Let the bull lead where it must."

"I studied hangings once I found out about Buddy's death."

"Okay," Two Bucks pushed.

"Then there's the dreams."

"I'm sorry?"

"People think dreams are bullshit, but dreams are your brain working through stuff, to serve witness, to present different scenarios. What Rose Petal said makes sense. I dreamed about Buddy a lot, and when I do, he's fighting the rope."

"I never saw Buddy's body. If I did, I'd put it together sooner. But I drug Larry's corpse to shore." I looked at Grandmother. "Drowning's supposed to be peaceful."

"And," said Rose Petal.

"Larry looked terrified. I mentioned earlier, Buddy appears in my dreams. Each time he tries to show me he did not kill himself. I'm not sure if his specter shows up or if my brain creates that image. But Larry acts the same way in my dreams. He wants me to understand something specific. I can't piece it together. Larry tried to show me more in the dreams, but I'm too afraid or dense to piece it together. In every dream, he's terrified. Not hard-fast proof he didn't kill himself, but enough for me."

"Who killed my son?" asked Rose Petal.

"Not sure, but I'm getting close."

"When you find out..."

"I tell you first."

She nodded.

"That's all I got."

Rose Petal asked, "Two Bucks, you said Larry didn't kill himself?"

"No," he answered.

"But..."

"I didn't say Larry didn't kill himself. I said Tails' father didn't kill himself."

"What...?"

He waited for me to finish the puzzle, not offering too much, making me work for it.

"But..."

My head swiveled back and forth, remembering the day I rested my head on Two Bucks' shoulder, the games he attended, practices he coached.

Drunk, but present.

"You're..."

He nodded.

"But how?"

"Your mom..."

"Don't call her that."

"Brandy drove into town with Larry the first time. 'Zactly the kinda woman Larry, the golden child, was s'posed to marry. Beautiful, connected, Texas royalty."

"And..."

"In Austin, at UT, Brandy considered herself the center of Larry's world. She pushed to visit where he grew up. Larry never wanted to bring Brandy home. Not 'cuz he was ashamed, but..."

History slipped into place. "He didn't want Brandy to meet Chic."

"And vice-versa. You, sir, win an ice-cold beer," Two Bucks said, rising to fetch his beverage.

"Don't want a beer."

"Wasn't gettin' you one," he said, popping the top. The bottle started sweating seconds later. No worries, beer wouldn't expire in front of my uncle—scratch that, my father.

"When Brandy arrived, Chic pouted 'round the house. Brandy watched Chic, figured something was up. Like any woman, especially an insecure spoiled debutante like your mom...sorry, Brandy.

"Everyone seemed tense. I suggested we go to the swimming hole. I packed a cooler of beer and off we went. Larry hung near the cooler, drinking, feet in the water. The rest of us, even Brandy, wore out the rope swing.

"Now Chic fills up a bathing suit like a repentant sinner fills up the church offering plate. Brandy looked mighty fine too. Since I grew up with Chic, I peeked a time or ten at Brandy when she was swinging or climbin' out the water. She didn't give a crap 'bout me peekin'.

"Brandy busted Larry snakin' ganders at Chic once too often, or just once, which was too often. 'Bout thirty minutes in, Brandy started steaming. Once we returned home, Brandy runned Chic off."

"Chic 'id be a threat to most women," I offered.

"Brandy done got used to being belle of the ball. Tough findin' out you're number two."

Two Bucks idled.

"Guess...I got used to it. Anyway, Chic left, and Larry followed to make sure she was okay. He stayed gone too long for Brandy's liking. So she ahh..."

"Ugh." I sounded, knowing what came next.

"Mom was shopping. I hopped into the shower to wash off for dinner. And in Brandy hopped."

"Ffuuuf," Rose Petal expressed disgust.

"And you..."

"Took her in the shower, my bed, the floor, frontward, backward, upside down. Wished I was a better man. But I was twenty, a fool. Brandy may be a bitch, but she looked damn good soaped up. I loved Chic my whole life, still do, but she'd never be mine. My brother won her heart long ago. Putting it to Brandy was my way of getting back.

"When Brandy got pregnant, Larry assumed you wuz his. Brandy pushed for a quick marriage. God knows her family held a figurative, maybe literal, gun to his temple. Larry discovered Chic was pregnant, few weeks after he married the redheaded she-devil. I suspect Chic got pregnant same day Brandy did, while I was ah...bathin' with Brandy, Larry and Chic danced the horizontal two step.

"Chic never told Larry he fathered Rooster. She never wanted to trap 'em, but he figured it out.

"I wanted to be Larry. Who wouldn't? He had everything...looks, the girl I loved, a perfect job, ambition. I was just Two Bucks. Number two, even in my name."

"Larry must'a slept with Brandy too. How do you know I'm yours?"

"Oh, you're his," answered Rose Petal, obviously disappointed she missed the clues in the past.

"Lot of unimportant things," said Two Bucks. "Way you stand, walk, eat your peas."

"Not very scientific."

"Ya want scientific. As a runt, when Larry held ya, ya never stopped hollering. When I held ya, ya stopped right away. Came to me for comfort, not him. My smell drew ya to me. All the science I need, Tails."

Two Bucks enjoyed a long pull of the longneck, then looked down.

"Dad," I said, trying it on for size.

"Yeah, Tails."

"I love you."

"You too, Tails. Always have."

"Nice to finally meet you."

"Yeah." Then I understood. Not Two Bucks, not anymore. First in my heart. I committed to never say Two Bucks out loud again. Eliminating the well-trod name from my mind presented a tougher challenge.

I reveled in my discovery.

A crap-nado pelted my brain. Another man might be in trouble. A man who believed Buddy and Larry Detals' 39th birthday curse. Larry's oldest son, only son, the cursed one. Today, on the birthday we shared.

I needed to locate Rooster.

The Search for Rooster

"Where's Rooster?" I asked Two Bucks and Rose Petal.

"I know where he'll be tonight. But good chance he swings by this morning."

Based on the premise of Rooster stopping by, like he usually did, Two Bucks and I powered through the most pressing chores. I repeatedly glanced over my shoulder, hoping to spot Rooster and Chic stepping into the clearing. Each minute, my worry climbed.

"Can we swing by Chic's house?"

"They're not there."

"You sure?"

"Yeah, son, sure."

The word rolled over me—*son*. Son of a living, breathing man. A man who loved me. Perfect, far from it. Sober, no, not even now, but present. Present was enough for today.

We worked side by side. I watched him, soaking him in, really, for the first time. Brute strong, a force of nature, not as coordinated as his brother, but stronger. Even though Brandy swam competitively, she possessed a petite frame, smaller and lither than Two Bucks. I resembled both.

Around 2:30 PM, impatience overtook me. "Hey, Two...I mean hey, Dad."

"Yes, son."

"Something in my gut's screaming I need to find Rooster."

"Clean up, we'll hunt 'em, but we have places to be. We're meeting Rooster and Chic later."

"Something you're not telling me?"

"Smells like someone needs to shower, 'cuz you smell like the shit we've been shovelin'. Dress in the fanciest thing you brought. I'll hop in the shower first. Be out in five."

We parted ways. I walked to my bedroom. In a small home, you hear everything. The shower pipes groaned to life. Serenaded by sounds of my newly minted father showering, I examined Larry's old bedroom. Studying pictures, images, and memoirs of the dead man seemed important. Looking, searching, investigating everything, and finding...nothing.

True to his word, Two Bucks emerged from the shower five minutes later.

"You're up, Tails," he said as he left the bathroom.

• • •

I emerged from the steaming shower and dressed. When we stepped off the porch, I asked, "Why don't we swing by Braelyn's bar first?"

"Well, ahh, he's not there."

"You sure?"

"I...ah...I called."

"Didn't hear you call."

"I called when you were showerin'."

"Why don't I believe you?"

Shell crackled under boots, walking toward Two Bucks' truck. It occurred to me I knew little of the man I thought was my father, Larry Detals. Successful at sports, school, business, finance. Shitty at fatherhood. What else did Larry suck at?

The dream floated back to me. Larry Detals' bloated carcass tried to tell me something. "A question's rolling around in my mind."

"K," he answered. We talked, both leaning on the hood of Two Bucks' pickup.

"For my entire life, townsfolk told tales about Buddy. War hero, lucky at life, great farmer, pillar of the community. Folks have been repeating his eulogy for decades. All the good stuff."

"You getting to the point?"

"Today, I get the gossip. He cheated on Grandmother..."

"Apparently, like it was an Olympic sport."

"No wonder she's been pissed at the world."

Two Bucks nodded.

"Not the best father," I said.

"Not to me, Larry wuz Buddy's favorite. Don't seem like it, but I was a Momma's boy."

"Funny, after all these years, I finally see that. So clear now. She was tough on you but pushed you. She also spoils you rotten. Have you ever cooked a meal?"

"Nope."

"Washed your own clothes?"

"Not yet," he said and laughed. "Don't suspect I'll be gettin' to it soon."

"Also, looks like Buddy got the glory, but Rose Petal ran this place."

"Dad made things happen, deserves some credit, but Mom makes this place tick."

"Following the same thought process. Everyone talks about Larry like that. Good at school, football. The king of raiding small publicly traded oil companies. Made millions, spent millions, left Brandy millions that she blew in less than a decade."

"Still waiting for your point."

I huffed. "Everyone talks about Larry like a god. Was he a terrible brother?"

"The best brother," Two Bucks said in reverence.

"I'm asking, what'd Larry suck at?"

"Selecting a bride."

"No shit. What else?"

"Best athlete in the county..."

"You're not getting to the point."

"He's my brother..."

"And," I demanded.

"Okay, water."

"What?"

"Yea, your dad...sorry, getting' used to you knowin', Larry...your uncle...shitty swimmer, never took to it?"

"How's that possible, growing up here?"

"We all got quirks. Family drove to Crystal Beach after Dad went off to the war, 'round 1942. Packed the car full'a aunts and uncles. I'm dusting off rust but thinkin' it was Larry's and my fifth or sixth birthday. We roughhoused near shore 'fore a wave whipsawed us. Took us tumblin', twisted us every which way.

"I remember the light brown, warm water surroundin' me, bubbles and froth. 'Bout ten seconds underwater, seemed longer, always does. Kinda like a carnival ride, the best kind, 'cuz I didn't need tickets to keep ridin'. Ended up sittin' on my ass, sand and shells in my hair, face rubbed raw from being pulled 'cross the ocean bottom. But I remember laughin'.

"Larry must'a been on a different ride. The Gulf spat 'em out five seconds after me, 'bougt forty feet 'tween us. Shook up, like a beer bouncin' 'round the cooler. Gulf popped his top and he started spewin' tears. He steered clear of deep water for years. Like most kid's he forgot 'bout it. Years later Larry 'bout drowned in the Neches. You got told 'bout that, right?"

"No, I didn't."

"Let's see. Dad was back from the war. We'd met Chic by that point, but she wasn't with us. Larry and me must'a been eleven. Family was out enjoyin' the river. Larry and I wrassled near shore. Tossing each other 'round. Mom and Dad seemed happy, or happy enough watchin' us, sittin' on shore. I stepped toward my towel to dry off, turned away for a second. Larry lost footin' or fell in a sinkhole, right when the current came callin'. Got holt of 'em. Dragged 'em to the bottom at first, then downstream. Some reason when he popped up, he called for me...not Dad or Mom. *Barry, Barry, help*. Weird, still remember that as the biggest compliment of my life."

"Barry?"

"That's my real name, remember."

"Yeah, I guess."

"Rose Petal labeled me Two Bucks later, but I was still Barry that day."

"Weird hearing you say it. Barry."

"Lawrence and Bartholomew, Larry and Barry. We were twins, remember?"

"Bartholomew?"

"Want to get back to the story?"

Before going back into the story, I took a moment to appreciate the surroundings, soaring pines, interlaced Saint Augustine grass, and the incongruency of my father's given name—Bartholomew. Epic.

I laughed. "Back to the story."

"Anyway, when Larry called, I dove after 'em. Stroked with every fiber of my being. Caught 'em a few hundred yards downstream. That Crystal Beach memory reclaimed him, brought 'em back to flip-floppin' in the tide, no air, thinkin' 'bout dying'. He shoved me under water, used me as a float. Fear got holt of 'em. Full tilt.

"I battled back up. Got face to face. 'I'm here, I'm here, I'm here,' I repeated, head bopping up and down in the water, Dad chasin' after us. He wuz smart, 'stead of divin' in, Dad ran 'long shore to make up ground. I started whisperin', 'Float, Larry, just float. We're okay. Float.' Everythin' happened so fast..."

Two Bucks lost track of the story and stepped out of himself. Darkness overtook his face.

"Then I felt the crack." Two Bucks rubbed his shoulder, triggered, caressing a phantom pain, no longer present. An injury that obviously held the lease of his soul.

"What?"

"I was calming Larry. So, the current pulled us blindly, my back turned the wrong direction to spot trouble."

Two Bucks stared at the tire-crushed shell and gravel of the Old Place's drive.

"Funny, my one valiant act happened so young."

"Most people ain't got the one."

He shrugged. "We crashed into a pine that fell into the river, sheared limbs porcupined out."

His lips turned down like a wrangler tugged them earthward. "Limb impaled me, blew up my shoulder." Two Bucks looked down, remembering his past tormentor in the present. "The sound and pain arrived together. But I remember two things."

Two Bucks unbuttoned his shirt. He motioned where the pine pierced him, showing the size of nature's impaler. "I remember the limb," he said.

"Yes," I pressed.

"Jagged. Covered in pine bark, even after it skewered me. Funny, at the time, felt like an outgrowth of the tree."

"And."

"I remember Larry's face...limb shish-ka-bobbed me, but I'm the calm one."

"Maybe because you saved your brother's life."

"I didn't know that yet. The current kept pullin', jerkin', grabbin', but damnit if we weren't jammed up. I held onto Larry with my one functional arm. Experiencing the horror, knowing, I'm 'bout to tell my brother I can't hang on, I'm so sorry, I can't...

"Just like that, two hands jerked Larry by the shoulder, tossing him to shore. I never saw Dad enter the water; guess I wuz distracted. He took time to ask Larry if he's okay."

Two Bucks stared into my eyes, allowing the moment to sink in.

"Only after Larry answered 'im, did Dad jerk me off the pine and carry me up the bank. Got lucky, I got impaled." Two Bucks stared at the soaring pines surrounding us.

"Gave Dad a chance to catch up, save Larry. I wallowed 'round in pain while Dad told Larry, 'Just breathe, son, slow down, just breathe.'"

Phantom pain washed over him again, but this time not from his shoulder.

"How do I not know this?"

"Larry never talked 'bout it, never got over the shame."

I added, "Rose Petal wouldn't talk about it."

"No. And I never talked 'cuz it wuz the best and worst day of my life. Best 'cuz I saved my brother, worse 'cuz everythin' changed."

"Everything?"

"Before that day, Larry and I stood on equal footin' with everyone but Dad. Larry learnt better, but I kept up. I proved to be the better athlete, bigger, stronger, despite bein' the second out the chute. Both of us popular, with the farm crowd at least. Most importantly, we wuz dead equal with Chic. Least I thought so. First, I got stuck in St. 'Lizabeth Hospital for weeks recovering. Next, back and forth for surgery after surgery. Then stuck in bed for months more. Larry and Chic still played together, did chores side by side, everything. Chic wuz sweet. She checked on me every day, but Larry had'er to himself. So, I lost that battle."

His stance, demeanor, and expression telegraphed the battle's cost. Two Bucks considered that loss incalculable. "Funny, I remember somethin' else..."

"What?"

"Layin' in bed, hearin' Dad bitchin 'bout the hospital bills."

"Wow, sorry."

"Thanks, kid." He held up his right arm. "Arm 'came useless for years after that, so I became left-handed. Relearned writin', throwin', even chores. Still, never the same. Never played sports again, spent years healin'.

"Larry shined. Dad cheered every step. We became the golden boy and the gimp. Case you're wonderin, I wuz the second one. My injury didn't stop chores. If anythin', Rose Petal piled on more. Mom didn't want no invalid. I found ways to do things, one-armed. Over time, I used both. Decades later, I figure the chores were her way of lookin' out for me.

"No college scholarship offers for the gimp, but Larry got plenty. Signed with Texas, played football like Dad. Those two became tight as trousers Thanksgivin' evenin'. By the time I wuz twenty, no one could tell, I'z injured. But I missed so much, I..."

"Tell me..."

"Missed loads of school. Ended up graduating a year behind Larry. Surrendered into being Two Bucks, I guess. Never wanted second place for you. Did my best...probably wasn't good enough..."

"You did fine, despite everything."

"Maybe I try parentin' with a few less longnecks goin' forward."

"Not your worst idea."

Two Bucks still stood in front of me, but his thoughts drifted back to the Neches. "Still hear voices over the current sometimes when I'm near the river. Can't explain it."

"Sounds like bullshit, but I do too. The voices call for me."

"Don't listen, Tails, don't let her take ya."

"I won't."

"The Neches, she finds funny ways of flirtin' with ya. Taunts ya. She's a liar, though. Lots of dead bodies've floated downstream."

"Guess so."

"Back to where we started. Larry never recovered from his second tumble with water. When the family swam in Neches, Village Creek, or the Gulf, Larry hung tight to shore, kept his feet under 'em. I'm not takin' nothin' from Larry. I loved 'em. On solid ground, the baddest man on the planet. Outworked everybody, studied hard, blessed with Dad's luck and Mom's work ethic. Water wuz the only thing Larry feared. Funny he drowned. People pull up close to their darkest fears. Guess that's why he killed himself the way he did."

"Or why he didn't."

Two Bucks shrugged.

"Dad, we gotta find Rooster."

The Rooster's Call

Late afternoon gave way to early evening, bright blues surrendering to rich blue-purples. Humidity recanted the threat of nonstop torture, surrendering unwillingly to subtle coolness accompanying sunset. Two Bucks' truck traveled all over Silsbee hunting Rooster.

An hour after we hit town, we pulled past the Pinewood Inn. Rental cars littered the parking lot. Easy to spot by their license plate guards, branded Avis, Hertz, or National.

"Some kinda convention in town?"

"Don't think so."

"The Pinewood's booked. Strange."

"Yeah, strange."

Two Bucks' brain stayed stuck in earlier conversations. Still, we scouted for Rooster. According to J&M's Grocery manager, Chic shopped hours earlier, but the trail died there.

After covering the whole town, we surrendered.

"Can't speak for you, but I could use a beer."

"I'm skipping booze tonight."

"Your call, son."

Ten minutes later, Two Bucks steered into Braelyn's parking lot. He smiled over his shoulder before sauntering inside. Hmm, the rental cars from the Pinewood now jammed Braelyn's lot. Strange. I followed Two Bucks' lead and walked to the bar.

"Surprise," the bar echoed, as I entered. Backslapping and hugs ensued. Dozens of long-retired teammates, out-of-work coaches, and one ancient umpire, long ago forcibly retired by Major League Baseball, mixed with the locals to celebrate my birthday.

I forgot. My 39th birthday, the dreaded landmark, or landmine, arrived, and I lost track. Rooster worries washed away by the tidal wave of well-wishers, backslaps, and hugs.

Twenty minutes later, each reveler returned to their seats and only Braelyn remained. She greeted me, dressed in similar attire as my first visit to Braelyn's. She hugged me before planting a pink neon kiss on my cheek. "Marking my spot to make someone jealous."

"Okay," I answered, befuddled.

"Happy Birthday, Tails. Rooster told me you never enjoyed a proper birthday party before. He wanted to make this one special."

She pointed to a picture of my best friend and me from decades before. A homemade poster read:

Welcome to Stephen "Tails" Details' Birthday Party, Featuring a Performance by the Rooster

Braelyn grabbed my hand propelling me toward the bar. I recognized old friends I did not greet at the door. The Mauler crew offered shots when we passed. I declined despite disparaging remarks about my manhood. With each interruption, Braelyn stayed at my side, kept her hand on my back, and kept pushing me forward.

"How did this happen?" I asked.

"Rooster willed it into being. Had little time to organize, but we did our best. Rooster's team reached out to your friends. My staff and kids decorated."

Biscuit stopped me next. "Happy birthday, bro."

"Thanks, Biscuit."

"Braelyn, girl, you *still* lookin' good."

"Still?"

"Just looking good then," corrected Biscuit. "And Braelyn, girl, the new bartender is smoking."

As we continued toward the bar, I added, "I doubt any bartender outshines you."

"Ahh, thanks, Tails."

I remembered my mission. "Wait, where's Rooster?"

"Just played a warmup set a few minutes ago. Probably getting the band ready."

"The Curs are here?"

"With Rooster, nothing's half-assed."

Her relaxed smile assured me everything, everyone, was all right.

"Like Biscuit mentioned, I hired a bartender for one night."

"Seems strange."

"Wants to say hi to you. She's real pretty."

Then I spotted the new girl, dressed in the same garb as Braelyn. Even turned away from me, bent over, the tanned legs proved unmistakable. Blue jean short-shorts framed her backside to perfection. "She borrowed one of my outfits. She's longer than me, so her backside peek-a-boos. Don't think the boys mind."

Confirming Braelyn's theory, men pressed to the bar, fighting for viewing angles. As she turned, I admired every inch before she spotted me. Unlike Braelyn's hat that was tipped back, the new bartender's hat tilted to one side.

The pink T-shirt she wore ended at her rib cage, showing off her lean stomach. Most onlookers never noticed, their eyes lost in appreciation of other assets.

"Not bad, for a Yankee."

"Not a figure of my imagination, not a figure of my imagination," I mouthed.

"Excuse me?"

"I thought she might be a figure of my imagination."

"Two things."

"Okay..."

"If she is, we're both seeing the same thing."

"Good. And?"

"Based on the way she fills out my cutoffs, you have a hot imagination."

"Yeah," I mumbled.

"The drooling peanut gallery thinks so too."

Finally, Elora Banks spotted me. She waved. The bar patrons turned and stared at me with venomous envy. To her credit, Elora looked at Braelyn. Her boss, for a day, nodded and Elora sprang from behind the bar.

I watched every step with the joy of an eight-year-old receiving a new set of Crayola Crayons, the 64 pack, with built-in sharpener. Magic.

On our flight to Houston and dinners, Elora dressed beautifully but professionally. Seeing her in this outfit, so out of context, and so graphically different, brought parts of me embarrassingly to life.

"Why hello, stranger," she said before kissing me.

Not a figure of my imagination, not a figure of my imagination, I repeated.

I gripped her and held her to me. She stepped back so I could take a full view. "I got into town without a birthday present for you. Braelyn suggested you might like this." She spun around. "She mentioned you liked her outfit when you two crossed paths."

I said nothing in shock.

"Braelyn, 'bout ten guys stuffed twenty-dollar bills between my..." Elora looked down at her decolletage instead of finishing. "They said it's okay because it goes to your kid's college fund."

"Damnit. I didn't warn you because you're just here for tonight. It's not okay, they always try something on new girls, I'm so sorry. I can guess the culprits." Braelyn stormed off to address the offenders. I heard but did not view Braelyn's departure.

Elora smiled before nodding toward the bar.

"I need to head back. Working the bar's part of your birthday present."

"Un-huh..."

"You monosyllabic now? Braelyn didn't mention a head injury."

"Sorry, just catching up."

"Hey, who left that big lipstick mark on your cheek? That's my job." I forgot Braelyn's earlier kiss. Elora paused, removed a lipstick tube from her cutoffs, coated her lips, then marked my other cheek.

Elora turned my head to one of the beer-branded mirrors and smiled. Braelyn's bright pink lip marks decorated one cheek, and Elora's dark maroon accented the other.

"I look ridiculous," I said and reached to wipe it off.

A hand stopped me cold. Braelyn, who returned to finish guiding me to the bar, held my arm in check.

"You an idiot? Don't wipe that off, you've been branded. Look around, stupid." Most male eyes focused on me. More accurately, the heartbreakers to my right and left.

"These rednecks would give up drinking, hunting, country music, pickup trucks, and tobacco to switch spots with you. So, shut up and leave my brand intact. Elora's too."

"Okay," I relented.

"Elora, I know we hired you for only tonight, but we need your talents at the bar."

Elora grabbed my hand. "Come have a drink. As the birthday boy, we'll get you a seat." I followed, Elora's backside drawing stares like lightning bugs draw kids with Mason jars. Irresistible.

Tig Mauler, one deliverer of Andrew Jackson to Elora's cleavage, smiled guiltily, shit-eating grin adorning his face. Still, as I approached the bar, he ceded his seat to me with flair.

"How...why...?" I asked. Elora turned to grab Silver Bullets for one of the throng jamming the bar. She nodded to another barkeep, who marked down the purchase. Elora already fit in.

She turned again and grabbed four longnecks popping the tops. Cool, frosty smoke rose from the bottles, as Elora and the other barmaid repeated the billing process.

"Cliffs Notes version," she screamed over the bar noise.

"Sure."

"I got a call from some guy named Biscuit. He said hold for Rooster."

"That had to be an experience."

"Yes." She turned, reacting to a patron holding up four fingers and pointing to his Budweiser. Elora popped four tops, then handed them off.

"Did I mention when I tried to be a screenwriter, I tended bar?"

I nodded.

"It's coming back to me. Anyway, Biscuit transferred me to Rooster. He got me here, bought tickets, everything. Said it was an emergency. Your birthday. Said you wanted me here. He also said something haunting."

"We get that a lot 'round here."

"He said sometimes you need 'your' people around to survive your birthday."

"He's right, but I'm better now."

"Forgot to ask, want a drink?"

"I'm not drinking...right now, at least."

She bent over the bar delivering the greatest kiss of my life. I'm sure catcalls, whoops, and ah's filled the air, but I retain zero memory of anything beyond her.

"There's one of those kisses waiting each time you tell me that."

I remained in stasis as she returned to her one-night job. Braelyn swung through and smiled appreciatively. "If you need full-time work, you'll have a spot."

A wink served as Elora's answer. The two women already possessed kinship. The distraction allowed me time to process. When Elora returned her attention to me, I culled my words to the few that meant the most.

"You disappeared..."

She smiled sadly but answered with playfulness to hide her guilt. She motioned like a magician. "Poof."

"Why?"

"Lots of reasons..."

"Care to share?"

"Well, first when I woke up, I freaked out."

"And."

"Give me a minute." She popped six Lone Stars, shoved them in an ice bucket, and passed them to Tig Mauler.

"You're not really employed here. You don't have to work so hard."

"Brings back memories."

"But back to the Houdini act."

"Dad didn't know I traveled to Houston to help..."

"I found that out when I called looking for you."

"Yeah, about that..."

"You got in trouble?"

"Not at first. But only because he didn't believe you. Later, he talked to another agent in Arizona. Found out I arrived late."

"Then you got busted?"

"I got the mother, or in this case, father of all lectures, about dating our clients. Especially an idiot...sorry."

"It's okay."

"An idiot who threw all his money away."

"Seems fair."

"But then you retired. Dad said you called him from a pay phone?"

"Long story."

"So, technically, we don't represent you..."

Elora shifted weight from one foot to the other. The shift led to, "Hey, stop looking down my top."

"If I didn't, I'd be the only guy here who's not."

"For the record, you've seen 'em."

"I need further study to finish my thesis."

"About?"

"God's two greatest creations."

"Men."

"Did I mention it's my birthday?"

"I can guess what you'd like."

"Wouldn't take a scholar."

"Well, if it's the one thing you want..."

Elora motioned to Braelyn, tapping her watch. Braelyn shrugged then held up ten fingers.

"The boss gave us ten minutes," Elora said.

"I'll take it."

Elora led, I followed. Thoughts of Rooster, hanging grandfathers, floating uncles, and my 39th birthday crowded out by thoughts of Elora's birthday suit.

Elora, who picked me first, despite the ire of her father, and honestly, a ton of better options, led me through the crowded bar. Men parted for Elora begrudgingly. Stares confirmed their eagerness to swap places with me.

I remembered the deserted boy, left abandoned at the Old Place, watching the man he thought was his father drive away. Lonely, lost, a suitcase and nothing else. My faculties fought to reach through time to tell that child, "Crap's in front of you, kid, I get that. Embrace the smell, shovel it, turn it into fertilizer, and plant your crops. All that crap delivers you here. This sober moment...the best moment of your life. Not because of the pleasures you imagine. Trust me, they'll be great. But for a far different reason. This woman, using logic you can never comprehend, picked you first. Her first-round draft pick."

I peeled my eyes from Elora's backside. *Braelyn's Realm* branded an old oak door. As Elora opened the door, tantalizing thoughts ravaged my brain.

A half-step short of paradise, a small, firm hand held me in place. I turned to see Chic, but a version I had never witnessed. Rooster's mother looked crazed, terrified. She vibrated fear.

"She's got 'em, Tails, she's got her claws in 'em again. Please, God, Tails, I need your help, or Rooster'll be dead before midnight."

Looking in the Rearview

My birthday party now lived in Two Bucks' truck's rearview mirror. I imagined Rooster's band breaking down their setup, drunken revelers settling bar tabs, Biscuit and the bouncers herding guests, and Braelyn explaining Rooster's mysterious family emergency. Elora, my dream girl, cleaning up spilled beer, half-eaten burgers, forgotten fries coated in ketchup, and grease-stained bar-naps.

The greatest evening of my life abandoned for the mission to save my best friend.

Truck lights cut through the night, white lane dividers flew by us as the truck rumbled toward Rooster's Houston penthouse. Two Bucks and me, in our spots from the ride over, Chic now wedged between us in the truck.

My cast rested in my lap, but I brought my left wristwatch arm up, 9:47 PM.

My 39th birthday had two hours and thirteen minutes to claim me...or worse, claim Rooster...both of us...or all four of us. Real or imagined, the curse changed all four of us.

With Rooster minutes ahead of us, but still on the road, it hit me. The curse's final foursome now drove I-10 to Houston. The remaining child, two grandchildren, and, in Chic's case, the unofficially adopted child of Buddy Detals all occupied the Interstate. Together, an easier target, all in one spot, for the curse's final axe...sorry, *act*.

"You okay to drive, Two Bucks?" asked Chic.

"Yeah, got caught hustlin' pool with Pop Mauler. Never grabbed a second beer."

Destination set, Two Bucks' sobriety confirmed, I dug in.

"Chic, Rooster promised to be there for my birthday."

She nodded.

"Rooster would never desert me, how'd Charla get to him?"

"Charla called Biscuit. Biscuit got Rooster on the phone. I watched from across the bar. Rooster turned ghost-white and put down the phone. He mumbled something about getting to Houston then just left. I followed Rooster out. Begged him to stay."

Two Bucks asked, "What the hell we walkin' into?"

"No idea. But it's something big."

Chic looked back and forth between us.

"I'm so, so, sorry, Tails."

"For what?"

"I love you so much, but I had to pick."

"I don't understand."

"After your father died, I had to pick."

"Still confused," I said.

"After your father killed himself on his 39th birthday."

She paused, deciding if she could share her secret, a secret Two Bucks spilled earlier. "Rooster is Larry's son too."

"I know Rooster is Larry's son."

"How?"

"It's new to me, Two Bucks told me."

She turned to Two Bucks. "You knew?"

"Course." He paused, understanding Chic needed more. Two Bucks' head stayed locked on the road. "I know everything about you, the way you take your coffee, the way you protect your son, the way you walk..." Two Bucks paused, needing time to gather. "God, the way you walk."

Despite everything, Chic blushed before returning to her story.

"Rooster was born first, few hours before you. Like Larry was born before Two Bucks. When Larry died on his birthday, like Buddy, I understood I could lose Rooster. So, I never told him. After Larry killed himself, I pushed you away. But Tails, you did nothing wrong. It's not about you…never was. I had to protect Rooster."

"What?"

"I tried to seal myself off, put a wall between us, because for Rooster to live, you had to die. The curse was coming. I didn't want it to claim my son. If everyone thought you were Larry's first son, even Rooster, maybe he survives."

"Wow."

"Sounds harsh, Tails. But a mother'll do anything to protect her son."

"That's screwed up, Chic," said Two Bucks.

Then I exploded. "Look, we're from Texas. Secrets, sugary-sweet, passive-aggressive behavior, and lack of in-depth conversation rule the day. Did it occur to anyone, a little fucking communication would stop this shit?"

"What do you mean?" asked Chic.

"Buddy Detals didn't kill himself," I screamed.

She stared at me, stunned.

"It's true," echoed Two Bucks.

"But…" Chic started.

I recounted the truth of Buddy's demise.

Chic sat, stunned. "How did I not know this?"

"No one did, but Rose Petal," I answered. Next offering details about why my grandmother hid the truth for so long.

"This lie, legend…whatever, controlled us. And Rose Petal, one of the unwilling architects of the story, never shared its foundation. So, the lie got piers under it. Cuckold men strung Buddy Detals for diddling their wives. That's dark, it grew, supported by the foundation of our lies and silence. Now the myth got into the town's consciousness."

"But Larry killed himself," said Chic.

"If he did, he bought the bullshit story. But I'm not so sure he killed himself."

"But…" she started.

"Oh, for the record, I'm not Larry's son."

"How can that be?"

The truck swerved; Two Bucks cleared his throat.

"Two Bucks, you screwed your brother's wife?"

"They weren't married yet. She climbed in while I was showerin'. Buck naked."

"And you screwed her?"

"Yep."

"How could you?"

"'Cuz her future husband was otherwise occupied," Two Bucks answered.

Awkward silence dominated the truck's cab.

"We've established you were both where you shouldn't be. Let's move past that?"

"Okay..." she agreed.

Two Bucks added, "Sure..."

Two Bucks and Chic exchanged sideward glances. We approached my favorite landmark on the drive from Silsbee to Houston, the picturesque Old and Lost River. The beautiful views, accented by moonlight. Seeing the standard-issue green highway sign stirred memories. *Old and Lost River*. The white letters glowed and dimmed as cars passed ahead of us, causing a strobe effect.

The name added mystique.

Old and Lost, Lost and Old, Old and Lost.

I remembered what Two Bucks shared, the call of the river. Children's voices intertwined with the current, calling you, welcoming you to join, become one. Creeks lead to rivers, rivers to oceans, oceans to oblivion. I looked to the sign as we passed. The truck's headlights enlivened the white words, *Old and Lost River*.

For years, I shunned the hanging ghost of Buddy Detals and the floating phantom of his son. Now I focused on the son, asking the water-bloated body to share secrets. Begging for dead company.

"*Old and Lost, Lost and Old, Old and Lost*," I chanted.

When you request your uncle's carcass attend a party in your subconscious, try not to act surprised when he accepts the invitation.

What's Lost

Old and Lost, Lost and Old, Old and Lost, I continued.

Larry Details' death, now old news, the why lost forever. Or was it?

Old and Lost, Lost and Old, Old and Lost.

Unsure why the words' rhythm comforted me. The Old and Lost River remained a childhood mental marker. A totem representing departure from rural Southeast Texas, the demarcation line. Ship channels, refineries, and warehouses served as Houston's eastern gateway. The river marked abandonment of the old and lost ways of living, as vehicles transported passengers into the modern world, Houston's industrial sprawl.

At this moment, the words translated differently. Embracing old and lost ways of trusting yourself. Listening to your body, dreams, falling into the...ether.

The darkness welcomes, the passing car lights lulled, assuring my journey, the bouncing of the car rocking me to...

Gratefully, bloated, rotting Larry did not appear. Something far more disturbing greeted my fall. I watched Larry, Brandy, Chic, and Two Bucks arrive at the swimming hole all those years ago. Larry, trying to look relaxed as he hugged the shore. Not telegraphing his fear of water to his new girlfriend. Brandy, Chic, and Two Bucks taking turns on the rope swing. Laughing and giggling at first.

I watched the woman who birthed me nine months later understand her true position for the first time. Brandy caught Larry stealing glances at Chic. She noted the easy familiarity of a couple. Laughing gave way to observation,

observation to jealousy. No, not jealously—stronger, vicious, tangible hate, not for Chic, but for Larry.

Suddenly, Brandy hated Larry for daring to place her second. I watched her plot punishment...demise. Evil formed behind her spoiled, entitled eyes.

A frequent dream traveler, I understood. My mind created these events. Using Two Bucks' tale, my knowledge of Brandy Detals filled in the blanks. Correctly or incorrectly, my mind harshly processed any news of the woman who pushed me out of her vagina, then treated me like a canned ham.

The beautiful dream foursomes swirled away. Echoes of children's dark laughter bounced in my ears. The daytime gone, night surrounded me, and the call of my name. Tails...Tails...Tails.

Larry Detals, or his carcass, now sat at water's edge. Back to me, eyes not leaving the pond. Dead, long abandoned, alone.

I walked forward, not afraid of the bloated monster from childhood dreams. Thankful for Larry's return. Not turning to greet me, Larry's face remained locked on the swimming hole, watching, no...monitoring.

His arm reached to the side. The dream phantom sat something on the ground, inches from him, meant for me. I stepped closer, examining the object, shiny, a coin. Without turning, he held it up. No, not a coin...a medal. A medal hanging from a ribbon.

Larry, so alone, here only to warn me, needed me to grasp his message. Enough so he turned, losing focus on the water he so feared, his monster, his demon. The pond creature, sensing distraction, attacked. Not hideous claws, but two darkly beautiful hands emerged and snatched Larry into the abyss.

I heard the phantom scream...or was it me?

"Tails, Tails," she called. The abyss called my name. Now she jerked me. How did I drift too close to the swimming hole?

"Tails...Tails, wake up."

Chic's firm, little hands jerked me awake. "You're dreaming, Tails."

"Was I?"

"I think so," she answered.

She still rode shotgun, jammed between Two Bucks and me. Out the truck window, I spotted the Anheuser-Busch Brewery off of I-10, almost there, almost to Rooster.

I held the dream close, almost choking it, not allowing the images to fade. Forcing the message back to my frontal lobe. Larry put Brandy second. No chance she fared well in the two spot. Also, Larry dies, she inherits everything, or thought she did.

Brandy remembered the swimming hole, knew how to get there. Clues circuited through my brain. Surely, Brandy learned of Larry's fear of the water. His area of incompetency was especially tantalizing to her. Brandy swam at a world-class level. Water, the one place Larry's physical tools failed him.

Brandy Detals killed my father—scratch that, *uncle*.

Lost no more. Found you, Larry Detals.

I waited to speak, wanting to reassemble the pieces. Maybe my mind fooled me. I accepted my hatred for Brandy Detals prompted my brain to construct her as the villain. Because who knows Brandy Winthrop Detals better than the child she chose not to raise?

Who else reevaluated every conversation to find meaning behind abandoning a child? Who processed every action and reaction thousands of times in their brains? Each time she did not call, every game she failed to attend, painted a portrait of my birth mother. Not just her inability to nurture, but a disturbing view of her soul.

"Sure you're okay, Tails?" Chic asked patting my knee. I considered Chic, a woman who offered me up as a human sacrifice, to save her son. A screwed-up high-water mark for motherly devotion.

I turned my thoughts from Chic to Brandy Detals.

Imagining the poor parenting Brandy endured to metamorphosize into a soulless monster. Did her father, mother, or uncles molest her as an innocent? Or did they indulge her every whim? Unsure of why, positive of the result, I turned from Brandy's upbringing to Larry's death.

Did Brandy do it? How was it done?

First, I recounted every swimming hole memory and my hundreds of times there. The muddy banks might leave clues of an escaping murder.

However, the swimming hole resided in the Piney Woods. Let's assess the facts.

Pine straw blankets the east side of the hole

Pine straw covers most of the surrounding area.

Even a warped Texas family like mine cannot keep secrets with the consistency of a pine straw-covered forest floor.

Brandy Detals may be a city girl, but acres of oaks, pine trees, and the bayou surrounded her childhood home. Possibly childhood adventures taught her pine straw's penchant for privacy.

How did she draw Larry to the swimming hole? Did Brandy do it? I'll never know.

Was Brandy the person with the most motivation to kill Larry Detals? Yes.

As a swimmer, did she possess a custom-made skill set, or kill set? Absolutely.

Why did no one else make the mental leap?

I was a teenager when Larry died, but I remember everyone accepted his suicide as fact.

If local police questioned Brandy, which I doubt, I'm positive Brandy created an ironclad alibi. Additionally, her father's money and influence could dissuade any investigation.

Rose Petal hated Brandy. However, my grandmother believed in Larry's suicide. She blamed herself for not helping Larry process his father Buddy's death. Rose Petal assumed her secrets contributed to Larry's suicide. *Why?*

Self-blame and loathing become all-encompassing when allowed to run amok. Hell, I understand that better than most. Chic and Two Bucks, before today, bought the suicide myth, sidelining their brains from doing any investigation.

There was little reason to consider foul play. The local police, not the biggest fans of my family for numerous reasons, usually displayed competency and professionalism. No one considered murder.

No murder, no murderer, or in this case murderess. Follow the money, follow the money, follow the money.

Upon Larry Detals' death, my mother received what she thought at the time was her husband's entire estate. The house, the vacation homes, his car collection, and even his company. Showing greed, or lack of inclination toward work, she liquidated the company's assets for fast money. Laziness and her desire to quickly disassociate from Larry Detals meant she received a discounted value.

Brandy burned through her blood money, as if Larry presoaked each dollar in gasoline. Years later, after her father's death, Brandy's financial tornado tendencies ripped through the Winthrop estate. Brandy's family wealth weathered generations, over 120 years before it fell victim to Hurricane Brandy's destruction.

But back to Larry's death. Brandy possessed reason, emotional inclination, and financial motivation to kill her husband.

Larry Detals probably foresaw his demise. Likely, not on his 39th birthday. Still, I wonder, did the cosmos warn him of Brandy's plot? With the Detals' bloodline, did Larry grasp death's periphery?

Men who feel death's proximity keep secrets or a secret. In Larry Detals' case, he shared his secret with one person—me. Unfortunately, Larry weaved his secret into a decades-old legal puzzle. A puzzle I finally possessed the tools to navigate.

Detals Spelled Backwards

"She killed him," I blurted. No varnish, no warnings or setup for the listeners.

"What?" Chic asked. Her thoughts ran to Rooster. "What does he mean?" she asked Two Bucks. Two Bucks, not looking from the road, managed a shrug.

"No, not Rooster," I answered, translating Chic's concern. "I mean Larry, she killed Larry."

"I don't follow," she answered.

Adding the varnish back seemed important now. "Brandy—she killed Larry. She lured him from the Old Place to the swimming hole. She drowned him."

"That's absurd," said Chic.

"Is it...really?" My words settled in the truck. Because of sixth-grade science class and the overuse of the saying, even below-average students understand heat rises. No one uses the term "cold falls." Dive into any lake, just below the surface, cool water embraces and even invigorates your body. Still, the deeper you dive, the colder the water. Chills greet you at lake bottom, where water hides her secrets. The sunken, forgotten, and discarded rest there, cast aside, hidden under the beauty the lake's pristine surface presents.

People, like lakes, hide secrets.

Secrets are cold.

They pull you to the bottom, where darkness awaits. I reevaluated my Alcoholics Anonymous visits. Yes, I only attended because my former teams mandated my participation. Still, I learned, despite the indentured nature of my attendance. Secrets are the bane of alcoholism and all addicts. Secrets keep us wallowing in the addiction.

Sharing our blackest secrets allows us to step from darkness, out of the cold into the light. Light warms, heat rises, stepping into the sun heals your soul. Often, we discover our secrets were not that terrible after all. Shared secrets weigh less.

I stepped away from philosophy, back to the present. I continued, "She killed Larry for the money. Oh, and because of you..."

"But..."

"He loved you. Larry never loved Brandy the way he loved you. Brandy hated him for it. Larry spent his birthday at the Old Place...with you. That'd push her over the edge."

"Got proof?" asked Two Bucks.

"Proof...no."

"Dreams talkin' to you again?" he asked.

"They've talked to me my whole life. Sadly, I made it about me. I thought my dreams called me to kill myself. I couldn't face them. But now, I've stopped blaming the past for my poor decisions, *my poor decisions*," I repeated. "That meant something. Facing Rose Petal, accepting her flaws, and understanding her love, changed everything. My dreams never pushed me toward the grave. They served as signposts, warnings, messages. Buddy and Larry visited my dreams to save me from myself."

"But they didn't," Two Bucks said. "My dead father and brother didn't rise from the grave and talk to you."

"It's my brain's way of processing. I thought the worst thing in the world was killing myself. It's not."

"What is?" Chic asked.

"Secrets. Secrets will trick you into throwing away time with the people you love...or push loved ones away. This family's secrets almost killed me. Now we gotta stop them from killing Rooster.

"Chic, Larry loved you and Rooster more than me. At the time, I didn't understand. It hurt. Unfortunately, I inherited Brandy's jealous gene. But Brandy and I are different. The Winthrops raised Brandy to be the belle of the ball, spoiled and coddled. You made Brandy number two in Larry's heart.

"Everyone made me feel like number two, or worse, number zero. Brandy, 'my mother', deserted me. When Larry came around, he spent more time with Rooster than me. Rooster's a better athlete, more famous. I always finished second to him. I didn't know he was Larry's kid then. Now I do. But I always had...I have number two disease. I get that now. I never felt good enough. Ever. Not once. So, when I read Larry's will, it crushed me."

"What about his will?"

"All the money..."

"I thought Brandy spent every cent."

"Every penny she got her hands on. Even she and her team of piranhas couldn't get to all Larry's money."

"But how?"

"Great estate attorneys, I guess. He left Brandy millions in the will. But he sat aside money for me...sort of.

"Larry wrote a letter to any future judges, arbitrators, or mediators about his will. Larry's letter stated that if Brandy spent the millions he left for her, it served as proof she should not manage her child's estate."

"Slick," said Two Bucks.

Chic added, "Not a terrible secret. Your father left you money..."

"Larry's not my father, but I'm not sure if he figured it out. That's not my secret."

"Cut to it, Tails. We're running short'a windshield time."

"Larry's lawyer flew to Cleveland on my 25th birthday. I was with the Royals by then. We played the Indians that night. Flying into town seemed excessive, but I agreed to meet him. The lawyer handed me a note from Larry. Larry left twenty million."

"Even with your baseball money, that's a nice bump," said Two Bucks.

"There's more." I paused, ashamed. Mentally, I returned to the lake bottom, the cold, the secret's weight holding me in place.

"Remember, Charla had just left me for Rooster..."

"I'm sorry, Tails. Rooster is too."

I pushed the weight aside, then kicked, propelling myself to the surface. I rose from the lake bottom, puncturing the surface, ready to be free from the lie. Warm water and sunshine met me. Cleansed at the surface, knowing the truth offered resolution.

"I'm sorry Rooster and I lost ten years together, not sorry Charla left me. Screw her. I'd just been traded for the third time. Alcohol held sway over most of my decisions."

"Seems like you're stallin', son."

"I am."

"Get to spittin', kid."

"When Larry wrote his will, he didn't predict I'd play professional baseball or Rooster'd be the biggest star in country music. He understood I had Rose Petal, Two Bucks, and the Old Place. Now that we know Rooster is Larry's son, it's Rooster's home as much as mine. Really, it's always been."

"Anyway, based on the information he had, he left one million to Two Bucks."

"Whoopee, I'm a millionaire," said Two Bucks with no enthusiasm.

"Two million to Rose Petal. And two million to me. But only if I managed his trust."

"And..."

"And I refused because the rest of the money..."

"What?" said Chic.

"The rest of the money went to you and Rooster."

"But..."

"Larry never thought I'd turn down two million."

"So..."

"The money's sitting there..."

"I've kept it there, stuck, by not signing his papers. Larry didn't plan for that. Larry's lawyers protected the money from Brandy. I kept it from you. Me, I did that because I felt second, again."

"I never wanted Larry's money, Tails. And I'm sorry you dealt with that."

"But it's yours. I'll sign the paperwork and get you the money. Even the two million he left me. I don't want a damn thing from Larry. I have a father now."

"Damn right you do, Tails," said Two Bucks. "Screw all that. Let's rescue Rooster."

Would Rooster live to crow another morning? He was, after all, the son of Larry Detals, the grandson of Buddy Detals, and tonight, Rooster Brewster was...39.

The Tower and the Fall

Two Bucks pulled his truck upfront. He appeared confused when a red-coated man in a bowtie walked toward him expectantly. I snatched the keys from Two Bucks and tossed them to the building's valet.

Two Bucks stood befuddled.

"He's the valet," I said, turning and hurrying toward the building entrance. Two men dressed similarly to the valet held the door.

"Not sure what that is," Two Bucks said.

"I'll tell you later."

Chic raced past the front desk, toward the elevator. She pressed the elevator call button twenty times. I asked the front desk manager, "Was a woman here earlier with Rooster?"

"You mean Miss Charla?"

I nodded.

"She left ten or twenty minutes ago."

I assumed Charla spent the night here often, before Rooster broke it off days ago.

"Shit," I said joining Chic at the elevator. She continued pushing the already lit button.

Two Bucks walked beside us as the door opened. The three of us entered the elevator, followed by the front desk manager. He slid his key into a brass slot and selected the penthouse button before stepping off. The elevator jerked to life, propelling us to Rooster. Chic's stare volleyed from Two Bucks to me, seeking assurance we failed to offer. Two Bucks' eyes transitioned from floor to ceiling, then back. Hands jammed in my pockets, I focused on the digital panel, ticking off each floor.

The elevator glided to a stop and the doors slid open. From my visit, I remembered the penthouse opened to a lavish hall with one door, Rooster's.

Door open.

Lights on inside.

Dead silent except...running water?

A rivulet crept slowly from the open door into the hall. The water pooled on the marble, expanded, then flowed again.

Chic looked at me and Two Bucks. No one moved. Both surrendered the forward scouting job to the out-of-work, alcoholic baseball player with a broken arm.

"Sure, right, I'll...ah...go first," I offered.

I peeked inside. Everything appeared in order. No change in the furniture. No sign of fight or struggle. I checked the mantle. Grammys and CMAs in place.

The running water guided me. I walked toward the kitchen, following the widening stream and the sound.

Spotting his boots, my heart sank.

Boot tips pointed to the sky, water pooling around him. Rooster lay dead or dying. I checked...dead.

Chic's scream, earth-shattering, heartbreaking, rocked the room, but unfortunately failed to wake the dead. She flopped onto Rooster's corpse weeping. I felt him, still warm.

Shoving her aside, I started trying to resuscitate Rooster.

I heard Two Bucks on Rooster's phone. "There's a man here, he's dyin'..."

Pause.

"I don't have a damn address but we need...oh, you got the address..."

Push one, two, three, hold his nose, breathe into him. Wait, nothing, push one, two, three, breathe into him, wait, push one, two, three.

Two Bucks hung up the phone, then tried to comfort Chic before she shoved him away.

Push one, two, three, hold his nose, breathe into him. Wait, nothing, push one, two, three, breathe into him, wait, push one, two, three.

At some point, Two Bucks turned off the running faucet. He sighed, opened the fridge, and popped a longneck open. "He's dead, kid...you done did all you could."

Push one, two, three, hold his nose, breathe into him. Wait, nothing, push one, two, three, breathe into him, wait, push one, two, three.

I'll never know how long I leaned over my best friend, hoping to resuscitate Rooster. As I pushed, failing to bring my best friend back to life, I choked down my emotions, focusing only on the task.

Push one, two, three, hold his nose, breathe into him. Wait, nothing, push one, two, three, breath into him, wait, push one, two, three.

The medics pulled me off. My arms throbbed, especially the one in the cast. My body surrendered, all of it, and after the medics took over, I collapsed, weeping.

Every emotion poured out, I screamed in frustration, interrupted by Father Time. The clock chimed once, twice, three times, a fourth, then a fifth, sixth, seventh, eighth, ninth, tenth, eleventh, and finally, the twelfth time. My birthday ended. Thirty-nine years and one day old. A milestone Buddy, Larry, and now Rooster failed to reach.

I joined Chic in tears. Her son followed his grandfather and father to the grave.

Police showed up, counselors arrived. Everything got investigated.

No signs of foul play. Opened bottles of pills sat by the sink. One tipped over, a lone surviving red pill rested outside the rim. Rooster took no chances. He emptied every pill bottle in his home. Dead.

I sat at Rooster's dining table, repeating to a female officer the same script I uttered to her male counterparts. My words, a mantra now, "Charla James, his former girlfriend, left before we got here. She did this. I know she did."

Charla James...I'm...scratch that, *we're* coming for you.

. . .

I woke, sore from crashing on my stylish, but not meant for sleepovers sofa. The plush gray couch, too short for my frame, left my knees grumbling and lumbar wincing. As a man who struggled with nightmares, I *prayed* last night was simply a dark trip into dreamscape.

Chic's sobbing echoed from my suite, evidence of my failed chat with God. Two Bucks snored in my guest bedroom. A half-dozen empties littering my granite countertop confirmed my unanswered prayer. The beer bottles, not the countertop dwellers, but the iced longnecks in the fridge whispered my name, promising numbness.

Alcohol served as my security blanket for twenty years. Sobriety left me emotionally exposed, naked, but also aware, crisp, raw. Those emotions offered the best chance to survive today. I needed all of me, not the drunken facsimile.

Worse than a nightmare created in my screwed-up subconscious, Rooster's death, by overdose, promised hundreds of future visits into my psyche. Truthfully, nights with him haunting my dreams disturbed me less than thoughts of life without him coloring my days.

Time to assemble facts.

Rooster's dead.

Evidence confirmed, my best friend killed himself on his 39th birthday, following his father and grandfather to the grave.

Police questioned, then released Charla late last night.

Charla admitted she visited Rooster's penthouse. Yes, they fought. She said Rooster begged her to stay. Maybe that's why he killed himself...heartache.

My ass.

Charla killed Rooster. The question was how. What leverage did she possess?

I realized last night I had no way to contact Elora directly. She left the bar by the time Two Bucks called Braelyn with the news. I imagined her heartache, losing her husband, then losing the one man who might help her heal. Rooster left a huge void in all of our lives: Braelyn's, mine, Chic's, Two Bucks', his band, his fans, hell, even Rose Petal's.

His music all that was left now...

I repeated that thought in my head...his music was all we had left.

Then again...

The solution clicked into place. I understood the game plan, but a coup d'état takes planning and time. Time for authorities to move to another case, for me to get right, and for my allies to lose hope, surrender, and wave the white flag. But most importantly, time for Charla James to let down her guard.

Mountain of Hope, Addiction Center, Los Angeles

My 6:00 a.m. group meeting hours behind me, I inhaled to power through the last minutes of my morning run. Running served as my TAWG, time alone with God, the highlight of each day.

Sweat coated me, despite the cool air and altitude. The downhill run from the facility near Griffith Park Observatory, started—*me time*. The return run, or climb really, back through Griffith Park, featuring posh home-scapes and the Hollywood sign, became my favorite daypart. My first week in residence at Mountain of Hope, I joined the running group populated by fellow addicts and two counselors. After the first month, the facility leader told me I earned one alone run. Each run, where I returned on time and sober, earned one more day. One day at a time.

Even the first few runs I completed the downhill portion of the course with ease. Almost anyone could, gravity propelling you to valley's bottom. The second portion, the uphill climb, started as a walk, then walk/jog, and over the last few weeks became a run.

For my healing, I chose the strictest program. For sixty days no outside contact, period. None.

Time passed slowly but deliberately. Finally, I tackled the Twelve Steps of Alcoholics Anonymous. An overdue assignment.

1) I admitted my powerlessness, alcohol controlled me—my life jumped the rails.

241

2) Next, I understood, only a greater power could restore sanity.

3) I turned my life over to that power, completely surrendering.

4) I completed a moral inventory, shining a flashlight into my darkest places.

5) After praying, I told Ted, my group's discussion leader, everything.

6) I prayed to my higher power, asking him to remove character defects and aid my battle with alcohol.

7) Next, I attacked my shortcomings: avoidance, commitment issues, feelings of not being good enough, etc., asking my higher power for help there too.

8) With Ted's help, I assembled a list of people I harmed. I planned amends for each one.

9) I planned each amends, writing letters to people I harmed, keeping the letters for now.

10) I no longer let my mistakes fester, admitting missteps daily.

11) Praying daily, in my case during morning runs, transformed into my favorite time.

12) Now refreshed and unencumbered by secrets for the first time in decades, starting the day I found a dead body under my grandmother's home, I committed to helping others fight the fight. Not waiting, I asked for responsibility at the center. Ted tasked me with leading a new group. I committed to thirty more days onsite to jumpstart the group.

•   •   •

I finished the run, admiring the hills of Griffith Park, a whole man. Run completed, I walked toward the clinic's entrance for check-in, to earn tomorrow's run. Today presented a new challenge, my sixty-first day. Guests could request time with me, one guest per day, coordinated by the staff.

I cooled down by stretching in the guest parking. Even below-average Sherlocks could guess the identity of guest number one. He told me he lived in L.A., but this license plate assured me of his identity—BIGBUTZ.

No wasted moments, not quite 9:00 a.m.. I checked in with the guard, then avoided the lobby, taking a back route to my room. A note dangling from my door informed me of a waiting guest. I sniffed myself, a quick shower smelled in order. Under the showerhead, I thanked God for a chance to share my first letter, my first amends.

Imagining but failing to select a more unlikely first guest, I walked to the lobby. There he sat, reading the *Sporting News*. My last big-league manager. The man who informed me my time with the Astros ended, Lonnie "Butz" Butzkowski.

He stood, hand shook/hugged/double-tapped and released me in one masculine-encased movement. Before Butz sat, I handed him my letter. He nodded, signaling familiarity with the ritual, before sitting to read my amends. Neither of us spoke, both settled into the comfort of silence.

He read with the detailed orientation of a former catcher/current big-league manager. "Thanks, Tails, I appreciate you putting this in writing for me." Butz smiled. "I ahh...did time here."

"Shit."

"Yeah." He pulled a sobriety chip, passing it to me. The brass coin, far different from the plastic three-month chip in my pocket. I turned it, feeling every groove, a ten-year sobriety chip. I returned the coin. Butz slipped the chip into his pocket, patting his pants to ensure the coin's safe return.

"When you joined the Astros, I thought I'd get more time to...ah, talk about getting sober...but the injury," he said.

"Not your fault," I offered.

"After the at-bat, the one that ended your career..."

"What about it?"

"You showed the team what toughness looked like. We won eight in a row, sixteen of the next twenty. The boys discussed that at-bat the rest of the season. Propelled us into the playoffs. Unfortunately, we ran into the Braves' pitching staff."

"Followed the team, when possible...from here."

"Hell of a season." Butz paused, assembling his words. "The Astros'd like you back."

"I'm sorry."

"Not as a player, but a minor league batting coach. You'll start in the low minors. But with your approach to the game, you'll be coaching in the bigs one day."

Butz reclined, allowing me time to process his words. Then he laughed. "Relax, Tails, don't need your answer today." He had to witness relief wash over me.

"Get right, tell me when you're dry for good. We'll find a spot then."

We talked baseball for hours with no pressure or agenda. Time passed quickly, but the conversation cemented in my brain, as a talk to remember on my deathbed. Every half hour or so, a baseball-loving staff member, not allowed to approach me for autographs, because of my status as a patient, approached Butz, interrupting our talk. My former manager handled each intrusion with grace. Then our time together ended.

Butz and I repeated the shake/hug/double-tap/release when he departed. Overwhelmed, I watched him drive away.

Every few days, to give me time to recover, my past came calling. I followed my process with each visitor, giving my letter of amends first.

No one explained who or how they decided the visitors' order, but Two Bucks, my father, came next. He announced two weeks of sobriety.

"Hopin' for a few more," he said. He asked to take the letter with him, read it later. "Don't wanna get all weepy in public."

Rose Petal, my next guest, traveled to Los Angeles with Two Bucks. My father took her to Disneyland days before. She chronicled her first roller-coaster ride, Space Mountain.

"Fancy place to ditch the sauce," she started.

I laughed, then agreed. She read my letter seated in the lobby. In a surprise move, Rose Petal hugged me when she left.

Elora visited next, dressed in a skirt accenting her goddess legs. Like Two Bucks, she requested to read her letter later. I asked for a future date, explaining I had business to handle before I would be ready. She agreed, leaving me with a kiss. When we walked to her car, a male staffer chronicled every step of her departure.

I addressed Rooster in letters to Rose Petal, Two Bucks, and even Elora. Still, I did not—could not—speak about him yet, not avoiding the subject but preparing.

Old teammates, managers, and even an ex-girlfriend swung by, but my last visitor proved most important—Chic.

She read my letter, thanked me, but remained walled off, unapproachable. Like me, she proved unable to say his name, and I understood. After forced pleasantries and obligatory "I'm sorry's," I asked for one huge favor.

"Chic, when I'm out, can you get me into Rooster's penthouse?"

"I'm not sure."

"You can't just walk into your son's penthouse?"

"No. I can't say much. Your counselor asked me not to pile stress…"

"I asked. I can handle it."

"Not this whirlwind you can't. For now, focus on you, Tails."

She smiled sadly, stood, and said good-bye.

The final thirty days of my stay grinded by with the speed of a three-legged turtle. My last week, the center allowed phone calls to arrange my return to the real world. Only one call needed to be made.

"Chic," I asked when she picked up the phone.

She answered my question before I asked. "My lawyer negotiated an hour in the apartment. All I could get while the attorneys work a settlement."

"Settlement…who else would get anything of Rooster's besides you?"

"Long story, Tails. I'll tell you when we meet at the Old Place."

"Just friggin' tell me."

"Not over the phone."

"Can't you just meet me at Rooster's place?"

"No, we need time to talk. Get to Silsbee. We need you here."

"Ohh…shit."

• • •

Days later, I found myself at the Old Place. I rocked on the porch swing next to Two Bucks. The creaking chain complained about the 400 pounds it endured. Chic and Rose Petal resided in rockers, their usual spots.

Chic started. "Charla's pregnant with Rooster's baby. Her lawyers sued for everything of Rooster's…every penny. His penthouse, his royalties, everything."

"Let her have it, Chic," I said. "You have the money coming from Larry."

"Charla knows about the will somehow."

"I can guess who told her."

"Charla can set the money on fire and toast marshmallows. I don't care. But in the lawsuit, she's demanding sole custody of Rooster's baby. I'll never see my grandchild."

"Knowing Charla, I can't believe she wants the baby."

"Sound like your mom," Two Bucks said, referring to Brandy Detals. "Using a child for negotiatin'."

"It's not about the baby, it's about revenge, control, proving she's right," I said.

Rose Petal remained quiet, rocking steadily.

"I know she killed Rooster. I just can't prove it," Chic said.

"Just get me to Rooster's apartment."

I considered each person on the porch. My home team, ready for battle with Charla, a battle I alone understood required nuclear options.

Chic, Two Bucks, and I started toward my rental car when Rose Petal announced, "Give me a sec to turn off the lights and the air-conditioning. I'm coming."

The four of us traveled in silence, each bearing the weight of our thoughts. When we arrived at the tower, topped by Rooster's penthouse, I tossed my keys to the valet and we stepped inside.

The front desk manager stopped us, pulling Chic aside. "I'm sorry about Rooster, Ms. Brewster. And I'm sorry about what I have to tell you." The manager examined his feet before reciting his next words. "Ms. James' attorney called. You are allowed one hour and one hour only in Rooster's suite."

"Ahhh..." Chic bemoaned.

"All we need," I said putting my arm around Chic.

Anger radiated from her pores.

Then the manager finished his orders. "Also, I have to check when you exit. You're not allowed to leave with items from the apartment."

"The hell you…"

"Chic, it's okay," I assured. "Let Charla win her petty battles; let's use our hour wisely."

As we continued to the elevator, Rose Petal seemed awed by the lobby's grandeur. She dismissed my assumption. "What a waste'a marble, brass, and money. No need for this ho-ha," she said, waving her hand.

The elevator arrived, and we stepped inside. The manager followed. As I remembered from before, he inserted a key card, allowing us access to the penthouse.

Moments later, Chic produced a key card and we stepped through Rooster's door. Everything appeared clean and in order. I marched to Rooster's recording studio.

"It's been months. Why here, Tails?" Chic asked.

"Needed the police to move on."

"Why? We know Charla killed 'im but there's no proof," Two Bucks said.

"What if there was?"

"Why didn't you tell us sooner?" Chic demanded.

"You don't battle the Devil without weapons of mass destruction. If the police found it, I'd lose my leverage. The threesome nodded. I turned to Chic. "Needed Charla to let down her guard. Wanted her to think you were just a grieving mother." Then I turned to Two Bucks and Rose Petal. "You two were country trash, and I'm a drunken fool. Wanted her eye on the prize, not on me. My time in rehab got me sane, sober. Most importantly, it made that monster feel safe."

I continued. "Rooster got song ideas all the time. The bathroom, shower, even in bed."

"We know that, Tails, even me," Rose Petal said.

"Yes, but Rooster wanted to capture tunes right when they struck him. So, he installed a recording system to capture every noise, sound, every word said in this apartment."

"There's a sound system that recorded Rooster's conversation with Charla?" Chic asked.

"I think so."

"Wouldn't the cops see the speakers, find the tapes?" Two Bucks asked.

"They'd see speakers and guess they led to his recording studio. Which they did."

"Still not following."

"There're two systems here. The old system you see." With turns of my head, I led their vision. Scattered tapes, CDs, a mixing board, and full recording studio sat in front of us.

"The cops listened to every tape and CD here. But they'd find nothing. Nothing except Rooster laying down album tracks. No evidence here if you don't know what you're looking for.

"Rooster became jaded after his song ideas showed up on rival artists' albums. He guessed someone got greedy, sold ideas out from under him. But he couldn't prove it. So, he spent 100K on modern technology to capture his late-night ideas and date-stamp them. Proof of the origin and date of his songs. The system's top of the line, no tape. 100% digital. You need a password to access the file. Watch this."

I walked to the recording studio's entry. A panel, similar to a phone dialing pad, occupied an area to the right. "Everyone assumed this panel locks the door, which it does. That's the trick...it does more."

I typed in the code. A code only two residents of Planet Earth knew. Technically, only one currently with a pulse. The birthday Rooster and I shared, and then the last two digits, 39. I typed in the code and a panel slid. The laptop was still there, plugged in.

"It's all here, all right here."

My limited computer skills meant it took a few minutes to locate the recording. But we heard it, every word.

Chic shook with anger. Two Bucks stared in disbelief. Rose Petal seemed to understand something the rest of us did not. My grandmother's secret remained hers alone, until months later.

Still, we had a big'ole problem. "We can't get the laptop out. There's no way," Chic said.

"Maybe we can sneak a disk out."

"They'll still search us," said Chic.

"How big's the disk?" Two Bucks asked.

I held up an example.

"You make the disk, I'll get it out," Two Bucks said.

"How?"

"Don't ask questions you don't want answers to, Tails."

The Long Play

Two Bucks' two butt cheeks served as the smuggle mechanism for the disk and plastic cover sleeve.

We reconvened at the House of Pies on Kirby, the location of my last meal with Rooster. Two Bucks went to the bathroom, returned, and sported a toothy grin. He held the mini-CD, hopefully protected from its surroundings.

No one offered to take it from him. With my direction, he dropped our proof on a napkin. Chic napkin-wrapped the disk, careful not to touch the surface.

"God, I hope you washed your hands," Chic said.

"No promises," Two Bucks offered. I prayed in jest.

"I'm not hungry, for lots of reasons," Chic said.

The four of us birthed our plan to rescue Rooster's child from Charla. Unfortunately, our plan's nature demanded time, money, and patience.

To execute our plan, Charla James would remain free to enjoy the spoils of Rooster's murder...for now. Time was not our friend but served as the arbiter of our plan's success.

• • •

Harris County Civil Courthouse, Eleven Months and Seventeen Days Later

I watched the 6'4", 400-lb. robed man shift in his seat. Judge Luke Loving looked perturbed. Despite his professionalism throughout the three-day trial, the judge hinted at his rooting interest, warmth offered despite his position.

"Mrs. Brewster, I am a big fan of Rooster. I am sorry we are here."

"Thank you, Judge," Chic offered.

"Are you sure...?"

"Yes, Judge," she answered, stopping him as if she considered letting the question enter the world a travesty.

Loving breathed deeply.

"Mrs. James." Charla looked up.

"*Ms.* James," Charla corrected.

The judge continued without acknowledging her. "Mrs. Brewster surrendered to your demands. Your son, Charles James Brewster, is the sole beneficiary of the estate of his father, Cole Michael Brewster. All real estate, royalties, investments, licensing rights, and all other manner of income outlined by your attorney. Rooster's mother will receive no part of this inheritance.

"The estate will release $1,400,000 each January 1st, for you to use at your discretion, for the care of your son. You and only you supervise how this money is spent. In addition, Ms. James, you will receive an immediate disbursement of $2,000,000. You can use this money how you wish.

"Per your request, Mr. Brewster's former business manager and executor for his estate is present. She has the $2,000,000 in her possession.

"Ms. James, you retain 100% custody of Charles James Brewster and are his sole guardian. Do you accept this responsibility?"

"Yes," Charla answered.

Chic started sobbing. I sat right behind her, so I reached for her shoulder. Her hand reached back, taking mine.

"In return, Mrs. Brewster made two requests. Charles James Brewster will visit his grandmother two weeks each year..."

Charla's lawyer stood. "Judge?"

"Yes, Mr. Conn."

"To be clear, two weeks at a time convenient for Ms. James."

"Yes, your team drove that point home. Please sit, Mr. Conn. You won, show grace."

Charla's lawyer, the buzzard who stripped every dollar from the financial carcass of Rooster's estate, smiled. Yes, the judge chastised him. But the Armani-enrobed attack dog accepted his censure to showcase his complete victory. He crushed Chic's claims with ease, questioning her ability as a mother, attacking her character, and stressing she did not possess the financial skills to manage her grandson's estate.

The judge continued. "The other condition requested by Mrs. Brewster, if you die, are incapacitated, arrested for a felony, or detained from your parental duties, she takes over as Charles James Brewster's guardian, full-time custodian, and manages his estate. Finally, at the conclusion of this trial, per the agreement, Rooster's mother will be allowed custody of Charles James for one month."

"Do you find these terms suitable, Ms. James?"

She nodded toward her attorney. He smirked. Next, Charla spun toward the back of the courtroom. Spotting Petra Klein, Rooster's business manager, and eyeing the suitcase of cash, Charla embraced her victory. Petra, per Chic's instruction, waited.

Charla's nanny entered the courthouse moments later. I spotted Rooster's son for the first time, so beautiful, full of life. I vowed to protect Rooster's child with every ounce of my ability, to be his father figure, if allowed.

As any hostage exchange is handled, and yes, I considered Rooster's son a hostage, Chic signaled Petra to release the money once the business manager held Charles James. After Petra handed the child to Chic, the new grandmother collapsed into her seat, weeping and beaming.

The judge completed the formalities. I studied as Charla thanked her attorney. Next, a man who I assumed was her hired bodyguard, stepped toward Charla.

Charla glowed, clapping, accepting congratulations from her team. The black widow, exactly where she planned to be, from the moment I met her. Wealthy beyond imagination, vindicated by the courts, on top of the world. No doubt she would find a path to this moment...no matter the cost.

Luckily no one paid attention to the losing table. Because Chic and I shared a smile, our victory ensured.

• • •

Two Bucks did not attend the proceedings. No chance he mustered the ability to filter his emotions. Rose Petal planted herself in the front row, listening to every word, chronicling every moment. Her glare seldom left Charla James. She looked away anytime someone entered the room, searching for Charla's secret conspirator. As if my grandmother grasped a plot point the rest of us missed. Again, Rose Petal proved herself a woman not inclined to share secrets.

In what I remember as one of the strangest and most enlightening periods of my life, Rose Petal stayed with me during the trial. She left the Old Place in Two Bucks' care. Grandmother treated the late afternoons, after the judge dismissed court, as the vacation she never enjoyed in her youth. Each afternoon, I planned events for her.

Because she was born into poverty, she never allowed herself time to relax or any semblance of a vacation, afraid everything would be snatched away if she rested. Rooster's death changed her, softened her. Rooster got into her heart, like he did mine and Two Bucks'.

The small-town girl, who never visited a metropolis, marveled at Houston's wonders. Tears overwhelmed her when she witnessed her first ballet, *Giselle*. Awe engulfed her when viewing a Monet at the Houston Fine Arts Museum. She even enjoyed viewing the opulent mansions in River Oaks. Yes, Rose Petal grumbled about the wasted space and unnecessary architectural flair, but her exuberance disclosed her appreciation. I wonder if for the first time she considered a different life.

She soaked in everything the city offered in those weeks.

The last week of her visit she opened up, telling me everything about her past, understanding that only I could carry her history, *our* history, forward.

• • •

"How many copies of this disk exist?" asked the detective.

"More than this one," I answered, not revealing our position.

"I'll let you get away with that...for now. Play the disk once more," said Amanda Pena. The HPD detective sat, dissecting the tape a third time. Instead of going into the station, Pena came to my Houston apartment.

The sound proved surprisingly clear.

First the sound of the door opening, then Rooster stating, "Hey, I'm speaking now to make sure the system is on, yep, there's the green light, we're recording perfectly."

The next few minutes, only sounds of Rooster's boot steps marked time. He sang to himself, maybe to ensure the recording apparatus remained engaged.

Then the knock, the sound of Rooster's boots walking to the door, followed by high heels striking marble, intermixed with Rooster's steps.

"You're not offering me a drink?"

"I just left my best friend's birthday party. This better be important," Rooster said.

"You should do a better job picking friends."

"Screw you, Charla. What did you do? You in trouble?"

"No, but you are...or your child is."

"Excuse me?"

"I'm pregnant."

"Can't be. We were careful. You were on the pill."

"You weren't careful enough, and I got off the pill months ago."

"Seems like something you should mention."

"Want to see the proof?"

Pena and I listened but could not extrapolate what proof Charla offered. Did she show Rooster an ultrasound or raise her shirt and model a baby bump? I'll never know what, but something convinced Rooster.

"What proof do you have the baby's mine?"

"Do you think I'd let anyone sidetrack this opportunity?"

Seconds of silence heightened the tension. Then acknowledgment. "No."

"I'm getting an abortion."

"What?"

"Told you the call was life or death. It is."

"But…"

Again, silence.

"I want the kid…I'll take 'em," said Rooster.

"No, you won't. I'm aborting your child tomorrow. Not bluffing."

"I know you're not."

"Unless…"

"Anything."

"Funny word. Anything. You mean it?"

"With my body and soul."

"Good, because that's what we're playing with."

"I don't understand."

"If you…kill yourself tonight, I'll let the baby live."

"What the fu…"

"You heard me. You will kill yourself tonight."

"No, I won't."

"I can promise you will. Guaranteed."

"What guarantee do I have if I kill myself, that you won't abort the baby?"

"The most basic emotion. Greed. This baby's my link to controlling your estate. My meal ticket. The baby's safe, because without your child, I get nothing."

"You don't need to kill me to get that. I'll take care of you and the baby."

"Yes, but in your scenario, you control me. You're in charge."

"Look, I'll have my lawyers…"

"I thought this through. At best, I get half of your estate. My way, I control everything."

"I'll give it all to you, all of it."

"Then accuse me of extortion, or lawyer up and fight me. No, thanks, I'll take it my way. You die tonight or the baby dies tomorrow."

"You bitch."

"I can live with that. Besides, killing yourself is in your blood."

"What the hell do you mean?"

"You stupid country bumpkin. You still not figured it out?"

Just the clicking of the tape for a full minute.

"Who do you think your father is?"

Silence.

"Come on, Rooster, you know. Chic tried to shield you from it, but you do. You die tonight...family tradition."

Rooster said, "Bullshit."

"You're Larry Details' oldest son. Oh, and something else? The man you think is your friend isn't."

"What?"

"Tails, he screwed you and your mom. Larry Details, your dad, left you and Chic a fortune. Tails administers the will. He kept that money from you. Sold you out."

Nothing. Only silence. Then Charla turned the knife. "Your best friend sold you out. Not much of a friend. Your father and grandfather killed themselves on their 39th birthday, and you're going to honor the tradition. Or tomorrow..."

Again, silence. Charla sounded chipper. "Okay, I'm heading out. It's a big night. Your last night, or your child's. You pick, Rooster."

The sound of high heels marching out, then the door shutting behind her. Then Rooster spoke, "Tails, I don't know the deal with the money, but I forgive you. But I need you right now, Tails. If you're hearing this. You're the only one who can save my kid. Sober the fuck up, get straight. Make sure my mom and kid are okay. Please, Tails. I love you and I'm trusting you, brother. Please.

"I'm turning off the system...no need for you to hear this part."

The last recorded sounds of my best friend, his boots striking tile, walking to turn off the system, then, "Bye, brother."

Amanda Pena seemed lost in thought. I looked around my apartment.

Chic chose not to attend. She enjoyed baby CJ, whom she called Bantam. Unlike when her son Cole received the moniker Rooster, Chic bestowed the nickname. Charla James' ode to herself, naming her son Charles James sickened us all, considering what we knew.

Days ago, Rose Petal returned to the farm. My three allies left the task to me and me alone. Only I could end this forever.

"And you used to sleep with her too?" Pena asked.

"Had her claws in me once."

"Why didn't you share this with police earlier?"

"Well, Charla was pregnant with Rooster's baby. Her body, her choice. If we accused her, she might abort Rooster's child for revenge. So, we waited for the baby to be born."

"Then..."

"Getting Rooster's son away from that monster became our obsession. We assumed Charla would use Rooster's child as leverage. We understood that. Possession of the baby was her strength, money her weakness."

"We fought hard enough in court to make her feel we were oblivious. We guessed she'd put the baby in our hands for quick cash. The baby's with Chic now at the Old Place, with Two Bucks and Rose Petal protecting him. An army couldn't harm that child now. How you use this disk is up to you. We have more. I'm hoping to see the arrest of Rooster's killer in the papers."

"You will see an arrest, I promise," said Amanda Pena. "She'll do time. I can't promise for murder, but we'll try. Extortion most likely, we'll see."

"We'll take it. We'll never allow Rooster's son to be controlled by that woman. That's all that matters."

"She's going to jail, but that doesn't mean she can't fight for..."

"Doesn't matter. She cares more about the money than Bantam. We don't."

"Bantam?"

"That's what we call him."

The following weeks blurred. Amanda tipped me, and I sat outside Charla's luxury townhome when police knocked on her door. Watching Amanda lead out Charla, dressed in handcuffs, high heels, and Halston remains a treasured memory.

Somebody—okay, *I*—released the disks to newspapers and TV stations. Chic, Two Bucks, and Rose Petal needed assurance Bantam would never be under Charla's influence again.

• • •

Rose Petal solved the riddle instantly. Took me a while, but I solved it.
You see it now, don't you?
I'm sure you do.
I'll wait for you to say it out loud. No rush, I have time.

• • •

Charla could not have done it on her own.

A dark mentor spoon-fed Charla the information to target Rooster's wealth. A subhuman who always calculates her closest path to financial gain.

Think about it, you got this. You have the whole time.

Why did Charla James demand a suitcase of cash? The money could have been deposited in her account with less risk. Same result. Why cash?

Funny thing about cash, it sure is hard to track.

Unless someone is stupid enough to purchase a Porsche the next week, then throw a party for 200 people catered by...

Afterlife

Charles James (Bantam) Brewster's 18th Birthday
The Old Place, Under the Devil's Oak

Bantam, or CJ as he preferred, sat in front of me, butt on the picnic table, feet on the bench. Per habit, I rocked in the swing attached to the oak's lowest limb, occasionally pushing off to continue the soft rocking rhythm.

This spot, the Devil's Oak, no longer haunted my family. The goliath's protective shade was now my favorite spot on the Old Place. Two Bucks hauled off the old tractor. As a catharsis, I built a courtyard here.

"So why tell me now?" CJ asked, his speech rhythms matching that of a man he never met, his dead father.

"You're a man today. Wanted you to know everything. No secrets, no hiding."

"But I don't know everything."

"Not quite, no. So, ask."

"Brandy Detals, my grandmother, she helped Charla?"

"Yes."

"How'd you figure it out?"

"A new Porsche 911 arrived in Brandy's driveway days after Charla James received a suitcase of cash."

"Oh."

"Yep, and when we listened to Rooster's conversation with Charla, Rose Petal guessed instantly. How'd Charla get her information if Brandy didn't tell her?"

Even from this distance, the creak of the Old Place's screen door pulled me from my story. I pictured Two Bucks holding the door for Chic. They would arrive soon to join us. Minutes later, Chic placed lemonade in front of us. She hugged Bantam before cuddling next to Two Bucks.

Two Bucks, like me, eighteen-plus years sober. Happier than ever, Dad settled into the position of family patriarch. Silver hair and sun-darkened skin suited him, but not as much as the smile permanently plastered on his face since his first date with Chic.

"Why didn't you turn her—Brandy—in?"

"Well, one, we couldn't prove it."

"And two?"

"Rose Petal had no intention of Brandy Detals going to prison."

Chic added, "Brandy went missing two years later!"

"Missing...yes," Two Bucks said. Chic squeezed his hand and smiled.

"What can you tell me?"

"Like her namesake, Grandmother had her thorns," I said.

"Oh...wow. They've never found Brandy's body?" CJ continued.

"Ah, the Piney Woods..." Two Bucks said and smiled, offering nothing else.

"What do I do with this?" CJ asked.

"You realize there's no curse. You gotta long life ahead, son."

"And?"

"And we'll be around to help. As long as we can. Life's worth living."

The screen porch signaled another resident exiting the Old Place. I awaited Elora's arrival to continue. "Especially if you have folks that love you. Folks who protect you no matter what. Don't give up on family. I did, screwed up. Lost too many years with her."

"Rose Petal?" CJ asked.

We smiled at the mention of her name. "Do you remember her, son?"

"She died when I was six, but Rose Petal was not a woman you forget, Dad."

"No...no, she's not." A tear raced down my cheek. Memories of jalapeño cornbread casserole, chicken fried steak fingers, and creamed gravy warmed my heart.

We sat in silence as the Big Thicket's night opera began, watching blue skies embrace the orange, then fade to evening purple, awaiting the fireflies, our evening's host, to illuminate the path...home.

The End

About the Author

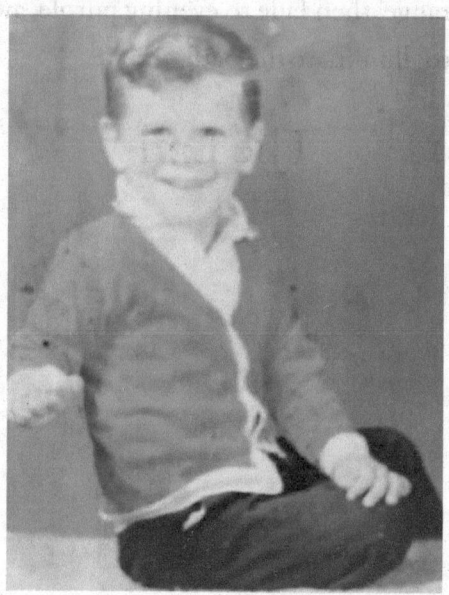

Sojka is a child of addiction, and an addict himself. He's been lost in the Piney Woods, witnessed death intimately, and swam the Neches River in the very spot others drowned. He is a member of a darkly secretive family.

This story is fiction, but these characters are real to him. Sojka trapped snapping turtles in their ditches, stole pecans from their yards, and dug night crawlers from under their homes. In *39, Sojka*, did not just write what he knew, he exposed who he is... the warts, the wins, and most importantly, the losses.

Sojka lives in Southeast, Texas, runs so he can eat Tex-Mex and paddle boards for stress relief.

PS: Tim's mother and grandmother were fantastic and in no way resemble Rose Petal or Brandy.

Note from the Author

Word-of-mouth is crucial for any author to succeed. If you enjoyed *39*, please leave a review online—anywhere you are able. Even if it's just a sentence or two. It would make all the difference and would be very much appreciated.

Thanks!
Timothy Gene Sojka

We hope you enjoyed reading this title from:

BLACK ROSE
writing™

Subscribe to our mailing list – *The Rosevine* – and receive **FREE** books, daily deals, and stay current with news about upcoming releases and our hottest authors.
Scan the QR code below to sign up.

Already a subscriber? Please accept a sincere thank you for being a fan of Black Rose Writing authors.

www.ingramcontent.com/pod-product-compliance
Lightning Source LLC
Chambersburg PA
CBHW010515100726
47903CB00009B/2762